COLLIER SPYMASTERS SERIES

Consulting Editor: Saul A. Katz,
founder 999 Bookshop, New York City

Also by Theodore Wilden

To Die Elsewhere

EXCHANGE OF CLOWNS

Theodore Wilden

COLLIER BOOKS

Macmillan Publishing Company

New York

To
Lord Alastair Londonderry
for his generous friendship

Collier Books
Macmillan Publishing Company
866 Third Avenue, New York, NY 10022
Collier Macmillan Canada, Inc.

This is a work of historical fiction. Names, characters, places,
and incidents relating to non-historical figures are either the
product of the author's imagination or are used fictitiously.
Any resemblance of such non-historical incidents or figures to
actual events or persons, living or dead, is entirely
coincidental.

Library of Congress Cataloging-in-Publication Data
Wilden, Theodore, 1936–
Exchange of clowns / Theodore Wilden.
p.   cm.
ISBN 0-02-038311-8
I. Title.
PR9115.9.W5E94   1988
823′.914—dc19   88-15977   CIP

First Collier Books Edition 1988

10 9 8 7 6 5 4 3 2 1

Printed in the United States of America

"You say that Caesar Borgia suffered the just punishment of his crimes. He was destroyed not by his misdeeds, but by circumstances over which he had no control. His wickedness was an irrelevant accident. In this world of sin and sorrow if virtue triumphs over vice it is not because it is virtuous, but because it has better and bigger guns; if honesty prevails over double-dealing, it is not because it is honest, but because it has a stronger army more ably led; and if good overcomes evil it is not because it is good, but because it has a well-lined purse. It is well to have right on our side, but it is madness to forget that unless we have might as well it will avail us nothing. We must believe that God loves men of good will, but there is no evidence to show that He will save fools from the result of their folly."

W. SOMERSET MAUGHAM
Then and Now

— I —

Berlin again

She alighted into the next seat in just the way of young females when they have well-to-do parents and an erotic future as well-stocked as their wardrobes.

"You going to Berlin too?" she asked when I enquired if she minded my smoking.

"I'm going to be written off, young lady," I replied.

"I expect you've got interesting connections," she said.

"Have had for centuries. And where are *you* going?"

"Berlin. And then beyond. Some other place. I've fixed myself a holiday. I'm sick to the teeth of Germany."

"Why are you going back there then?"

"I'm not going back. Just refuelling, if you see what I mean."

She was German even if her English was good. She was young, but she did not wear jeans. She had a certain *esprit*, but without a shred of arrogance, and she was better than just sexy because she had breeding.

Her hair was long and blonde. Her eyes were green. Her trim figure that of a mannequin you would like to see re-trained as a stripper; she rejoiced in the sacred name of Veronika and doubtless had the right sort of friends (not my sort). She was probably twenty-five, smoked Winstons, and occasionally gave a light click of the tongue as if she had just remembered something. Her lips were like two neatly cut-out little cushions and there was no hint of suffering at the corners of her mouth.

"But you could have written to your parents for the money."

"I've really only got a father. My mother divorced him because he was forever on the move. Lives in Westphalia now and gets a new Volkswagen every year."

"Who does?"

"My mother, of course. My mobile father can't stand Volkswagens. He calls them pan-German hot-water-powered buses. Runs a Jensen himself, though he hardly ever uses it because he's only home at weekends and then not every weekend. Two months I've been waiting for an answer to my last letter. His office wrote to say he's away on his travels, so I'm going to have to touch his secretary for some cash. Maybe Daddy will have come back in the meantime."

"What does your father do?"

"Exports. I expect he exports goat kids or Bibles, or those tapes where you can hear heavy breathing and *je t'aime* and *moi non plus*."

When she spoke, it was as if she was telling you something terribly confidential, for your ears alone, something she had never told anyone else before. As if she were recounting the confessions of the mistress of one of the three musketeers.

I smiled and forgot the roar of the plane's engines, and all the way till we landed at Tempelhof we chattered away; I with the sheer delight of a middle-aged man who has left forty behind him and will never cease to regret it.

We were sitting in the bar of the Intercontinental, and I knew it would be a long time before I would be able to go to bed. As a man grows old, his pillow becomes a kindly nursemaid serving him during the intervals in his journey to the long, final sleep. In earlier times dying was more peaceful, more dignified even; in the bosom of the family.

Nowadays they just torment you to death in hospital; and anyway, I did not have a family in whose bosom to die.

Veronika was drinking Tia Maria Café with the expression of a gourmet. She was wearing a light-green dress made by Laroche's ex-midinettes; she looked slimmer, her breasts even more innocent.

"And what do *you* do?" she asked me.

"Export," I said almost tenderly, and I felt as if even in my grave I should still be repeating the lie. "I used to export sugar-cane. Sugar, I mean. Ever since there've been problems in certain countries . . . I'm not fussy about what I export. But, tell me, why did you come here, to the hotel?"

"Why did *you* come here?"

I smiled.

"We came into the city together, didn't we? It's not that far from Tempelhof. But you ought to be with your family. Or that secretary . . ."

She heaved a sigh.

"The problem is that we've got so many homes. My uncle has a large house at Pullach, and Daddy often goes there. Then there's one in Frankfurt. I've got to find out first where Fritz is. That's the secretary."

Unlike her, I knew she would be spending the night alone, but I left her free to chatter of this and that, just as when you work slowly through a box of chocolates, waiting for the one with the brandy filling. She was going to have to wait too, because then I saw Whitfield. I had not seen him for quite a number of years. He took a stool opposite us at the other end of the bar and opened the *New York Herald Tribune*. Then he folded it again, started on the *Süddeutsche Zeitung*, and ordered a whisky on the rocks.

It was fifteen years since I had held him bound in a

cellar in Havana, and I was pleased to see he had not got any younger either. He held his cocky little head slightly to one side and occasionally wiped his nose. Got a cold, poor journalist, I said to myself. Shouldn't drink things with ice.

I glanced at my watch. Seven o'clock. I excused myself from Veronika and went over to the phone. Three hours had passed since my plane had landed and it was time to contact Mottey. I knew he was a British agent, that he was perfectly at home in Berlin, and they had once told me at Gonzales' place that he promised everybody more money than was in the Bank of England.

I knew my orders. I knew the value of time on this mission. I knew that at first I would have help, but that in the end I would be alone. In the end I am always alone.

2

"Mr Mottey?" I asked, when a slightly hesitant, wry voice answered the phone.

"Yes. What d'you want?"

He'd been drinking. No doubt of that. London had not warned me. They had not done a blood-alcohol test on him.

"It's seven o'clock. Rise and shine. You're going to have breakfast."

"Who's speaking?"

"Her Majesty wishes to be remembered to you."

That was the agreed cue – a play on Queeney's name.

"Aha. Where are you?"

"At the Intercontinental. Will you come over?"

"Yes. About half an hour. You alone?"

"No. But it depends what you mean."

"You haven't spoken to anybody yet?"

"Not to any of those you mean. Do you really propose to go on over the phone?"

"Wait. I'm on my way."

He hung up.

I lit a cigarette and thought for a moment. Then I went back to the bar. Veronika looked up and handed me a visiting-card.

"The man said it's for Mr Lima. I told him you're not Mr Lima. That you're called Therrick."

"You should set up an information bureau," I said.

"He said not to worry and to give it to you. He's sitting over there."

I picked up the card. Sure enough it had Whitfield's name on it. I shrugged.

"I'll have to leave you for a little while longer; try to behave yourself. Then I hope I'll be able to invite you to dinner."

I went round to the other side of the bar and sat down next to Whitfield. He raised his head and gave me a crooked smile.

"You saw me, didn't you?" he asked.

"Yes, but I didn't notice that you'd seen me. I didn't want to disturb you."

"I saw you when you went to the phone. What's your name these days?"

"Therrick. Does it matter?"

"No," he conceded. "I've got a hunch there's something up; you being here."

"Your paper pays you too much."

He blew his nose and said:

"When the history of this city comes to be written, there'll be a place of honour in it for you."

"You're exaggerating. Everybody gets to Berlin sooner or later."

"You've gone up in the world. You must be on good money by now."

"Our relative finances would make a tortoise laugh," I smiled. "Is there something you're after?"

"Information. And I've got some as well."

"I wouldn't doubt that. But there's a bit of a snag about doing a deal with you, wouldn't you say?"

"I must write something from time to time."

"Okay, but you keep going off at half-cock. You'll turn into a liberal. I admit there is still some difference between a Soviet agent and an American liberal, but not a great deal. And it'll get even worse."

He smirked. "We'll get the President."

"Yes," I said, "you probably will, and you'll get medals for it. You'll weaken your country, you'll lose your client states, then your credibility and then your friends. You'll betray your allies for some irrelevant principle because for a long time you've had your priorities wrong. I suppose you're on the band wagon."

He took a drink. Then he rattled the ice in his glass and ordered another.

"You drinking?" he asked me.

"Hadn't you noticed I've got charming company?"

"Hm, anyway . . . So if you do have anything for me . . . I've been here since yesterday and I'm in 315. Don't feel shy about giving me a buzz."

"I might. If you've got something in return."

I left him to his own devices at the bar, an ageing veteran of the Pentagon and the White House, not wanting in courage, but inclined to steadily apply his energy to ends which, in this divided world, have disastrous consequences.

"Dinner will be somewhat delayed," I said sadly to Veronika, who had become a kind of oasis in my cheerless mission, a *fata morgana* and an obstinate illusion in which I placed no trust, but which I intended to keep, despite the rules. After all, who knows . . . Something might come out of it . . . In my experience unimportant things often lead to useful contacts, to strange encounters and to the unexpected. Of course, sometimes you meet a person, just a character who struts about on the stage for a while and disappears. You never know what happened to him or why.

The bar was filling up. Mostly with businessmen and their mistresses of the moment; here and there an Arab of the lower echelons (the Arab big shots don't use the Intercontinental, a sort of motel to them) and a handful of newsmen, killing time between seven and eight before going off to the Renz.

"Are you working very hard . . . at your exports?" asked Veronika, playing at being a little girl, but making fun of her own game.

"Just keep blathering," I said tenderly. "I've got to keep my eyes open for some people."

And so I saw Mottey.

3

Oscar Mottey had sleek black hair, what there was of it, a longish skull and prominent jaw-bones. Fortunately, he did not have a moustache, otherwise he would have looked like a graduate gigolo. He was wearing a dark-blue striped suit, a polka-dot bow-tie, and there was a mass of purple handkerchief at his breast-pocket.

Mottey sat down and looked at Veronika with distrust.

"This is Mr Mottey, Veronika. I'm afraid he'll kidnap me now," I said, and Mottey did just that.

I noticed Whitfield's eyes following us.

"D'you know Whitfield?" I asked the purple handkerchief.

"Yes. You were supposed to be alone." Mottey frowned.

I gave him a pat on the shoulder. The days were gone when his sort could lecture me. Gone for good.

"Queeney gave me *carte blanche*. Do you know that?"

"They phoned me today from Bonn."

"Phoned?"

"It's okay. We use scramblers on the phones and change the frequencies every day."

"Nichols," I said.

"I know," he said laboriously. "It's . . . most unpleasant."

"It may get even more unpleasant."

"That exchange mustn't come off. He really is one of ours."

I kept my expression neutral and he added:

"I know him. Know him well. We were at Cambridge together. He's a couple of years younger. Got a wife and . . ."

"I heard all that in London." I didn't bother to say that I'd even gone to see Nichols' Lana Turner.

He ordered a Campari and I had the feeling it was to rinse his stomach out before the next whisky.

"I wouldn't drink Campari if I were you," I said, "but I don't mean that as advice."

He nodded, grumbling into his glass. "Nichols isn't in Berlin any more."

"You know that for certain?"

"No. Only fairly certain. They've moved him."

"Where to?"

"No way of knowing."

"Who talked to them?"

"We did first. Then the Consul. Jeremy had a Soviet passport."

"What?"

Mottey glanced at me and then nodded painfully. "He went to Odessa not long ago. By boat. He needed to get into the port and a bit beyond. They found it on him."

"And that's why they insist he's a Soviet agent?"

He heaved a sigh and brandished his glass of Campari.

"Cheers," he said and tossed it down. "That's what we can't make out. The passport is probably forged. Our handiwork, I expect. They must have discovered that by now. This has been going on for a week."

"Must be a fine old scare if London roped me in. Can't your own people do anything with it? The normal expulsion, and Bob's your uncle . . . ?"

"It's being handled by a special section of the BND, the Sonderabteilung Colonel Koerner; and one other colonel. They're the ones who have taken him away. Now they want to trade him for their own man. All they're waiting for is the Soviet negotiator."

"What else do you know?"

"That's all. It's not my department. I feel terribly sorry for Jeremy."

"Me too. Who'll give me more information?"

"Someone who's in contact with STASI."

STASI was East German security, as opposed to the West German BND.

"Who's that?"

"Nighton. Cyril Nighton."

"Ours?"

"Ours."

"Hm."

He ordered another Campari and said, as if uttering a prophecy, "I know that yesterday Nighton tried to get in touch with Koerner. I've been ringing him all today. No reply. But he must turn up. Here's the key to his flat. It's a safe-house. You'll find it easily. Wilmersdorf. At the corner of Berlinerstrasse and Briennerstrasse. Dead opposite the crematorium."

I took the key, and put it in my pocket.

"How long should I wait for him?"

"Just wait. None of our people can tell you more."

He finished his Campari.

"I'll have to have a Scotch. What's yours?"

"I'll have to push on."

"Can I ask you just what they told you in London?"

"You can. They don't think that negotiations are possible. They told me to get him out. At all costs. By whatever means."

Mottey smoothed down his hair and ordered his Scotch.

"The entire Sixth Fleet couldn't get him out. Koerner's got him and that's that; it's not like the days when we locked up Blake."

"Be seeing you later on this evening," I said ruefully. "Pick me up here in two hours' time." Then I turned and asked, "But before we meet, tell me, what's STASI's interest?"

"BND want to swap Jeremy for one of their own men STASI are holding." Mottey raised his eyebrows. "Or they just want to keep him . . . Because he knows something. That's only Nighton's guess, mind you. But by now Nighton may know what it is that Jeremy is supposed to know about. Does it make sense to you?"

— II —

Cyril Nighton,
the agent

Veronika made eyes at me.

"You're treating me like some unwanted kitten," she said.

"If I were younger, I would fall in love with you just for the way you said that."

"You aren't as old as you feel."

"I'm just as old as I feel. Come on, eating time."

I decided to change quarters. This hotel was getting on my nerves. We found a table and Veronika ordered melon, smoked salmon and a Wiener Schnitzel and said she'd have Moselle to go with it. I nodded agreement, ordered much less for myself and said I would have the Moselle too.

"Two bottles then. I'll get through one in no time," she said.

"And then you're off to beddy-byes."

"And what about Berlin by night?"

"Not tonight. Tonight I've got things to do. Maybe tomorrow."

Veronika smiled happily. We talked about food and colourless dishes in colourless prefabricated hotels in dull cities. Veronika drank like a fish.

"And now I want to put this child to bed."

"Eight o'clock's not my bedtime."

"It'll be nine by the time we're ready," I said.

It was too, and Veronika let herself be hauled off to her room on the second floor, and with a string of tolerably comely oaths, accepted her sentence: go to bed, or be locked in.

"I'll keep you locked up here. I like you, and until your father's secretary comes to fetch you I feel responsible for you," I told her. "Get a move on!"

"Do you mean I've got to get undressed with you here?"

She did not seem particularly unwilling to start.

"No, you undress in the bathroom."

Of course, I imagined her undressing. Of course, I imagined what it would be like if . . . but the shadow of Nichols' fate kept intruding and I suddenly heard the rattling of the ghost train carrying him round and round the corridors inside the House of Horrors. Instead of skeletons it was displaying the faces of agents finished off in the bureaucratic no man's land between the enemy's lines and our policy of détente.

My mouth went suddenly dry. When Veronika came back and slipped into the bed, I bent over her like a father and gave her a chaste kiss on the forehead.

Instantly her arms seized me and she hugged me close.

"I like older men," she said softly.

"So do I," I said and left the room.

2

I settled down in Mottey's Mercedes.

I looked sideways at his face, briefly lit up by the head-lights of a passing car. It was motionless.

We drove through the streets of Berlin, the only German city I liked . . . Why? What sort of magic had it for me?

Was it because it was cut in half by the Wall, a hostage island in a hostile sea? Was it really because of Checkpoint Charlie? Or was it because the Berliners knew the true meaning of solidarity on earth? Or because every word here had, or could have, a double meaning? Because you could never know who was who and who was behind him and if his backer today would not become his enemy tomorrow?

Or was it because it had witnessed Hitler's triumphs and Hitler's end, the final desperate, useless fight against reality? Or because of the Berlin of the twenties I had heard about – *jenseits des Guten oder Bösen*? Maybe it was because this magical, shady, stubborn city did not belong anywhere – like myself?

My work for Gonzales' Agency hardly encouraged a settled life. It was a highly private "Informations Export-Import" service, centred on Lisbon, which worked on CIA assignments among others. It had some agents of its own as well as some 200 not always reliable "correspondents" all over the world. Gonzales' Agency employed people who did not want to work for any particular service, or whom no service wanted.

I'd been with Gonzales for the last fifteen years, from the moment David Bleyhart, himself an ex-mercenary and Gonzales' agent, pulled me out of Algiers and brought me to Lisbon. My first assignment was Cuba at the end of 1958, shortly before Castro took over with American help, and even if it was a wash-out I at least learned how irreversible their short-sighted foreign policy could be.

Gonzales' Agency wasn't exactly a cosy nest for an agent who was definitely getting on in years, but it was a living.

Only the prospects were bleak; no savings, no pension, nothing to look forward to. And on top of everything, since the beginning of this blessed year, 1973, there had been persistent rumours that Caetano was on the way out and every agent knew that Portugal would become a mess. No wonder Gonzales was quietly packing his bags. That might have been the reason he had no objections to my working for the British, this time on my own.

It began to drizzle.

Mottey turned into Kurfürstendamm and slowed down. "Tell me more about Nighton."

"Very able, fairly young. The CIA has tried to rope him in. But he's stayed. He's got excellent contacts with East German security. He looks after British interests when it comes to swapping people with the East."

"Agents?"

"No, the Swiss business."

"D'you mean Lehling?"

"Yes."

Lehling was based in Switzerland, and whenever the East and West Germans could not come to an agreement, for 70,000 marks he would spring from East Germany anyone you cared to mention. Or nearly anyone.

"Where's this all leading us?"

"Kraus. The British put in the order for him. Chemist. Cost 'em a packet. Lehling got him out in the end. Nighton took him over in Zurich. He'd organised the entire deal."

"So STASI has it in for him?"

"Yes and no. He's got friends there. Dollars work wonders." He stubbed out his cigarette.

"This black market in people has been going on for years. The East Germans 'release' certain names and offer them to the West. And the West buys them. 40,000 marks a head on average."

"And Nighton?"

"He's often arranged a spot of *Trinkgeld*. A tip. Even STASI people will accept one from time to time, but not as much as here. It's harder to do business in the East than in the West. Stiffer controls and more faith in the system. Also more fear of reprisals."

"What's Nighton like personally?"

"Above all, intelligent. Woman mad, like any English-man on the Continent. He went out with Sheila Rae for a time, before she hit the big time and went off to Holly-wood. He knows Nichols well. In 1968 they did the report on the wave of suicides among the West German Intelli-gence. You know the story . . . autumn 1968. Eighteen of them in all, including an admiral. They put a pistol in his hand. Eighteen of them, and all working for the East Germans. For the sake of United Vaterland. In the hope of a centre-left State."

"Nothing is as lethal as hopes," I remarked. "What's Nighton's standing with the West Germans?"

"The way they politely ignore Soviet agents – and they've got about 15,000 of them in the country – they're not going to do much about the British ones. There are not more than a couple of hundred here, not counting the illegals."

I lit a cigarette.

"The rain's stopped. I'll get off here and get a taxi."

Mottey pulled up at the kerb.

When I opened the door of the Mercedes the noise of Kurfürstendamm hit my ears; as if emerging from the underworld the bright lights of Shanghai and Nicky-bar made me blink. Suddenly here was the sound of high heels hurrying along the shiny pavement. Here was the sound of German voices; the sound of cars and the sound of the night. So I almost missed Mottey saying:

"Have a good journey to the cemetery."

3

The journey from the Kurfürstendamm to Berliner-strasse by way of the Hohenzollerndamm took a few minutes. In the taxi, I thought over the situation. First and foremost I needed to know Nichols' new "address". I might be able to get that from Nighton.

In London Queeney had warned me: "Don't count on any official help. You'll be on your own." Queeney was as prudent as an old owl, and he sat on his branch very firmly. The British were quite unlike other outfits I'd come across in the intelligence business. And I couldn't afford to forget that I was not British myself. That meant I had to succeed. They wanted Nichols back. They were prepared to pay for it. Why had they not approached the German government through the Foreign Office? The Foreign Office would have pulled a face and said they didn't want to know about any agent; still less in a friendly country like Germany.

Koerner's department would probably be somewhere near Munich. Or would it? Nighton might know . . . but I'd find that out shortly if he were in. But what if he weren't in? Should I wait?

Things being as they were I decided I would. There was no sense in deciding what to do next before I had seen Nighton.

"That's the cemetery over there, and that's the crematorium," said the taxi-driver, as I paid and got out.

Berlinerstrasse was long and wide. I crossed it and entered the house on the corner. Nighton lived on the second floor.

There was a note on the door: BACK SOON.

Of course, that could have meant in an hour. Or two. I dug the key out of my pocket and walked into the flat; into that mixed smell of perfume and coffee and cigarettes. I took off my coat and hung it on the stand, and then, as was my habit, I knocked lightly on the door that I thought would be that of the living-room. I opened it, but it led into a bedroom. There was a woman asleep on the bed. She was beautiful, and completely naked. She had fantastically shaped breasts, almost as beautiful as Marika Zou, whom I had once seen in Paris at the Shocking Club. This woman would be a close second to her.

I just looked at her for a while, then regretfully closed the door and crossed the passage to the living-room. The light was on.

There was a man lying on the settee, his mouth gagged and his hands tied behind his back. I couldn't be sure whether it was Cyril Nighton. But I could be sure that he wouldn't be talking to me, because from the left side of his chest protruded the hilt of a knife sunk deep into the body.

— III —

Nighton's mistress

The first thing I did was to take out my handkerchief and carefully wipe the door-handle. The second thing I did was to wipe the door-handle of the bedroom where the woman was sleeping. Then I put my gloves on and, after a moment's reflection, my coat as well. Then I went to the telephone.

But I didn't dial Mottey's number. I had to decide whether to wake the woman. That meant almost certainly getting involved. Could I afford to?

I walked up to Nighton – if Nighton it was. I assumed so. He was cold. How long had he been lying here like this? Who had left the note on the door saying BACK SOON? Nighton? Probably. For the woman? Hardly. She would have had her own keys. Or would she? How had she got in? Had she been waiting for Nighton, and fallen asleep? Had they made love, and had Nighton then got dressed and left? He was bound and gagged. Someone had been afraid of noise. The murderer hadn't been alone. There'd been at least two of them. Neat work. Had they been waiting for him? Were *they* the ones who had left the note?

I made up my mind. I went out of the room and knocked on the bedroom door. I had to be certain that it really was Nighton. Silence. I opened the door and went in. Only now did I take in that the light on the bedside-table was on.

I looked at the woman's body. I forgot the perfection of its curves, as I realised she was not breathing. I bent over the bed, right across, and saw a deep gash through her hair. The blood had run down behind the pillow and behind the bed, so I hadn't been able to see it from the door. She was dead and cold.

2

I suspected the phone might be tapped, but that couldn't be helped. Going out to a public phone and back again was an even greater risk. I lifted the receiver and dialled.

It was a while before he answered.

"The friend whose key you gave me won't be telling me anything. I'm waiting for you at his flat. Right now. Okay?"

"My God!" was all he said; then the line clicked.

Again I carefully wiped the inside handles of both doors – the bedroom and the living-room. I took a look round the flat, but there was no sign of disorder.

I sat down in the living-room and wondered whether the murderers had given the police a tip-off. If they found me here it would be unpleasant, even though both of them, the man and the woman, must have been dead for some hours and I did have an alibi. But getting involved with the West Berlin police was the last thing I wanted.

It was close on eleven when there was a short ring at the door.

It was Mottey.

I led him in silence into the living-room.

"Nighton," he said. "Nighton!"

He looked at me as if he had just lost more at cards than he could afford, and ran a hand over his sleek hair.

"That's not all," I said. "Follow me."

I opened the bedroom door and pointed to the woman.

He raised his eyebrows. He, too, apparently thought she

27

was asleep and didn't know whether he ought to be looking.

"Get closer," I said, and he did.

He stood over her naked body, touched it reluctantly and I pointed towards the head. I saw his face twitch: he understood.

He stood there a moment, then turned and came back over to me.

"You haven't touched anything?" he asked softly.

"No."

"We've got to get out," he said. "The flat is clean. He often used it just overnight. Sometimes someone else slept here . . . if necessary. They won't find anything."

"Don't you want to make sure?"

"No need," he said with conviction. "I myself slept here two days ago . . ." He broke off in mid-sentence. I just managed to stop myself asking him if it was a safe-house for the sexual needs of British agents.

"That's it, then?"

"That's it," he said. "I must inform Bonn at once."

"And what about London?"

"I don't have a direct link. Bonn will see to that. If I went through our resident here it would take just as long. Let's go."

We closed the door and left the note as it was.

3

At Mottey's flat, also in the British sector, on Pariserstrasse, I let him get on with fixing the scrambler to the phone, dialling Bonn and passing on his information. I took my coat off, lit a cigarette and let my eyes roam the book-shelves. It was a modern, impersonal flat, fairly large, with a terrace overlooking the street. Mottey was asking for instructions for both of us. Bonn promised word within the hour.

I held out no great hope. Although they were already on British Summer Time in London, it would still take a while before Queeney was informed, and there was no one else with the authority to change my instructions – or recall me, which wasn't what I was hoping for. The death of a British agent was bad, and outright murder even worse, but that couldn't alter the fact that Jeremy Nichols was in a German jail and that his captors were all set to hand him over to the other side.

No, London would still want Nichols.

Even more than before.

Mottey put down the phone and cleared his throat, but I spoke first.

"I've got a few questions to ask you. Perhaps you can answer them here and now. London isn't going to cut back my authority. Be sure that from now on they will, if anything, extend it."

He nodded. He was agitated and found it hard to regain his composure. On top of that he was working off the alcohol, which he did by surreptitious head movements. He must have gone on drinking after I'd left him and then driven home to bed. It was thanks to the amount he'd drunk that I'd found him at home at all. If he'd been out on the town . . .

"Nighton keep a notebook?"

"He'd a good memory. If he did have a notebook, it'll be at his home."

"Where's that?"

"Munich."

"Is there anyone at his Munich flat?"

"No. But Bonn'll take care of that."

"Who was the woman?"

Mottey seemed not to have heard the question.

"Do you know her?" I asked.

"Yes."

He was disinclined to say more.

For an Englishman he did seem rather more agitated than I would have expected.

"Was she Nighton's mistress?"

"Yes."

"For long?"

"No. Few months."

"What was her name?"

"Michaela."

"German?"

"No."

"You're not saying much."

"No."

"English?"

"Irish."

"What was her surname?"

"Mottey."

I gaped at him.

"She was my wife."

Mottey was Anglo-Saxon to the core.

4

"I am very, very sorry, Mr Mottey," I said after a moment. "Do you mind if I nevertheless go on asking questions?"

"Go ahead," he said.

I lit another cigarette. I waited for him to offer me a drink, but he wasn't going to. He didn't seem thirsty any more. I scrutinised every movement of his face. If he were suffering, he didn't let it show.

"How long has this . . . ?" I began.

"Nobody knows about it," he said. "A month or two."

"Was that why you started drinking?"

He raised his head. "Yes."

"And nobody knows about that either?"

"Not yet. And I'm giving that up now. There's no reason for it any more."

Had he hated her? Did he feel avenged now? To what lengths was the spite of this crumpled purple handkerchief capable of going? What lay hidden behind those thoroughly British features? What eluded me, a mere Continental, when confronted with the secret passion of an Englishman? Michaela Mottey had been a most beautiful woman. Did he feel hatred towards her now, lying in the bedroom of the flat in Berlinerstrasse, which for both of them, for Nighton and for her, was so close to the cemetery?

"Had she left you?"

"Yes and no. She . . . worked at the Military Mission. That's how I met her. Two years ago. I could never understand what she saw in me. But we got married straight away. I'd already been divorced once. She . . ." He hesitated, as though considering what he should tell me; or as though he wanted to know in advance just what I wanted to hear.

"Nighton . . . whenever he was in Berlin, he came here, of course. Michaela . . . knew what I was doing; or she suspected it. We never talked about it. You know what the married life of a spy is like. You married?"

"No."

Muriel was not marriage. She was an unfulfillable dream hidden away in Athens, eternally waiting and eternally provisional, for days snatched in a year that was too long for my holidays not to be too short. And even when time shortened with the years, the length of my holidays only shortened with them. Days became hours, hours minutes,

31

minutes seconds. Ageing is a malady. The ageing of dreams is gradual murder.

But I could imagine the marriage of a field agent. I could imagine the divorce of a field agent. The grounds: de facto separation. I could imagine the hopes with which Mottey had started his second marriage. He must have been crazed with desire for that body. That face. He must have felt powerful when he saw the changes wrought in that face by ecstasy. Or must he?

"It was a sort of game between us. She never asked what I thought about it. She stayed on at the Mission. We'd sometimes go out to a night-club with Nighton. In the days when he was still dating the Rae woman. He was a marvellous dancer. The playboy of British Intelligence. He was extremely able. D thought especially highly of him."

"D? Who's D?"

"Our resident in Bonn."

He explained to me that the residents in each state were designated by the initial letter of that state. I nodded. Every intelligence service has its quirks.

"There was quite a difference in age between us. I'm forty-eight. Michaela was thirty-two. Nighton forty. He didn't seduce her. It was the other way round. He took it as a passing episode. He resisted at first. And I . . . she stopped sleeping with me. She was Irish. They're a rather volatile race. You never know . . . Two days ago Nighton went to Hamburg. But Michaela didn't come back here. I knew where she was. I had a key to the flat. I went over. Gave her a hiding. Then I raped her. She never said a word. Except: 'I've never enjoyed it so much as with him'. I lay down on the floor and fell asleep. I was finished. I haven't seen her since then. Until tonight."

Had he been capable of murdering her?

"Nighton had been trying to contact Koerner, you told me."

I was trying to divert his attention.

"That's right. He told me so before he left for Hamburg."

"But Koerner's in Munich, isn't he?"

"No one ever knows where he is. He moves around Germany like a pike in a pond. He's the head of the Sonderabteilung. Some people call it 'The Twins'. Probably because there's two of them in charge of it. Both colonels. Him, and a chap called Groller."

"What's known about them?"

"Next to nothing. The department was set up shortly after it came out that Gehlen's right-hand man was working for the Soviets. It's meant to sort of keep an eye on everybody. We've got one in our outfit too, but it works differently. Here they're an all-powerful gang."

"Gang?"

"That's what we call it. They're the only ones who dare make an arrest. They've got close links with the Prosecutor General. They're not afraid of the press. They're not afraid of anything."

"That's the first time I've heard of it."

"It'll be a long time before you hear about it again. The few of us who do know aren't keen on talking."

"Hm. Do you think Nighton died at the same time as . . . as your wife?"

I riveted my gaze on him.

"I don't know," he said simply. "It wasn't me who did it."

"You could have killed *her*. They could have killed Nighton later."

"I'll be in it up to the neck either way." He took out his cigarette case and lit a cigarette. His brain must have been swirling with different thoughts. "They're almost bound to suspect me."

"You might have an alibi. Me. But I won't give you one. I'm sorry."

"I understand." He was well aware that I could not risk contact with the police.

"You'll deny it, of course."

"Yes."

I shrugged. "Even if it was you who killed Michaela Mottey, it would be all the same to me. You can see that."

"Yes, I can see that," he said. "Your interest is in Nighton."

"*Our* interest."

"Not mine though. It's all the same to me."

He did not look dejected; he did not look anything in particular. I asked him to open the door onto the terrace – the room felt hot. He did so, then came back and sat down as before.

He looked obedient. I knew he hadn't killed his wife. I knew it through my sixth sense. I had watched him when I led him into the bedroom. I had seen *how* he looked at his wife's body. He had thought she was asleep. He had been thinking about her being naked. He had been thinking of the two of them making love before Nighton was killed. He had thought: They were making love. Then Nighton had to go out. They were waiting outside the door. Or they rang the bell. Nighton hadn't wanted to get up. But when he heard the bell, he got dressed and went to open the door. They gagged him and tied his hands. She was asleep, exhausted by love-making. Nighton was on his own. They dragged him into the living-room. There they despatched him like a trussed chicken. Those had been Mottey's thoughts as he looked at his wife's body. He knew nothing.

"It depends what time it happened." I paused. "It's possible the time will tell in your favour. It could be, the sooner they find her . . ."

"I was at home. Drinking. I've got no alibi. Except for

you. That is, for when I was at the Intercontinental. I didn't meet anybody there. Except you."

He went through it like the alphabet. He wasn't telling me anything new. They were in a shambles, the British service. Nichols in jail, Nighton murdered, Mottey out of action, neutralised by suspicion. Would they arrest him? Probably. Even if they weren't quick to find out how long she'd been deceiving him.

"There is one other possibility," I said.

"Really . . . ?" he said. "What?"

I looked at my watch. It was midnight. Bonn still had not phoned. London was either asleep or debating what to do.

Mottey was staring at me vacantly. But he was sticking it out, he wouldn't cave in.

"Didn't you report to London your wife's . . ."

"I reported there was a woman in the flat with him. That it was my wife . . . they'll find that out soon enough, won't they?"

"They killed her because she happened to be there. For no other reason. The police won't come up with anything much. We both know that."

"Yes."

"And it won't help us. Quite the contrary, it'll make things sticky for you. I won't be able to help and London will be in a pickle. What's the alternative?"

"Do you mean to say . . . ?"

"I do. I've been given full powers and I've made up my mind: At the very least we've got to get your wife out of the flat. Possibly Nighton as well. But perhaps two corpses is too great a risk."

He stared at me. "You're really serious."

"Deadly serious."

"You don't believe I . . ."

"I don't believe anything in the world. I believe myself,

35

and here and there my memories. And the extra senses I've got. But your lot can't handle this business. They'd know too much and you'd get hauled over the coals for it later. If I can work it, I'll fix things without them. And without you. You just sit tight and wait for them to phone you from Bonn."

"I should have met you before this," he said pensively.

I stood up.

"I've had the same idea about a number of people in my time. But generally I have decided it's too late even then. May I use your phone?"

— IV —

Everyone has a past

He smelt very slightly of Tabac Blond by Caron, his
dinner jacket was alpaca, the colour of anthracite, and his
gestures were alternately abrupt and languorous. Paul
Ludovico Veronese was an Italian, a Jew, and one of the
top men in the Berlin underworld. He was a tall, white-
haired *padrone* with aquiline features and tiny wrinkles
around the eyes. A man whom no one could have once
imagined capable of growing old; and yet he had done; a
man of a thousand memories and one of the last of the
generation which, with Humphrey Bogart at its head, had
had the gift of wrestling with life with strictly guarded
elegance.

Veronese was of the Bogart generation: it was there in
his every movement, in every facial expression, in the look
in his eyes, as they looked around and accepted with the
merest hint of regret the way things were.

His wife was sitting by his side: still beautiful, in silver-
black taffeta, a whole collection of jewels on her plump
fingers, and in her face the devotion and loving patience
of a woman who will not speak until her husband asks for
her opinion.

Paul Ludovico Veronese, despite his sixty years, still
kept to his daily custom of drinking a bottle of Cristal Brut
Roederer between midnight and one in the morning at the
Sorrento Bar on Kurfürstendamm.

Now I was sitting at his table, in a raised box above the

37

dance floor, where one girl was undressing another and both were sighing.

Veronese received me with courtesy; I kissed his wife's hand. The waiter brought another glass and I explained to Veronese in a half-whisper what I wanted.

I was tired and visualised Oscar Mottey, sitting alone in his flat, waiting for word from Bonn.

2

Veronese gazed at me with his head tilted to one side.

"I have a rough idea of what you want done. Perhaps we should get down to the details, if you agree that would be to the purpose."

I agreed it was to the purpose and we got down to the details.

"The man is not to be moved, if I've understood right."

"Right."

"The woman is to disappear . . . for good . . . or is she just to be found somewhere else?"

"The second alternative's the right one. But I don't want her to be found for a few days."

He nodded. "It'll be eight thousand five hundred marks. I can cash your cheque. What bank?"

"Neuflize-Schlumberger in Paris."

He nodded again. "Can you make it out right now?"

I did so.

"Write down the address and give me the key."

I preferred to dictate the address to him. Then he took the key and rose.

"I'll leave you now in my wife's company for a while," he said, and it sounded as though he were awarding me a medal.

On the dance floor, a juggler had replaced the two ladies and was working with bricks which flew like birds from hand to hand.

"Do you like the performers?" I asked, turning to Madame Veronese.

"They are part of the night life really, don't you agree?" she replied. "I like variety shows. Music hall. And the circus."

She spoke easily; she had an alto voice and not a trace of affectation. She must have been the perfect helpmate for Veronese and she certainly loved him.

"I envy your husband," I said. "And please don't take that as a cheap piece of flattery."

She looked at me questioningly. She was perfectly aware of her allure and of the charm which spilled over onto other men.

"I'm very old-fashioned, Mr . . ."

"Therrick."

"I'm very old-fashioned, Mr Therrick," she said in English. "In my day, women got married once only and they regarded that as one of life's successes. We knew our menfolk had the occasional adventure, but we would turn a blind eye, because, on the other hand, they had no illusions about their adventures; they were only trying to reassure themselves of their own masculinity and attractiveness. The main things, their emotions and tenderness, remained ours. That could well be what you envy my husband for, don't you think?"

She undoubtedly knew that I was *en pleine action* – otherwise we would not have been sitting here like this, and her husband would not have left us. She knew there were things going on in my mind and that I had problems. And she knew that I had no inkling of her problems. She knew that our lives were listing dangerously.

I took a sip of my champagne before replying.

"I envy him the way he must feel. His back so well covered by someone who loves him, who knows life yet who hasn't let herself be maimed by it. As for me, I've missed the boat."

She looked at me somewhat quizzically before she asked:

"Will you be staying in Berlin long?"

"A few days . . . maybe more. I don't know."

"I was wondering if you'd be able to come and have dinner with us. Or you can call in here any time . . . before you leave. I promise I won't ask you what you're doing. I'll only ask what you're thinking."

I felt I was back in that remote inner world which I had so often had to suppress for the sake of my profession. I forced a strained laugh and changed the subject. "The juggler is really outstanding."

"Yes," said Madame Veronese. "My husband bought him through an agency in Amsterdam. He is Dutch. He's a truly superb juggler." She smiled at my discomfiture. "What nationality are you?"

"European. With traces of Greek."

"Now I understand."

The chance to sit at peace and converse with Madame Veronese was as rare in the kind of life I lead as it was welcome and refreshing. She was not of the *grand monde*, but, by her own nature, she was a real lady, by what she had learned from living on the fringes of high society, and by what had possibly, indeed quite probably, been made of her by her husband. Without question he was one of those men who tames a woman first in bed, then in life, then by philosophy; then they introduce her to society and finally they allow her the freedom to evolve into someone whom others will envy. With womankind, beauty is learnt, fidelity acquired and nobility evolves . . .

"Have you any children?"

"Of course. Two. My son is a doctor in Rome – he's

40

finished his studies. My daughter's in Switzerland. And I assure you," she added with a smile, "if this is what you want to hear, they neither go in for drugs, nor wear jeans."

We laughed.

"And they're not trendy Communists either, I presume," I couldn't help remarking.

"No. But I wouldn't hold it against them if they were. Not at their age."

I invited her to dance.

3

Paul Ludovico Veronese was waiting for us in the box.

"You must be excellent company," he said. "She usually only dances with me. Isn't that right, *cara*?"

His wife stroked his hand and they looked at one another with the smile of long-standing conspirators who have withstood the menaces of the world and for whom it is nothing but a show which they look down at from the security they have created out of love, devotion, money, courage and ingenuity.

Veronese turned to me and said softly:

"In two hours she'll be in the boot of a stolen car and the car will be dumped somewhere at the edge of the French sector. Where do you want them to leave the key? We're off to bed. But there's nothing to stop you spending the time here . . ."

I reflected for a moment. "I'll wait here. That's the simplest."

"That's what I think," said Veronese and he got up. His wife rose with him. So did I.

"If you need anything . . . you know where to find me. And come and see us before you leave Berlin. Any man my

41

wife is willing to dance with is always welcome at my table."

I watched the tiny wrinkles round his eyes and the movement of his hand as he offered it to shake, and I bowed lower than I usually do.

4

It was gone half past one; the floorshow continued with striptease spots every twenty minutes; patrons came and went. I ordered a Remy Martin and some ham, a combination which helps me to get over my early-morning fatigue.

I was alone in the box, and I felt alone with the problems surrounding the fate of Jeremy Nichols.

A major part in his predicament was played, of course, by the Soviet passport, which, according to Mottey, the German authorities had found on him. It had been issued for his trip to Odessa . . . all well and good. Why had he kept it on him and not destroyed or returned it? That was against the rules. No one likes issuing false passports and they are always assumed to be used on a short-term basis only. What reason could Nichols have had – I ruled out carelessness – other than thinking he might be forced to use it again? What had taken him to Odessa? That I would never know – the British wouldn't tell me. I would never be able to see all the cards of my own side. For them I was a mercenary, a hired agent, nothing more.

I thought of Queeney, the head of the whole section. My meeting with him had been fairly brief. Queeney was a smallish man; his hair kept falling over his forehead and his light-blue eyes appeared to be mocking the whole world. He stammered slightly and had a liking for Italian wine. We had sat in his club in Mayfair; it was midday, and I had already completed the financial negotiations and the overall terms of the contract with Bride, the head of the German section. The fact that he had introduced me to Queeney was an honour of sorts and, at the same time, it revealed how concerned the British were about the entire affair.

For two days I had been through a kind of briefing with Bride; all very polite, of course. I had made contact with him in Hamburg that Spring, through a young British agent to whom I had been of some small assistance. Bride did not mention the matter. My having a British passport (Gonzales had bought it from a corpse somewhere) amused him.

"If there's trouble," he assured me in a grave voice, "we'll naturally insist it belongs to a corpse."

"Would you rather I had a different passport?"

"Oh no . . . this one's perfectly all right. As long as there's no trouble, you can be British. Why not?"

Then he filled me in on Nichols. Addresses, principal contacts, bank account . . . but not a word about the Soviet passport. Why not? Before I met Nichols' wife to learn something about his habits, I had to be inspected by Queeney.

"He wants to keep tabs on the operation," I had been told by Bride, who was more than halfway to retirement, knew the world, and saved his affection for his dog.

Queeney chatted to me in a jocular sort of way, as if he were trying to camouflage both the importance of his position and the importance of our meeting.

"So . . . hm . . . Gonzales . . ." he said. He had a rather ingratiating stammer. "And you've been working for him for . . . er . . ."

"Fifteen years," I said.

"Ah yes . . . of course . . ." No doubt he would read

43

Bride's report, even though Bride had scrupulously respected my condition that there would be no burrowing into details about the Gonzales outfit, and that the debriefing – the "interview" as they called it – would be concerned solely with my own role.

"Mr Bride assured me that I can deal semi-officially with representatives of the German authorities," I said.

"Yes, you can. We'll confirm that if they ever ask. But don't bank too much on them. They're convinced Nichols is a Soviet agent. They say they've got cast-iron evidence. They wouldn't say what that is, because it's a matter of national security." He grimaced. "Part of the 'evidence' is that the Russians want to do a swap for him."

"Are you absolutely sure Nichols isn't a double agent?"

Queeney gestured with a flourish reminiscent of the final hand movement of a virtuoso pianist who has just finished playing Rachmaninoff.

"I'm not sure of anything. On principle. But I haven't got the slightest reason for believing he is. No, I don't believe it and I do trust Nichols."

"Macmillan trusted Philby . . ." I objected.

"I'm not a Prime Minister who's scared of the House of Commons. I'm an intelligence officer," Queeney replied.

"All right. Can I use any means available?"

"Yes. Any at all. We expect you to."

"Do you want him alive?"

He raised his eyebrows. "How else?"

But he understood, the sly fox. I did not bat an eyelid. We didn't either of us bat an eyelid, so after a long moment I said:

"Suppose we get a situation like this: I can't get Nichols out and he's been handed over to the Russians or the East Germans . . . would you prefer him to be dead?"

"You must do everything and anything to get him out alive."

"You understood my question."

He looked me in the eye a little angrily. Suddenly he had lost his stammer.

"Get him out. At all costs. By any means. If he's exchanged, he's a dead man. But they'll make him talk first. That would be bad for us. If that happens we'll give him the DSO."

We stared at each other.

"If I said I wouldn't like to be a British agent, I expect you'd say I was being sentimental," I muttered after a while.

"We do and will trust you," said Queeney loftily. "We know you could make the whole business easier for yourself."

"In such a way that he'd get his DSO posthumously?"

"Yes. But we believe you won't do that."

"No. I won't do that, except as a last resort. But I'll need some first-rate marksmen at my disposal, just in case. I'm not good enough myself."

"You'll have at your disposal absolutely everything that *we* have at *our* disposal. But try to get by without it. Deliver him to us. Anywhere. At the Consulate, in the street, in Munich, Berlin or Hamburg. We'll go anywhere in Germany to fetch him. But he mustn't cross the line."

— V —

The private life of
Jeremy Nichols

Dovehouse Street, where Bride took me, is a longish, fairly narrow street in Chelsea. Nichols' house is opposite a hospital, and Bride remarked:

"It's quiet here."

He had not been keen to bring me, but it was one of my conditions. I wanted to know as much as possible about the man I was supposed to pull out of the mess he was in.

The door was opened by a pleasant blonde woman, who might have been a little over thirty-five and looked eternally young. When she saw Bride her face fell.

"Mrs Nichols . . . May we come in?" and when she nodded he said, "This is Mr Therrick, a colleague. We'd be very grateful for a word with you."

She led us into the living-room. The fireplace had been replaced with an electric fire and there were tall bookcases on either side of it. The carpet was light-coloured, the walls papered, and there was a wide window overlooking a small garden. Nichols had a nice home, a nice wife. From upstairs came the sound of children's voices.

"Caroline has two children," said Bride, when Mrs Nichols had gone out to make coffee. He did not sit down. "I'll leave you here for an hour. Then I'll come and pick you up." He explained this to Mrs Nichols, and she nodded a little uncertainly.

46

"Have you any news?" she asked me once we were on our own. She masked perfectly the tension that lay hidden behind her words. She had very fair skin and did not use make-up. She was a woman who lived for her husband and her children.

"I'm going to get some," I said. "I'm sorry I can't tell you anything encouraging, except that I hope to get your husband out of this nasty situation."

I didn't know just how much she knew of what I had called a 'nasty situation'. Bride had made it clear that I was free to ask questions, but not to offer information.

I wasted the first ten minutes in polite soundings. She was not forthcoming: "What do you actually want to know?" and "After all, I don't know anything about my husband's work . . ." and so on. It took a while before she grasped that I really was only interested in the paraphernalia, the details, of their home life. When she did understand, she took offence.

"First you get him into a mess, and then you come and ask what he has for breakfast!"

"I understand how you feel. I fully understand. But if I'm to help him . . . could I see some photos of him . . . ?"

I had one photograph that Bride had given me – I had to recognise the man I was faced with either getting out of jail or killing! But I could do with seeing more – and using memories is the best ploy for getting round someone.

She reluctantly produced one album but, as we leafed through it, she mellowed and began to explain that this was when he was a boy, that was when they first met in Sussex, this one is his parents, this was when they were in the Bahamas together, the pound was still worth something in those days, terrible what's happening today, Labour will be the ruination of the country.

The impression of Jeremy Nichols was of a tall, slim, well-educated Englishman, in good health, brought up in comfort with good parents and a good wife. There was nothing at all about him that marked him out as an intelligence agent, indeed as one of the best the British had in friendly Germany.

"At one time I used to travel with him, but since the children were born and now they're growing up . . . Jeremy wanted them to go to English schools and grow up in England, and because he couldn't be here all the time, I had to . . ."

I could well imagine the loneliness of months on end, sometimes two or three, without her husband. He would come home, for a few days, for a week, but then he would be off again. And when he did come home, he had to be out a lot, at meetings, and in the evenings various men, men Jeremy Nichols called colleagues, would come to the house, and he would shut himself up in the study with them. It was obvious to me that life with him had not been much fun. Had she been unfaithful to him? Did they have some sort of understanding? Or – like many English wives – did she see sex as an occasion to make her husband happy rather than as a need of her own?

I studiously avoided this area, of course.

"He came home once every six weeks or so, sometimes more often. Usually for a week, sometimes only for four days. Occasionally I went to see him in Basle while the children's grandmother looked after them."

She paused, then said: "Will you help him?"

What was I supposed to say? I had seen how he lived. Or at least how he lived one part of his life. It was very different from anything I would have imagined.

"My husband is not a Russian spy!" she blurted out when I did not reply.

"I'll do what I can," I said with conviction.

— VI —

The Commodore

The Sorrento Bar was slowly emptying. New customers were still arriving, but fewer of them. It was three o'clock. I ordered another Remy Martin, and looked around. After a while, I went to the phone and rang Mottey.

"Any news?"

"Where are you?"

"At a night-club. Have they rung you?"

"Yes. Are you coming here?"

"In about an hour. Go to bed. I'll wake you."

"I shan't sleep." It did not sound like a complaint.

I hung up and went back to my table. It was then that I saw him, I could not be mistaken. The same tall figure, the same springy step, the same carriage of the head. I caught up with him.

"Theo . . ." he said. Nothing ever moved him, he was truly unflappable. That was part of his image.

The Commodore. No one knew his name. In his time he had had any number of passports, dozens of names, many wives, scores of mistresses. He must have been well over fifty, but he looked ten years younger; he had the face of an ageing Don Juan in a B film, with the bearing of a *nouveau riche*. He knew the top people in Germany — lawyers, industrialists, politicians. He was received by them all, he had information for them all, but no one could boast of knowing much about him. His shortened biography would make comic reading: he had been the lover of a cigarette factory owner in Hamburg; he had driven for Auto-Union racing cars; he gained access to the Dutch Court through one of its dominant members; and he knew as much about horse-breeding as if he had been a horse. And, of course, now and again he even had a tip for Gonzales.

"Commodore," I said with a smile and held out my hand.

Then in unison we said:

"What are you doing here?"

We smiled and he said:

"I'm not here alone. Would you care to join us? Or are you here . . . on business?"

I hesitated, but then I shrugged. "On business. I've got problems. Perhaps you can help me."

"By all means. Can you give me an advance?"

"Of course. How much?"

"Let's say five hundred marks, if that's not too much, for listening."

I made out a cheque, because he knew it would be covered and I knew that he based his reputation and his contacts on his ability to keep his mouth shut. No information pedlar I knew was as reliable as the Commodore. Perhaps that's why he is still alive – he could be useful to anyone some day.

And so the Commodore lived on. He wasn't one of the jet set; he was still with the café society, moving between Vienna, Berlin, Amsterdam and The Hague. Now and again he would pop over to Washington and at other times to Rome. He knew the whereabouts of the Nazis, he knew the whereabouts of the Israeli agents, he knew who was where and who was who, and the only ones he despised and would have no truck with were the Palestinians. But he had good contacts in Egypt.

"You've heard about the arrest of one of the British?"

He smiled, and took me by the arm to a box where a very beautiful half-caste girl and two elderly gentlemen were sitting. He leaned towards them and said:

"Please excuse me for ten minutes." Then he took me by the arm again and asked where I was sitting.

We settled down and he lowered his voice.

"I've heard about the arrest of someone who worked for the Soviets. Is that supposed to be the same thing?"

"I dare say," I said. I could not imagine how this man, who looked like the routine card-sharper at the annual ball of the local nobs in Baden-Baden, could possess qualities so far in excess of his appearance. He was a man of many parts. He could discuss poetry with such enthusiasm that I had once suspected him of being a poet himself. He would remain an enigma to the end of his days.

"If it is the same thing, just carry on; I do know a little about it."

I did not mention Nichols by name, but explained that I needed to know something about him and something about his contacts. And something about the people from the Sonderabteilung.

"Well?" I asked when I had finished.

"Two thousand," he said, "will buy you the telephone number of Colonel Koerner's flat, his address in Hamburg, where he is at present, and a few snippets about your hero. And I'll throw in a background note on the Barthels affair."

Barthels was a well-known politician.

I made out the cheque.

2

When the Commodore spoke, it was as though he were flicking the dust off ancient secret service files and at the same time mixing a cocktail for an eighteen-year-old at her first ball: he relished words, he painted with words, yet the message remained clear.

Significantly, he spoke of Nichols in the past tense. He described him as an elegant, educated tramp among the secret services. Popular and reliable, with a sort of boyish curiosity and having apparently professional contempt for the Social Democrats – which might well have been the Commodore's own contempt.

We sat in the Sorrento Bar, there in Veronese's box, just the two of us, parasites on the history of the world and the lives of our contemporaries – he the cunning cynic, steeped in the colours of the world and staring at reality as if it were a mirror of everything he had failed to achieve in life, and I, waiting for the key to a flat in Berlinerstrasse and for confirmation that the wife of a British diplomat was in the boot of a stolen car (would they have put her clothes on?), waiting for a change in my life which would never come; and somewhere in Germany the fate of Jeremy Nichols, still ticking over . . . there we sat and talked as if time had stood still. I sensed that by the time I took my leave of the Commodore, the scenario would be even more complicated and, worse, even more real, and it would be a nice dollop of mud for the news agencies of the powers concerned to start slinging.

"Koerner will probably never deal with you direct," the Commodore continued. "He just pulls the strings and cultivates his image of a great hunter of Eastern agents. Most of them get quietly expelled. The Ostpolitik does make certain demands." He thought that wonderfully funny.

I took down the phone number and the address. The Commodore then treated me to a description of Colonel Groller making out an arrest warrant.

"They're great pals, Koerner and Groller," he added.

"What's the name of the lady Nichols used to siesta with?"

"Susanne Piermont." He laughed again his soft chuckle. "Susie has a tremendous clientèle. She does her best to see they never meet, but they still do. Nichols seems to have visited the lady in the afternoon, and Barthels shortly after him. Barthels hasn't got much time. They soon came to an agreement. They decided there was no point in trying to split the three hours of her time between them when they could spend the three hours all together."

I raised my eyebrows. "Do you mean . . ."

"Precisely." He grinned with satisfaction at my surprise.

"Barthels," he went on, "knew Nichols' private ways just as intimately as Nichols knew Barthels'. It had been going on for some time. Susanne Piermont apparently found things quite satisfactory. Barthels probably paid more and Nichols made it up by his performance."

"And if I were to ask you, Commodore, how you know all this, what would your answer be?"

"The usual one."

"The source of the information cannot be revealed."

"Correct."

I imagined Susanne Piermont having a peep-hole in her flat, and the Commodore having a key, so that he could be the third party. I did not say as much, of course.

"Does the German secret service know about it?"

"It's possible. Is Nichols married?"

"I don't know," I said.

"You do know," said the Commodore. "But be that as it may, I hope my information is of some use to you." He knew full well that it was.

I mentioned photographs.

He smiled. "The cheque for two thousand you've given me was for information."

But he did give me his phone number and address and

53

the phone number of Susanne Piermont. Then he told me how I might meet Barthels. He said that Barthels was keeping up his visits even though his partner was missing. Then he stood up, and we shook hands.

He slipped out of the box, a slim, superannuated ghost, burdened with the knowledge of the intimacies of his fellow-men, the lasting allure of women, the ambition of men and the money in their bank accounts.

I reflected. Oscar Mottey was waiting for me in Pariserstrasse, Veronika was at the Intercontinental sleeping the peaceful sleep of her father's daughter, and Barthels was probably asleep too, not knowing that soon I would begin to blackmail him.

Then one of the doormen entered the box and without a word placed an envelope on the table.

It contained a key and a small piece of card on which, in pencil, were the letters "O.K."

The band was having a break and the pianist was tinkering with *Misty*.

— VII —

A predicament

The voice on the phone was guarded.

I propped myself up on the pillows and glanced at my watch. It was half past nine.

"Is that Mr Therrick?"

"Yes, speaking," I said, half-asleep; I had arrived at the hotel at six in the morning. I had asked to be woken at eleven.

"I want to talk to you."

"Nice of you, I'm sure. Who are you?"

"The name wouldn't mean anything to you. Can you come down to the vestibule?"

"No, I'm in bed and I haven't had any breakfast yet."

By then I was wide awake.

"I can wait . . . shall we say half an hour?"

"Okay. But you must promise not to spoil my breakfast."

The man managed a slight laugh. Or that was what it was meant to sound like.

"In half an hour then."

He hung up.

I got up and staggered into the bathroom. I had a shave and inspected my face with disgust. I'm getting fat. And old. The rain is already falling on my grave, wherever it is.

As I dressed, the phone went again.

"I am missing you, old thing," said Veronika.

"I'm just going down to have breakfast with someone very nasty," I told her. "We might be able to meet after that . . . for a moment. I'm afraid I shan't have much time today."

"I intend to join you in the dining-room."

"Don't do that. Sit in a corner somewhere. I've got business to discuss and don't want you there."

"Will you come and sit with me afterwards?"

"Of course. For a moment."

I heard a little squeal and she hung up. One fun-loving girl. The mirror was right: I was getting old.

2

The dining-room was half-empty. No one approached me in the vestibule so I sat by a window and ordered breakfast. The man who came up to my table was wearing a brown suit that had seen better days, a tie a shade too gaudy and probably signed by Yves Saint-Laurent. His face was round, unwieldy; the eyes – brown, nondescript, full of water and blankness – looked at my chest; and his voice was obscure, as if he had spent three days bawling. He was very shabbily manicured.

"Can I sit down?"

"By all means."

He didn't speak until the waiter had deposited coffee and rolls.

"How long are you going to stay in Berlin, Mr Therrick?"

"What's that to you?"

He hinted a smile. A feeble hint. This man had no sense of humour. He had spoken in English, but he was German.

"I haven't come here to argue."

"Hadn't you better tell me who you are?"

"I've already told you my name wouldn't mean anything to you. But we know you."

"I don't like 'we's'. Speak for yourself."

He jerked his shoulders, as if trying to shed some burden.

"We'd be glad if you left."

"Mr Whoever-you-are, what the hell d'you take me for?"

Of course, I guessed the man knew what he was talking about, but he wasn't being very subtle.

"Nothing. My job is just to tell you that. We'd be glad if you left. Today." He coughed and reached inside his breast pocket to take out an air ticket. "It's in your name," he added. "London. Or anywhere else, that's up to you. Lufthansa will gladly change it to Paris or Vienna."

I had a good look at the ticket. "Mr Therrick" was written on it.

"You from the Red Cross?"

"Just take the ticket," the man said. "Take it and no nonsense, all right?"

"Is that all you have to tell me?"

"No. Two more things. If you don't take this one you'll have to pay your own air fare. That's the second item."

"And the third?"

"Not long ago you were in Hamburg. Remember who you went to see there and what you were doing. We know about it."

The Germans had been negotiating with some Americans about enriched uranium, and it was then that I had made contact with Mr Bride's young agent.

"Provocation gets nowhere with me," I said sadly, since I knew it was true. That too is a sign of getting old.

"Get out," the man said in German. "Get out of Berlin, get out of Germany, while there's time. You're not wanted here."

"You can tell your masters that you've given me the message; I'll be paying my own air fare when I need to, you can keep this ticket, and if you've nothing else to tell me, then please go."

The man looked at me in dismay for a few seconds, then rose. Reluctantly he picked up the air ticket and said:

"As you wish. I've said what I came to say."

"You've said what you came to say."

He turned and left, the slight, stooping errand-boy of someone somewhere in the wings, someone with rather more lead in their pencil.

3

I lit a cigarette. This was no joke. True, it was a clumsy effort but the fact remained that the day after I had arrived someone already knew about me.

I had enough experience not to waste time worrying who it might be. In my profession these things either come out in time, or not at all, and it's generally better if it's the latter. I just had to accept the facts that someone knew of me and that I was not part of his plans.

There was no question of my flying out.

The whole episode had spoiled my appetite. I lit another cigarette and considered. When I had been to see him earlier that morning Mottey had clearly said that London had confirmed my authority, that the order had been given to put me in contact with another agent, and, finally, that it was held necessary to declare a state of increased caution. Mottey did not elaborate on what that meant in terms of British practice, but I could pretty safely assume that all their agents would start "sleeping" except the one Mottey would put me in contact with today at midday. I decided to tell Mottey to get me a pistol. I stubbed out my cigarette and went to join Veronika.

Keeping half an ear on her bright chatter I could still hear Mottey thanking me. He had tried to be as off-hand as possible, but he meant it. Not even in the small hours could you have guessed how upset he was at the death of his unfaithful wife.

"I don't think you'll have any difficulties. But you'll have to report her missing," I'd said.

"I'll wait a day or two. When they ring from the Mission I'll say she's gone to spend a few days with her parents in Ireland. And then I'll act very surprised that they don't know anything."

"Didn't you go with her to the airport?"

"No. She took an early morning charter flight and didn't wake me."

"As you say."

I gave him the two numbers – Koerner's and Susanne Piermont's.

"Can you get these tapped?"

"Yes, not easy, but yes. Can you tell me whose numbers they are?"

"The Munich one is Colonel Koerner's office. The Berlin one belongs to a call-girl. I want reports daily."

"I'll do my best."

Then we agreed to meet at midday and I left him, the widower no one must know him to be.

"So do you like the theatre then?" Veronika asked.

"Sometimes," I said. "Usually only when I have a good dinner promised for afterwards. There's nothing as enjoyable as a good dinner after a mediocre play. In good company."

Veronika had started to get a bit high-brow but I let her prattle on.

I'm going to need that pistol, I was thinking.

4

At eleven o'clock I excused myself, promising Veronika I would ring her that evening, and went to my room. I packed my cases and rang to have my bill prepared.

I went through the vestibule at a hard canter and joined the porter with my suitcase and grip beside a waiting taxi.

"Tempelhof," I said and was driven off. Now and again I looked back. It was very hard to tell whether anyone was following. The cars behind kept changing.

At Tempelhof I had my bags taken to the departures hall and then put them in the left-luggage office. Then I went out and headed for the taxis standing in a long queue. Mercedes and Opels. I jumped into the one at the front and told the driver to go to the Reichskanzlerplatz as fast as he could. I could see a taxi following us, but I was not over-concerned about it. I know it takes time to shake off a tail and that there are ways and means. Mere routine. I don't enjoy it especially, but I'm quite good at it. At Reichskanzlerplatz I got out and ran into the U-bahn station. I hovered around on the platform for a while and only jumped onto the train at the last minute, went one stop to the Kaiserdamm, got out just before the doors closed and ran across Riehlstrasse to the Witzleben Park.

I was alone.

I walked round the lake and arrived at the hotel Am Lietzen See.

It's a small hotel by the water's edge, one that had often been my refuge before. The only problem was my papers. Here I wasn't known as Mr Therrick.

But it was a stranger at the reception desk and he took the hundred marks without a word, entered the name George Miller and that was that.

"My bags are at the airport," I said. I handed him forty marks and the left-luggage ticket.

Then I went to ring Mottey from a phone-box outside the hotel.

"Where are you? We're waiting."

"We can't talk. Take a walk outside the house. I'll pick you up two hundred yards from the entrance," I said and rang off.

Nothing was certain any more. I couldn't know where the leak was. I had to reorganise the whole system. I had to go underground.

5

The taxi drew up in Pariserstrasse and I had no alternative but to wait for them to reach me. The other man was corpulent and walked with a slight waddle. I let them come right up to the car and made sure they could see me, but I did not move a muscle to show I might care for their company. And so, without a vestige of recognition, they strolled on for a few more minutes. No one was following them. There might, of course, have been some binoculars at one of the windows.

I opened the taxi door, and they got in.

"Witzleben Park," I told the driver.

No one spoke.

That was awkward, because the taxi driver would remember us, but it was better than letting him realise that none of us was German – because the man who had come with Mottey was certainly anything but German. Close up I could see he had laughing ironical eyes; he was dressed with taste and for the morning, in a cashmere jacket and a brown-striped shirt. His handshake was brief, firm and reassuring: 'I know the rules, my friend,' was what that handshake said.

"It's going to rain," said Mottey as we left the taxi and we went into the park.

"This is Donald Peccarie, and this is Therrick," said Mottey at last.

We exchanged nods.

The park was practically deserted, with just the odd person using it as a short cut to Fischerplatz. We walked slowly, three gentlemen with time on their hands.

"What's going on?" Mottey asked.

I gave them a brief account of my morning meeting.

"D'you suspect anyone?" Mottey asked.

"No," I replied simply.

"Could you tell the man's accent?"

"He was German. From the North maybe."

No one spoke for a while.

Then Mottey said: "They've started tapping that girl. But with the Munich number things are a bit complicated. My man says he'll have to go to Munich himself. And even then he thinks the number will be protected."

I was annoyed. "Could it be linked to a special circuit? When shall we know?"

"Couple of days. But don't count on it. We'll do what we can. That's assuming he doesn't use a scrambler as well."

"He might not," Peccarie chipped in. "Anyway, we all live on hope."

He had a pleasant voice and knew it. He emphasised his words like a radio commentator. But the voice sounded somehow incongruous. I watched his lips. Suddenly I had the feeling he was very efficiently dubbed – was it a proof that he listened to our conversation with perfect detachment? So *that* was my new contact. Mottey was falling asleep.

We paused at the water's edge and watched a number of ducklings splashing their wings and squeaking. They had their own worries.

Mottey said, "I'll leave you here. You can make your own arrangements."

"We can," I said. "Good luck."

Peccarie gave a nod and Mottey turned and left us.

Peccarie and I gazed into the water for a moment. It was beginning to get warm, but the sky was overcast and rain was not far off.

"I'll need a pistol."

"Today?" Peccarie asked.

"Yes."

"Any preferences?"

"No."

"Silencer?"

"No, thank you."

He smiled. "Are you certain that number is Koerner's?"

"So I'm told. There's no guarantee."

He gave a sad nod as if he spent his whole life investigating solely on the basis of unconfirmed reports.

I told him where I was staying and under what name.

"D'you think they really did . . . lose you?"

"For the time being . . . definitely. But I won't stay lost for long."

Peccarie gave me his phone number, then took a key from his pocket and handed it to me.

"The flat's in Potsdamerstrasse. You'll find a scrambler there."

He added that I should take it back to the hotel and gave me the sequence of frequencies and the address. They were assuming the worst. I put the key in my pocket.

"Is Barthels in Berlin?"

"He's speaking in the Senate tomorrow. There's some uproar over it, on the other side. They say he's no business here as a member of the Federal Parliament. He couldn't care less, of course. He comes every month, for about a fortnight. Thinks his presence gives the Berliners moral support."

And Susanne Piermont some money, I thought. I told Peccarie to get anything they had on her. He told me Barthels' secretary was called Schiller and that they had a link to him. I gave him Koerner's address in Hamburg and asked if I could take a look at him there.

"He's constantly on the move. And we haven't got enough men. Still, we can give it a try. What do you want to do?"

"First, I want to hear what that girl says on the phone and find out when Barthels is alone with her. I'll need plenty of leverage for dealings with Koerner. At one time Barthels worked in the Ministry of Interior."

"That was some years ago," said Peccarie in a voice that made it sound as if I was talking about horse carriages parading under the lights of Unter den Linden. "No hope there anymore. Koerner's Sonderabteilung is something new. For the first time the Germans are making a sound job of something. Since the days of the Abwehr and the Sicherheitsdienst, that is."

"But he'll know someone there, "I said bluntly. "He'll have to."

Peccarie nodded again, indicating satisfaction, I thought. There could be no doubt he would be reporting on me to London.

"Can I use the flat whenever I want?"

"Yes. I have the only other key. Where do you want to play over what we've taped?"

"At the flat."

"Good. I'll pop in this afternoon with what we've got on Barthels and the Piermont girl. I'll be back at seven with the pistol. Is that okay with you?"

I gave him my hand.

He shook it, briefly, in a matter-of-fact way.

Then off he went in the direction of Neuekantstrasse – roly-poly, polite, calm, taciturn.

— VIII —

The network

The flat was very near the Wall. I wasn't pleased that its key also fitted the main entrance to the house, though in Germany this is quite common especially in modern blocks of flats. I felt exposed, as if these two rooms with bath and kitchenette, put at my disposal by British Intelligence, were open to the public. But doubtless it only *felt* like that.

I found the scrambler at once, next to the telephone. I stowed it in my attaché case and spent the whole afternoon reading through the two files. Barthels' file was comprehensive, describing his career, his wife and children, the schools they had gone to or were still attending, his interests, his taste. There was detailed information about his tailor and each of his servants. The file ran to over fifty pages and was certain to be of local origin – they probably had a good deal more in London.

The other file contained just two pages of text and some photographs and newspaper clippings. Susanne Piermont had had a short career as a fashion model, then photographer's model, later a few porno and sex films to her credit, as it were, and then she had set up on her own. She was twenty-six, a brunette, with high cheekbones, large lips, and eyes that seemed permanently amazed at the size of a penis. Her breasts were shaped for the gourmet. I mused sadly that life will have it that perfect breasts always belong to those women who will never fancy me. Or to those I have to pay.

Peccarie arrived at seven o'clock on the dot. He produced a bottle of whisky and poured for both of us, then a large piece of Bierwurst and some bread.

"I'm sorry you weren't stocked up," he apologised. "We haven't used this flat for some weeks."

Then he withdrew from his case a Walther PPK, and handed me some cartridges and a shoulder holster. He watched in silence as I put it on.

"The first lot of Piermont tapes will be here about nine," he remarked casually. "I've been thinking things over. I might have something in a day or two, but by then it might be too late."

It was the first time he had tried to warn me.

"It's not serious yet," I said cheerfully. "It's just that somebody knows about me and I don't quite fit his bill. But they don't want me dead or they'd have sent someone else. They know it's the first time I've worked for you."

He nodded, the muscles of his fat face moving as if he were chewing.

"Here's Barthels' timetable for tomorrow," he said and handed me a sheet of paper.

"Where did you get it?"

"From the papers," he replied. "As the Russkies say, in Germany it's enough to read the papers and you've got everything."

"Not only in Germany," I said, but with his English tolerance he let it pass.

For a moment we felt the frustration of secret service personnel who can do nothing about the whims of their bosses.

"Do you think that whoever it is who wants you out will believe you've gone?"

"Of course not. All I want is a few days' grace to reach Koerner."

A satisfied nod, as if I confirmed his suspicions. The

question why London had hired *me* didn't bother him. He had reached the same conclusion: London wanted to keep its nose clean.

"The Foreign Office didn't object then?"

"The Consul asked for a meeting, but he had it turned down on the grounds that Nichols isn't British," said Peccarie with ill humour. "And of course criminal proceedings haven't started yet."

"D'you mean Nichols hasn't asked to see the Consul?"

"Who's to know? If he has, it was a mistake in terms of the conspiracy. It's all highly complicated: we don't even know where he's being held. The Embassy in Bonn has tried unofficially to contact several lawyers; there wasn't a word from the German authorities that Nichols needed representation. If they charged him, accused him of something . . . something could be done. But they didn't. But even then it could fall within the jurisdiction of Bonn or Frankfurt or Munich. And that's not Berlin! Berlin has its own administration and jurisdiction. Here it's the British Military Mission that is the legal authority . . . The Germans are playing it by the administrative book, and there they can outdo even the French. Here they're capable of sending a file back, right down from the Minister, if there is a dot missing from an *i*." He bit into the sausage. "The Sonderabteilung is holding Nichols and, until someone officially admits that Nichols has been arrested, Nichols will just not exist. That's the game they're playing."

"And those from the Sonderabteilung, are they all mad?"

"Koerner's acting off his own bat. Last year he managed to knock out at least twenty Soviet and East German agents. And Brandt prefers things kept quiet; he doesn't like people spoiling his Ostpolitik. He even gave up boozing because of it."

"Can you give me a reason for Koerner being such a fanatic?"

68

"Well, he probably thinks he's landed a big fish. And then he's almost certainly got someone on the other side he wants to swap. It doesn't matter two hoots to him that Nichols is English. All he wants is to get his own man back."

"Any idea who he is?"

"No. But we'll find out."

"Let's hope it's not too late."

"You'll try and get to Koerner?"

"Yes. But I'm no more optimistic than you are. What's he going to do for me? If he keeps turning a deaf ear, shall I threaten him with a world war?"

Peccarie almost smiled. "Then why try?"

"That's what I'm paid for, isn't it?"

Peccarie didn't respond so I went on.

"I'm trying to do the one thing that seems logical, though experience tells me not to put much faith in it. Nichols' predicament is pretty hopeless and London knows that just as well as I do. Just as well as you do."

"I thought you hadn't realised," he said with a hint of an apology. "I thought they'd sent you for appearances' sake, and that they'd chosen someone who still believes in miracles."

2

He finished off the sausage while I smoked and watched him. He must be one of those who entered the service during the war. Then there was a change of enemy; disillusion and renewed uncertainty. He must have witnessed the growth of imaginary guilt behind which the West was hiding to avoid facing reality: the fact that it was at war, whether or not it wanted to be. I thought all this had worn out Peccarie. After all, the West is a mess, and a sorry sight; importance of family shattered, education levelled to the lowest denominator, discipline gone and upbringing as well. He must also have known that the new generation would have lost the Second World War. This generation would have licked Hitler's boots.

It never crossed my mind to go into all this with Peccarie. He would have been dismayed and probably shocked. Any experienced agent, whichever side he's on, knows three things: firstly, that justice on earth does not exist and will never exist; secondly, that injustice can only be tempered if there is good education, respect for a set scale of values, and a stable family; and thirdly, that the state can afford only as much freedom for the individual as does not jeopardise its own existence.

For the most part, the so-called free countries are headed by clowns who don't like to listen to the warnings of their secret services, because to do so would be to break their promises to their electors.

3

"What are you thinking?" asked Peccarie. He glanced at his watch. "Kurt'll be here any minute with the first recording."

"D'you use local people mostly?" I asked.

"Yes. Like everybody else."

Carefully he wrapped up the remnant of Bierwurst and put it in his case. Then he had a gulp of whisky, as if it were Perrier, and lit a cigarette.

"The Ambassador has worked out some sort of Note. Sober, very, very sober. They're at their best writing Notes. Something on the lines that, as the representative of the

United Kingdom, he has no grounds for the assumption that Jeremy Nichols' case does not involve a British citizen, and on the other hand that he has every reason to believe that it is all an unfortunate misunderstanding." He looked at me as if he had just backed a favourite and won. "The F.O. doesn't officially acknowledge the existence of the Nichols case, and certainly won't feel like defending Nichols by saying he was spying for Her Majesty in the land of the Hun. And poor old NATO is gasping as it is, so you can't make things even worse for it, can you? On top of that, our Prime Minister is having problems with the miners, in fact there's trouble all along the union front, and we know whose hands they're in, and there's the Common Market business. What's Nichols against all that? He only matters to us and the Ambassador knows it, and until he gets direct orders he won't lift a finger."

"And he won't get them," I said. "Or they wouldn't have sent me here."

"No, he won't get them," Peccarie concurred and asked if I didn't have at least some vague notion of what Nichols might have done to upset the Germans.

"It's the first time anything like this has happened," he added.

But I hadn't the faintest idea. In that respect London was being as close as an oyster. Poor bloody Nichols, I thought, not for the first time, nor for the last.

4

We were brought the first tape at nine, covering twelve noon to six in the afternoon, eight calls in all, two from the flat and the rest incoming.

A lot of names were dropped in the incoming calls.

Peccarie jotted them down and I knew he would have them checked and pass them on to me next evening, annotated where possible.

There was one short significant call.

– Hallo?

– Sigi. How are you, darling?

I raised my eyebrows and Peccarie nodded.

– I knew I'd be hearing from you. When did you get here?

– I'll perhaps come tomorrow, that okay? At six?

He wasn't going to go into explanations.

– I'll be waiting . . .

– Okay, 'bye.

– Tschüss.

Then a click.

Peccarie raised his blue-green eyes.

"That's him."

"Can we have it once more?" I said.

I switched on the light and lit a cigarette.

Barthels' voice sounded calm, almost flat. He might have been talking to the switchboard. Not a trace of libido.

"Again," I said. I wanted to learn that voice by heart.

Peccarie rewound the tape and played it again and again. It never occurred to him to ask why I wanted to keep on listening to this banal little exchange. He was used to keeping his thoughts to himself. I wondered just how concerned he was about Nichols' fate. I wasn't going to ask him if he knew Nichols – there's no point in asking the English too many questions.

We went back through the rest of the calls, but there was nothing to indicate that the Piermont girl was expecting anyone that evening.

A woman verging
on disquiet

It's always as well to have references. In life a reference –
that is, a good reference – is one of the most important
things. I had one. And it was very much a matter of
life.

The phone rang for a while before she answered.

It was the voice I knew, a trifle distant.

"Don't ask me my name. I'm an orphan in Berlin and
I've got to see you right away."

"I'm not particularly interested."

She had to be pushed, and quickly.

"Jeremy," I said. "Jeremy."

She came to the door wearing a tiger-skin bolero and a
long nightdress.

I gave her the smile that we over-forties assume belongs
to men of the world but which really conveys no more
than the anxiety that we are no longer twenty-five.

She had no sense of humour and she had a ghastly
modern hallway with glass and metal furniture, which dis-
tracted me for a moment from her neckline.

The sitting-room was a medley of the same metal and
glass, but here and there it was set off by that coloured
fraud that goes by the name of abstract painting. I wondered if Berlin whores were beginning to intellectualise.
Or only Susanne? She was now displaying a slender ankle

from beneath her gilded nightdress. I put on the noble expression of the slightly hungry client.

"You really are like the one Jeremy raved to me about," I said.

"Which one?" the dear thing asked.

"Might I ask your fee?"

She smiled as if to say, 'Good lad, that's the way to talk.'

"It depends on the services you require. What will you drink?"

She poured me out a whisky and sat me down on a divan with my back to the worst of her pictures.

"I wasn't actually expecting anyone today."

"Surprise is the unrusting weapon from my tenderest years. Every time I was picked up by someone I didn't care for I would piss myself."

"You horrid little boy," she said. "So that's what you like . . . And who's to piss on whom?"

I threw her a glance.

"When did you last see Jeremy?"

"Oh, it's some time ago. He didn't tell me about you. What's your name anyway?"

"Call me darling."

"Okay, *mein Schatz.*"

"And Jeremy?"

"What's up with him?"

"That's just what I'd like to know."

She had no idea I was trying to flush her out. She got up and began parading about the room. Her buttocks rolled like the swell of the Pacific.

"You know, I only have very select clients. Only the best references. You haven't actually got any references," she went on, and it sounded as if I were such a fabulous bloke that she didn't really mind. Provided I didn't want to pay by cheque . . .

I knew that what I was really after from her would call for some foreplay.

"Show me your thighs," I said.

2

She unwound herself from my embrace and asked if I wanted a cigarette. I shook my head and carried on getting my breath back. Where were the days when I wanted a cigarette *afterwards*? Now I would have preferred a massage and being fanned.

We ended up on the carpet and before we'd finished it cost me a lot in concentration. At my age I wasn't greatly interested in this mathematically mature bitch, who was too young to put oneself at her mercy, and too old to give one the delicious sensation of corrupting innocence. Her hand movements had the refinement of the professional, she kept her lips apart as if she were being photographed and, when she kissed, the customer might feel as if he were Cary Grant. But I've never had that experience and very likely never will. So the feeling I had was that I was sacrificing the remnants of my manhood for the glory of Her Majesty, and my consolation was that it was she who was paying the 700 marks. Only now did it occur to me, more or less exhausted, that the payment was coming from the pockets of Britain's wretched taxpayers.

"Do you think that taxes can destroy the development of a country like England?" I asked Susanne, once I'd got my breath back.

She goggled at me. She can't ever have been asked a question like that, certainly not in these circumstances.

"Oh, it doesn't matter what you think." I waved the matter aside and let my head fall back on the carpet.

75

"You had other things to talk about a minute ago," she remarked.

"You can't blame me! You were squeezing my testicles!"

She groped through her long bronze hair, her breasts jutting, slightly reminiscent of the maiden on the rock at Copenhagen, proud of her power and indifferent to the future.

I had paid in advance.

"Was it nice?"

I couldn't pretend it hadn't been. But I didn't want to tell her I'd had to imagine her pimp lying there between her nervous thighs before I could finish.

I drew her towards me. I really do enjoy paying a woman compliments straight afterwards. Not many men have the gift, but it'll work on any woman!

"You've got a fabulous body and such wonderful skin," I began. "Every movement you make is like the movement of a beast of prey that fascinates its victim first. I bet men are only too eager for you to devour them." When she snuggled up close, flattered and coquettish, I went on, "And if you don't want me to smash your face in you'll start singing. What does Barthels like?"

3

In the end she even gave me some photos. She had gone through the whole range of emotions: first, she pretended incomprehension and outrage, then came anger when I hit her, tears when I gave her a kick in the liver (only a little one – it would have been much worse if it had been her pimp), and finally genuine anxiety when I tied her up with the cord of her dressing-gown and made her believe I was going to brand her breasts with a cigarette.

If I hadn't made love to her first, the shock wouldn't have been so complete. But there are things that either have to be done brutally or you might as well not bother.

Now she was sitting in an armchair, her hands bound, and I laid the prints out in front of her on the carpet. The pictures were very clear and sharp. In most of them, Barthels was alone, generally in a state of erotic ecstasy. Only a few showed her hand or mouth, but Barthels' face was always visible. There were some thirty pictures.

"How long did it take you to make them?"

She said nothing. I kicked her below the left knee-cap.

"You're not from the police . . . are you?" she asked uncertainly.

"You're hoping to get off without a spell in the cooler, eh? But then the police wouldn't have much evidence. You know that too. They told you that. How many of them were there?"

"Ouch," she yelped when I gave her another kick. I knew that after the first surrender she was now gathering strength for some tactical opposition. She was trying to fathom what I wanted, where I was vulnerable and whether there was any hope of doing a deal.

"Listen here, sweetie-pie," I said in the vilest Berlin accent I could muster, "if you don't want your piss-hole jiggered for life quit thinking and get shitting like you had cholera. I'm not from the police, and there's much worse. How many of you were working on it?"

"Just Jens."

"And you."

"Yes."

"Got a two-way mirror somewhere?"

"Yes. In the bedroom."

"How long did it take you to make up this collection?"

"Several weeks . . . Jens said it's a bit tricky getting everything right."

"When was the last time?"

"About three months back."

"Where are the photos with Jeremy?"

"Jeremy?"

I kicked her.

"Where?"

"But there aren't any with Jeremy . . . Jens wasn't interested."

I was certain she wasn't lying.

"Does Barthels know about it?"

"No. He doesn't."

"Jens started by telling you you could make money out of it."

"Yes."

"And then he changed his mind, eh?"

"How d'you know that?"

I kicked her.

"Answer me, you cunt. Why did he change his mind?"

"He said we had to wait."

"What for? Till Barthels became Chancellor?"

"Yes."

I lit a cigarette. Who was this Jens? Was he working for himself? I looked at her. I could not afford to release her from the terror that physical violence had struck into her. Ten years before I could not have imagined doing anything like this. But now I was perfectly cool. If this was the fastest way of getting what I had to have, then so be it. Practice, instinct, and the knack. Had I found what I was after?

"How many clients have you got?"

"Eight."

"Any special cases?"

"Yes . . . two."

"Is Barthels a special case?"

"No. It all depends what . . ."

"Any photographs with other clients?"

"No."

"In a minute or two, I'm going to have a look round here. A thorough one. If I find any, I'll stub my fag out on your clit. What about it then?"

Surprisingly enough her fear did not increase. Either she was certain I wouldn't find more photos, or Jens had got them. Jens . . .

I stood closer to her.

"What time's Jens coming?"

And I gave her another kick without waiting for her answer.

She hesitated. Then she began to cry. "He'll kill me if . . ."

"What time?"

"What's the time now?"

"What time's he coming, cunt?"

"One. Maybe two."

"He always comes about then, doesn't he?"

"Yes."

"Does he ring first?"

"Yes. When I've got a client."

"So he's not going to phone today?"

"No."

"How long have you known him?"

"Three years."

"How d'you get to know him?"

"We were in several films together."

"You mean blue films?"

"Yes."

I looked at my watch. It was quarter past twelve.

"Has he got a key?"

"Yes."

"Was it he who suggested you set up on your own?"

"Yes."

"And he promised he'd marry you?"

"Yes. But he meant it."

"Naturally. What else did he promise?"

She was crying again. This time I left her to it because it had sunk in at last just how deep was the trouble she was in. It was all in her imagination, in point of fact, but she was past grasping that she could well come through unscathed except for the loss of one client, name of Barthels.

I went across to the drinks trolley and poured out a couple of brandies. I had a drink and then gave her one. It made her splutter.

"You can keep the seven hundred," I told her. "But I'll flay the hide off you if you try to warn Jens. Just let the old grey matter get to work for a change, you cow. Got it? And if I do have to shoot Jens, I'll shoot you too."

I showed her the pistol.

She stared at it wide-eyed. I sat down on the divan. She kept gazing at the pistol. Then she began to shake.

"I'm not going to hit you any more. It's your life at stake now. Have you got a bit of a clothes-line?"

4

But Fräulein Piermont had all her washing done at the laundry. I went into the bedroom and opened her wardrobe. I took out all the belts and girdles I could find.

Then I looked over the flat. The room they took the photographs from had originally been for the maid. It was furnished comfortably and the view from the peep-hole took in the bed and part of the room. A Nikon was lying on the little table next to the peep-hole.

When I went back into the sitting-room I found Susanne

unconscious. I slapped her face three times before she came round.

"Can you hear when the door of the flat opens? Think before you answer, I can't sit here aiming at that pretty little head of yours. Jens won't give anything for your corpse, and if he came in without a warning, I'd have to shoot. So, it's in your own interest for him not to surprise me. Got it, sweetheart?"

She nodded. "There's a chain on the door," she said after a moment.

"Yes, I saw it, but that's no good. Jens mightn't be alone."

"He's always alone. He's never . . ."

"Never introduced you to any of his fine pals, that it?"

"No. Yes. Never introduced any, I mean."

She was tamed at last.

I asked her a few more questions, but there was nothing else she knew. They had been using her – a poor little whore with no professional principles.

I opened the door into the hall so that I could hear Jens come in and sat down opposite Susanne. She couldn't move, the bonds were tight. Her mascara had run and there were streaks of it beneath her eyes and on her cheeks. Her body was going to show bruises here and there.

"And now, my child," I said almost kindly, "a few instructions. If Jens rings you up it goes without saying that you will speak to him as usual. If, as a result of the way you say anything, he doesn't turn up, I'll put my cigarette out where I said.

"If he calls to you from the hall, you will answer from here in a way that won't give him a hint of suspicion. Something like: 'Come here quickly, I've got something to show you.' Understood?"

"Yes," she said listlessly.

I released the safety catch on the pistol.

We settled down to wait.

— X —

Intrigue

It was five minutes past two o'clock when the door into the hall opened. Then it banged to, the chain was fitted, and I heard:

"Susie, you asleep . . . ?" It was a vulgar voice, too self-assured; and it had been drinking.

I aimed at Susanne and she called out, with a slight rasp in her voice:

"Come here quickly, Jens. I've got something to show you."

The footsteps in the hall faltered. Silence.

"Susie . . . ?"

This time the voice was full of tension. I twigged: Bunnikins didn't usually call him by his Christian name. I expect she had her own nickname for him or called him her gorgeous brute. I put the pistol to her temple and whispered:

"Cunt!"

But she didn't say a word. With women you never know. Hysteria had taken her to the brink of heroism. Or was she more afraid of Jens than of me? Not a sound from the hall.

I couldn't let things go on like this. Susanne's eyes were firmly shut, she was shaking all over, but she wasn't going to utter another word. She loved him, the cow. Several light steps took me to the half-open door into the hallway and then Susanne screamed.

A light switch clicked. The hall was in darkness.

Silence.

I dropped to my knees and let myself down onto my stomach. Then I started to wriggle towards the hall. I tried not to move the door, but I knew I would be betrayed by the rectangle of light shining through from the sitting-room. I waited.

I supposed he didn't carry a gun, but he could have a flick-knife.

Susanne sat silent. Jens was somewhere in the darkness of the hall. The situation had turned to my disadvantage. I could only wait to see what Jens would do. But he did nothing.

The seconds ticked away.

After about three minutes I heard a movement. I couldn't tell just what sort of movement, because the hall was carpeted and I had no way of knowing where Jens was – nevertheless it was the first sign that he was getting impatient. His instinct for self-preservation must have been highly developed, and by now it was obvious to him that something distinctly worrying was going on.

He must have been a good bit younger than me but he didn't have my training. And time was definitely on my side. He would not risk trying to come in; he would try to get out. That was all I knew for certain: Jens would not try to save Susanne. That is not the way with pimps.

Another minute passed.

Then I heard a bump. He must have jumped towards the door and misjudged the distance. Hectic grappling with the chain. But I was already on my feet. The door swung open. He was unlucky: the light in the passage was on. His dark silhouette was all I needed. I drove him hard into the door jamb.

The scuffle was brief, one or two jerks and then he felt my pistol against his neck. I twisted his arm back and hurled him inside. I shut the door and switched on the light. He stood in the middle of the hallway in a check overcoat, gasping for breath.

"Good evening, Jens," I said. "Shall we go in?"

2

Susanne's 'boy friend' was about thirty but life had done its work on him: he had the face of a real jail-bird, with a low forehead and broad cheekbones, which Susanne probably took as a sign that he was a 'wild 'un', pale blue eyes that could scarcely ever have read anything except the newspaper, a tiny receding chin on which he obviously had not yet taken enough blows.

There was something quizzical about his expression, and something repulsive; a combination of self-satisfied mediocrity with envy for those at the top. A real sod.

I kept a reasonable distance from him and made him sit on the floor, with his legs nicely crossed and his hands on his head, in his nasty check coat, beneath which he wore a purple shirt and a yellowish-brown tie.

The way he gazed at the naked Susanne spoke volumes. It expressed all the fury of someone whose property another has dared to touch, mixed with fear of what that property might do. What was missing from that gaze was pity.

I did not say anything. Jens would be a tougher nut to crack than Susanne, that much was clear. I sat down in one of those dreadful modern armchairs, lit a cigarette and aimed at Jens.

Then Susanne spoke quietly:

"I couldn't help it . . ."

He did not answer.

After a few minutes, when he had probably begun to think I was waiting for someone, he said:

"What d'you want?"

I said nothing.

So he said nothing either and Susanne said nothing for her part. I let ten minutes pass. Then I got up and went slowly over to him.

"Turn round," I ordered.

It took him a while, what with his legs crossed and his hands on his head. He swayed from side to side, but in the end he managed.

"Good boy," I praised him. Then I hit him lightly over the head with the pistol and jumped aside. He dropped his hands and gave a groan. Then my voice took control again: "Stay sitting, or it'll be a bullet."

I gave him a couple of kicks in the kidneys. Good ones.

"Before your friends come . . ." I remarked casually. "Just a little elementary dancing lesson, Jens."

I gave him another kick. Match of the Day, Berlin fashion.

Before long the squeals of pain gave way to soft groans.

I knew it needed time. I was tackling an unfamiliar field, and a good *mise en condition*, as the French say, was of prime importance.

After a while I stopped kicking him and sat down again.

"What d'you want from me?" he broke the silence at last.

I said nothing.

There are many theories on how to prepare someone for a speech. They take account of situation, the number of persons involved; and it is an entire science, one that cannot get by without chemistry, in which the Russians are supreme.

Being alone, I had to use the most complex version, which

needs time. While I could have knocked Jens out and bound him, that would merely have put him out of circulation for at least an hour and thus reduced the psychological impact, and then I would have had to start all over again. The only snag was that I badly needed to take a leak.

3

After soundly considering the courses open to me I decided with some reluctance to exploit the disadvantage and turn it to advantage; Gonzales had always held the view that execution should be preceded by degradation.

"I wouldn't move if I were you," I advised him and, keeping the pistol on him, I relieved myself nicely straight in his face with Susanne looking on. I rained on him from about a yard away, but I have to admit that despite the great urge I had felt at first, it cost me some effort before I got started. Once you get beyond forty the bladder doesn't work so well, I thought, watching him splutter and grimace.

Pissing on a pimp with his whore looking on is the ideal cure for a pedlar of intimate photographs.

"Right," I said, "and if you don't want to end up as a block of cement, you'll start answering questions like in school, or I'll have you taken somewhere else where they'll start the big game with your trigeminal, vertebrae and bone-marrow. That could leave permanent traces, and there'd be no more straddling your heifer. Who d'you work for?"

"Myself," he said.

"Okay, and who else?"

We were not long getting to the main item on the agenda. Everything depended on my being alert and cautious so that he could not start leading me by the nose.

"Nobody," he said, and it might have been true, but need not have been.

"Right, Sunshine, we'll have another little chat about that later, and without Susie here," I said loftily, and added, "How many girls d'you run?"

"Hm," he said, and it smacked of revolt. I jumped up and gave him a kick on the chin. He collapsed, or rather subsided, onto the carpet, and I returned to my seat.

"Right, once more," I said affably. "How many girls d'you run?"

4

The interrogation took till nearly four o'clock in the morning. Meanwhile I had been trying to decide whom to entrust Jens to. Peccarie? I certainly couldn't let him go, and anyway I was far from sure I had got everything out of him.

Jens could no longer keep his hands on his head and Susanne looked wooden. I stepped over to the telephone and told Jens he could rest his head on the divan.

I dialled the number Peccarie had given me. A woman's voice answered.

"Get me the man who gave me this number," I told her. I gave him the address and within twenty minutes I was steering Jens smartly ahead of me to open the flat door.

Peccarie looked at me and then at Jens (who once more had his hands fair and square on his head) and said good morning in German. He came in, closed the door behind him and drew a pistol. Jens footed it back to the sitting-room where I showed off the naked Susanne to Peccarie. He nodded at her, unsmiling, took off his trenchcoat and, pistol in hand, sat down.

"This guy hasn't done any talking yet," I said, still in German. "But it's draughty here."

Peccarie gave a nod and went to the telephone.

"This the only phone?"

"There's another one in the bedroom," I told him, and he went to see where it was. He came back in about five minutes and nodded again. We couldn't talk with those two there, so I just related the facts in brief and showed him the photographs.

He grabbed them, took a good look and put them to one side.

"I'll hang on to them," I said with a smile. "They're mine."

We exchanged looks. Peccarie said nothing and finally handed them to me. I wasn't doing all this just to give Queeney some stuff on poor Barthels. I was here to stop Jeremy Nichols being swapped across the Wall, and for no other purpose.

About half an hour later the bell rang and Peccarie went to the door. There were three of them, looking tough and almost merry considering it was so early.

They lifted Jens up off the carpet, handcuffed him, and bound his eyes.

Jens began squawking with fright.

I said: "As long as they bind your eyes, there's a good chance they're not going to shoot you, old son. If they were going to shoot you, they'd hardly bother with such niceties."

The three of them dragged him off, not without first treating themselves to long and thoughtful looks at Susanne.

I inspected the bathroom. No window. I started running hot water into the bath and went back to untie Susanne.

"Have a hot bath, you'll feel better, then you'd better make us some breakfast," I said and locked her in the bathroom.

Back in the sitting-room, Peccarie was smoking. He

didn't say a word, just watched me. I could read nothing from his features. He just sat there.

"How long can you keep that guy safe?"

"Long enough. Weeks. Months maybe . . . if necessary."
It sounded like a question.

"A few days," I said. "I suspect he's not just working for himself. But he might not even know it. That's the snag. He mightn't even know."

"I hope you're not taking things too far," Peccarie remarked. "Basically I don't care. London's orders are clear. But it'll block one of my flats and he'll know three of my men."

"He's no agent," I said. "Runs a few girls and someone's had him specialise on this one. Don't know who the some-one is, though."

"Any good beating him up?"

"Oh yes. Put the wind up him. Let him think he's really in the shit. Caught up in the big-time."

"And isn't he?" Peccarie returned.

I shrugged. "Maybe he's just a pimp who got big ideas and blabbed. Says he's got the negatives at home. I didn't search him."

"My lads'll see to that. Do you want them to go and have a look at his flat?"

"As soon as possible."

"Okay. And you?"

"I'll stay here. I've got to work on Miss Piermont here. Still got to get her sewn up."

"You want to see Barthels here?"

"Sure. Here and nowhere else."

He smiled. His smile was almost good-natured. Like an ageing dog, when he opens his mouth, hangs out his tongue and wags his tail – but a watch-dog still.

"Go careful with Barthels. If he finds it's us doing the stirring . . ."

"He won't find anything. Don't worry. It's not the first bit of blackmail I've done. I don't want much. But I've one request of you: London mustn't know anything about this whole business."

Peccarie grinned, then nodded.

"You can trust me. They'd only hold it against me for not taking the photographs from you. You're not going to let me have them, are you?"

"You bet I'm not," I said.

— XI —

I invite myself
to the ball

Barthels arrived dead on six. But even before that, events began to develop very fast. While I was spending the afternoon with Susanne, by now thoroughly quelled, Peccarie came back from Jens' flat. He gave me the negatives and shook his head when I suggested that they could have had copies made for their own use.

"There was no time anyway," he said. "They didn't find them till an hour ago." He looked at Susanne and turned back to me: "I want to speak to you."

"Shall I send her for the champagne?" I asked, and ordered her into the bedroom. Susanne trotted off and I sat down on the divan opposite Peccarie. He hadn't bothered to take off his coat.

"That pimp's called Baumgartner. Jens Baumgartner. My lads are still pumping him, but we probably shan't get any more out of him. He's spent some time in the army."

"Well I never . . . Since when have pimps been hatched out of the disciplined ranks of the Bundeswehr?" I whistled.

"He seems to have been contacted there by the East Germans. He's not too sure himself who they are . . . some fellow called Sichler – the name's assumed. Some girl answers the phone and says Herr Sichler's in Munich.

Anyway this Sichler first hired him as a bouncer. Then they saddled him with a girl, and then others. He was into this game before he joined the army. But they weren't interested in the army . . . He was only an ordinary rookie. What they were interested in was his sexual prowess. He can do it five times a day . . ." Peccarie grimaced somewhat wryly " . . . and they supplied him with flats which he could use. In the end he was left with Susanne and some other worthless package. He sees Sichler about once a fortnight. Baumgartner says it was Sichler's idea – to take shots of Barthels."

"Of course. Does he sense there's politics in it?"

"No. He was in for the money."

"So now you're trying to turn him round, eh?" I said.

Peccarie smirked, but what other course was open to him? They obviously wouldn't hand Baumgartner over to the Berlin police; they would take the plain man's way out. Sichler was still around and there was no need for him to find out about the nocturnal melodrama. I could well imagine the spin they'd put dear old Jens in.

But that was beside the main point; a parallel course I couldn't afford to follow. Peccarie went on ponderously:

"There's a problem."

We both knew that each of us knew what the other was thinking.

"You want to borrow those photos, right?"

Peccarie nodded.

"If Sichler wanted to see some . . ."

"Hasn't he seen them yet?"

"No."

"Does he know they exist?"

"Baumgartner says he does. But I'm not so sure. Baumgartner might have been trying to inflate his own importance . . . and price. He guessed that it wouldn't be Barthels paying, but someone else. He's not that daft."

"And so you want to put tabs on Sichler and sniff out who's behind it all, is that it?"

"Of course."

"Then why did you come back with the negatives?"

"You know as well as I do that the Nichols case comes first. If you need them for Barthels it can't be helped. I just thought a photo or two . . ."

"Aha."

He had the look of a man who knew beforehand that he would be turned down. But he had to try.

"Nothing doing," I assured him. "Barthels will get the whole lot. I feel like playing the part of a gentleman."

He nodded. He had known I'd refuse. He lit a cigarette.

"Okay, forget it then. Now, this will interest you: you caused something of a stir."

"What am I to understand by that?"

"Our Resident has been contacted by the French. Someone wants to speak to you. They didn't say who. But it's serious."

"Who contacted the Resident?"

"A liaison man from SDECE. They know you're on a solo trip for us and they know who you are."

"But I don't want to put my head above water just yet."

"Something can be arranged," said Peccarie.

"You're being suspiciously modest," I countered. "That means that it matters to you somehow. How?"

"Custom. Sometimes . . . we, sort of, cooperate. You see . . . with you not being one of us, and them knowing it. Besides, they made it clear they've got some information for you . . . I mean, there's something they don't like the look of . . . they just want a chat. One mustn't underestimate the French. I've already suggested meeting in a car . . ."

"What's the chap from SDECE called?"

"Dupont."

"Okay. Do it tonight. Pick me up here at nine. All right?"

He looked relieved. It clearly mattered to him to be on good terms with the French, even though the SDECE was not a service for which I personally would work and one which Peccarie certainly didn't admire either. We all preferred the DST, which, tough as it was, at least kept faith and didn't hire just anybody. France owed much to Wybot for putting it together.

"Anything else?"

He was silent for a moment, then said:

"Yes."

"What? Oh, come on, Peccarie, today's a queer day, isn't it? You look as if you're constipated. What's up?"

Peccarie reached inside his breast pocket. He took out a photograph. But he didn't pass it over. The look on his face betrayed considerable agitation.

"This came in the post today." Pause. "It was addressed to our man who's based at the Mission. Everyone knows he's one of ours. It's a sort of open letter-box."

"So where's the snag?"

"He gave it to Mottey and Mottey to me." He hesitated. "Unfortunately you have to know."

I reached across. Reluctantly he passed me the photograph.

It showed the revolving door at the hotel Am Lietzen See, and the man coming out was me.

"Hm," I said after a moment. "It's a bit distorted, isn't it? In real life I look younger, don't you think?"

2

Barthels was fifty-five but looked younger; balding, elegant, with blue eyes, and a half-smile of a reader of Grimm's fairy tales. A blue-grey striped suit and a silk tie, white handkerchief and shirt, a man who has come to enjoy himself – that was how he looked when I sighted him in the doorway of Susanne's flat.

He was standing there now with Susanne, his arm wound round her shoulders – Susanne silent in her negligée, he nonplussed at my presence. I was sitting on the divan and smoking. Because the door to the hall was open I had heard them exchange greetings. Susanne like the meek little lamb that she was, never opened her mouth, except to say "Come in," and she might have given him a kiss. I sat there and stared him in the eyes. The happy smile slipped from his face. I didn't speak.

"Who's that?" he asked Susanne, but she just followed her instructions:

"I'll leave you together . . . this gentleman will explain . . ." And added, a token extra: "I'm sorry . . ."

Barthels stepped into the room and I pointed mutely at the armchair opposite.

"What does this mean?" he asked.

Not even Fellini could have contrived it better; everything was working out a treat.

"Smoke?" I asked him.

He looked at me blankly. He was trying to conceal his indignation, but he still could not figure what was happening or how he should act. He had not expected to find a total stranger in the flat of his paid mistress. And her departure and my attitude plainly told him that there could be nothing pleasant awaiting him.

But he was an intrepid character and so he looked me straight in the eye and did not reply.

"Like a glass of something?" I carried on in my role of host.

"What do you want?" he asked tersely, and remained standing.

I had my speech ready, my whole course of action, but on impulse I decided on something else. I tossed him the photographs, which he deftly caught. He had a look at them, then tossed them back. His face remained unchanged.

"How much?" he demanded drily, still standing in front of the armchair.

I picked up the photographs and put them in order.

"Won't you sit down?"

"No," he said. "There's nothing for me here. Name your price. Either I pay or I don't."

Now things weren't going so smoothly. Here was a man of experience who wasn't born yesterday. I fished out a cigarette and said, as I lit it:

"Two million."

He smiled. "This might be the end of my career, but you're not getting a pfennig."

Now it was my turn to smile. "All right then. Not a pfennig. You really won't sit down now you've just saved yourself two million?"

He looked at me as if weighing me up and decided to sit. I couldn't quite guess who he took me for, but most probably he thought I was the one who organised the taking of the photographs.

"First, don't resist my congratulations," I said. "For a man in your situation your behaviour is remarkable." I meant it sincerely. The discovery that he has been photographed in the most intimate positions comes as a shock even to the greatest cynic. He hid his anger and shame superbly. "I am neither the one who photographed you, nor the one who ordered it. I am someone else altogether and I shall blackmail you very gently. There is even the chance you may thank me in the end."

He put his hands in his pockets and waited.

"I'm glad," I went on, "you aren't asking me who I am.

That I'm not German you've spotted already. Allow me to tell you first what has happened."

He listened without stirring. I told him briefly about Jens and Susanne.

When I'd finished he asked:

"Was it this Jens who was after the two million?"

"That was just a joke. No one wants two million. But the people who've been behind Jens till now would want much more."

"They wouldn't get anything. I'd risk the scandal."

"Perhaps. That's what you're saying now. I'm inclined to believe you. But anyway, allow me a word of reproach. Why don't you politicians have the common sense, when you've found yourselves a girl, to tell your own police about her? And why don't you take a flat for yourself, with you the only key-holder, where she can get in only when you open the door to her? Eh? And there'd be no scandal and no blackmail."

"There's always a way . . ." he began but I interrupted him.

"But never an easy one. The rule is: never in someone else's flat."

He agreed.

"And another thing . . . your own police. Why didn't you ring the superintendent of the Crime Squad, or the Vice Squad and make an agreement with them? Having a mistress isn't against the law, is it? Well, is it?"

He shrugged. "We all like some privacy . . ." he said.

"Some privacy," I returned deliberately loud. "A whore, a pimp and a camera. And all because you don't trust your own police. I suppose you must have a reason, eh?"

He sensed from my tone that we were getting to the point.

"What is it you want?" he said.

"It won't go beyond us two," I began. "I've got the

negatives and the prints, no one else will get them and I'll let you have them. But," I paused for effect, "what are you going to tell me about Jeremy?"

"Aha," he said, and that was all.

"So you know he's inside," I said.

"Yes."

"Do you know why?"

"Yes."

"Tell me."

"It looks as if he's a Soviet agent . . ."

"Do you believe that?"

He was silent.

"So the three of you are trying to make out he's a Soviet agent. Very nice too. I wouldn't have thought you so frivolous."

His hand travelled across his face. "You never know . . ."

"You're not sure of it."

He looked at me. "No," he said. "I'm not. But I could be mistaken . . ."

"You're not mistaken. Jeremy Nichols isn't a Soviet agent. Never has been. You can be sure on that score."

"What do you want?"

"I want to speak to Koerner."

"Aha."

We were silent. I gave him time to consider.

After a while he said, "Is that all you want?"

"Yes. Then you can have the negatives and these prints."

"Hm."

I knew I had won.

3

The car bowled along Perlebergerstrasse and into the French sector. It was a big Mercedes 600, with curtains, and it ran silently. The glass that separated us from the chauffeur was raised.

Peccarie glanced at his watch.

"Twenty past nine," he said. "I'll leave you here. My man's in the car behind, I'll join him. When you've finished I'll come back for you."

We were in Wedding, the main part of the French sector, which I didn't know. There was a slight drizzle and the asphalt of the road reflected our headlights. I hadn't the slightest idea whether the Mercedes and its chauffeur were 'ours' or French, and I hadn't wanted to ask Peccarie. In any case it wasn't my business; he had said he'd take care of security.

During the journey we hadn't spoken. I was thinking about the photo sent to the British agent at the Military Mission. So someone knew where I was. All that was left to me was the operations flat. But that someone was keen to frighten me. I assumed that these were the same people who had sent along the chap with the air ticket to the Intercontinental. They were serious, but how serious?

As for Barthels he had made an honest effort; much as he disliked my listening in on his phone-calls. They were very terse. He made eight calls before he got to the person who promised that Koerner would ring him next day. In Berlin.

He refused to tell me whom he had spoken to. "You want to speak to Koerner," he said, "so I'll arrange it for you. Nothing else is any business of yours." I nodded and no more was said. He left at eight and did not even say goodbye to Susanne.

The Mercedes turned off the main street into a square, the name of which I failed to catch, and stopped outside a post office. I looked at Peccarie but his expression was unchanged: we evidently hadn't arrived yet. After a moment the Mercedes set off again, and when I turned round I saw the lights of another car close behind. We drove down a narrow street, and stopped outside what looked like a cemetery.

"Is this a crematorium?" I asked Peccarie, and he nodded. *Décidément*, as our colleagues at SDECE would have said, there were plenty of crematoria in Berlin, and somehow they kept turning up on my route.

The chauffeur drove close against the kerb and Peccarie got out, closing the door gently behind him. The inside light was off and I could see his dark silhouette as he stood outside. Another car, a smaller Mercedes, had drawn up behind us, and behind that another car. It looked like a Mafia rendezvous. Then Peccarie opened the door and announced:

"This is Monsieur Dupont."

4

The stranger climbed in and arranged himself beside me. Without looking at me he tapped lightly on the glass separating us from the driver. The driver got the message and stepped out of the car.

We were alone. M. Dupont drew the curtains and switched on the light. He was looking me over. In his grey single-breasted overcoat and brown lace-up shoes, kid gloves and a light grey-striped shirt, he looked like a middle-ranking official of the Union des Banques Suisses.

After about twenty seconds he put out the light and said, with the voice of a one-time adventurer who has locked his pistols in his desk-drawer and changed his friends:

"I'm very glad you accepted our invitation."

With a glance out into the dark I asked, "How did you find me?"

"We weren't looking for you," he said. "You turned up."

"You want to introduce me to someone . . . or so I've heard."

For a while he said nothing. We spoke in French, but he had started by asking me if I spoke the language. I had no doubt he knew that at the end of the war I had deserted from the FFI, the French Army of Liberation, and that David Bleyhart had got me a job with Gonzales. That was fifteen years ago and since then files marked with my name had been steadily growing thicker at a number of services.

"It may not be necessary," he said after a pause. "In our line of business the less faces seen the better. You agree, *hein*? Maybe we two can deal with it together. And if it turns out that we can be of use to each other . . . we know how to contact you, as you can see."

"But I can't see how I can contact *you*, if ever I feel like it, which might never happen, but which is always possible."

"Through your colleague, through your colleague," he replied. "There and back the route's the same. You can't beat the agency route. A bit of bureaucracy can't do any harm."

I took out my cigarette-case and was about to light up.

"Would you mind not smoking, please? I don't want to open the window and I can't stand smoke. There's not much room in here and my eyes'll start watering before long."

I was touched. I snapped the cigarette-case shut and put it back in my pocket. M. Dupont made a gesture that wasn't very clear in the dark, but might have been of gratitude.

"The Nichols affair has attracted the attention of all those involved and informed." He spoke as if he were at a regional development conference. But there was something quiet and steely, patient and very purposeful about him. He wasn't to be under-estimated.

"Yes," I agreed.

He waited a moment to see if I would add anything but I said nothing.

Almost grudgingly, as if offended at my reserve, he took up the thread again.

"You really are certain Nichols has had no dealings with the Russians?"

I replied calmly: "Monsieur Dupont, you must know the way things work. *They* told *me* that Nichols has never worked for the Russians. I've had my instructions. That's all."

I wouldn't have thought Dupont capable of a smile. Perhaps, in the half-light, I was mistaken.

"What if the British just want to get their own hands on Nichols?" he hazarded. "Suppose they've just sent you along to fish the chestnuts out of the fire for them so that they can settle accounts with him later?"

"You can bet your Wellington boots on the chestnuts bit," I said. "That's all the British ever hire foreigners for. And you too, don't you?"

He waved this aside with quite evident impatience, like a man about to make love to his wife and not liking to be asked whether he loves her.

"Your job's simply to get Nichols out . . . and back home?"

"Monsieur Dupont, my job is my affair. Don't tell me you've invited me here to tell you what the British are up to. What does the SDECE want?"

At the sound of the initials of the French espionage service he gave me a look of disapproval, then controlled himself at once and said in a level tone, "We'll come to that."

— XII —

You scratch my back . . .

Growing old is exhausting. Time goes faster and faster and hope is diminishing. After sixty, and sometimes even before that, a good morning bowel movement is probably one's chief satisfaction in life.

Dupont had not yet reached sixty and I could not guess how he was getting on with his bowel movements, family, women, life and death. He looked like someone who believes in being active, and who refuses to ponder over anything that does not help push forward the barrowload of fortune. Thus he fails to see that the pushing of the barrow brings us all the time nearer to death.

You could tell just by sitting next to him in the half-light and listening to him convince himself that he had been through the mill of espionage, intrigue and deceit. In his heart he was probably deeply distressed at not yet having got to the top and at the prospect of never getting there. He must have been certain that he was more capable than others. But at the same time he had self-control and was probably treated by his superiors as a reliable and unfaltering actor in the plays they organised for nation and state. He, like others, was sometimes left wondering about his own identity, the inner sense of mission having slowly faded leaving nothing but weariness and cruelty. Dupont was undoubtedly cruel, though he would have been offended if anyone had said as much to his face. He was a professional Frenchman interested in the fate of a single Englishman.

He was looking at me thoughtfully; we had reached deadlock. I still had no inkling why it mattered to him that we agree Nichols *might* be a Soviet agent, but whatever the reason, no agreement had been reached.

I waited.

"We know as you do," he went on reluctantly, "that Nichols is being held by the Sonderabteilung. Maybe we know where. Maybe we can guess why."

"Are you going to offer me some help?" I asked ingenuously.

"Kagin arrived today," he went on unperturbed. "With Vorontsov."

Colonel Kagin of the KGB's First Directorate was the go-between for their 'illegals' and counter-espionage. A man of over fifty, he had the rank of Ambassador to the UN; he was as at home in Geneva as in New York and he was the main organiser of the exchange and sale of agents. Vorontsov was a slightly younger man, probably in his forties, also from the First Directorate, who had worked some years ago at the Department of Satellite Control Services and then been transferred to the Planning and Analysis Department. The last I had heard of them was a year before when they had turned up in Mozambique. In 1969 they had been in Prague. Dupont's terse little snippet was therefore far-reaching in its implications.

"Officially, Kagin is holding talks with the American Mission on the problems of access from Berlin . . . In recent weeks the Soviets have been making things difficult, using their East German stooges. Kagin is staying in East Berlin, but he'll be over here every day."

"I see," I said. "Do you know him personally?"

"My boss does. And you?"

"I've met him. Long time ago. In Havana."

"Does he remember you?"

"You'll have to ask him."

"Hm." He stopped to think (which was purely theatrical) and then continued.

"You are working for the British for the first time. You're keen to make a good job of it. There's not much of a future for you in Lisbon. Gonzales will be packing his bags before long."

I knew that, and he knew that I knew. On his part it was a bare statement of fact, but it had the ring of an overture.

"You might care to take out some insurance," he continued. "If you do us a favour, we can help you over Nichols, and there'll be something to your credit with us should you ever fall out with the British. That could be quite useful, couldn't it?"

It was the old, old song. Caetano was crumbling in Lisbon and the publication of General Spinola's explosive book spoke clearly of a change of régime.

"I'm not the double agent type," I said.

"But you've worked for all sorts of organisations. You've had to. After all, that was the basis of Gonzales' success. So?"

"What do you want?"

"A trifle," he said.

2

When a man is courting a woman he is witty, intelligent and attentive. It is only later that he does not want her to talk while he is reading his paper at breakfast.

When an intelligence service is trying to hook you, it never wants more than a trifle. At first.

"I shall be glad of your help," I said noncommittally. "But it depends what that trifle is."

"That I can't say until you respond a little more positively."

"*Vous avez peur de trahir vos objectifs?*" I asked, using the classical phrase.

"*Du baratin,*" he returned. "Well? Shall we shake on it?"

Suddenly he was a Texas cattle dealer.

I thought for a moment. They couldn't be after much: Dupont wouldn't have got to the point so promptly. There had to be a catch somewhere, but probably nothing that would be very important to me. What they were after was obviously information on someone, and considering my chequered career there was a fair chance that it was someone who would not matter much to me.

"Okay," I said. "In exchange for what?"

"We'll tell you where Nichols is at the moment. And – if we're satisfied – my boss will tell you what we've got on him in our files. And . . . we'll give you a hand if necessary," he added in English. He seemed to be amused that I had chosen to work for the British.

"I'm listening," I said with resignation.

"You married?" he asked.

"You mean you don't know?" I returned with surprise.

"Answer me," he said gently.

"No," I replied truthfully. How could I have been married? Muriel would be right to call me a 'husband with a suitcase'. It was like a piece of Emmenthaler cheese that longstanding nostalgic relationship of ours: too many holes in time. "But I don't feel inclined to make my private confessions to you," I added.

"You won't have to," he assured me. "I'm only asking for your sake. You do have the odd diversion . . . with women, don't you? Like . . . when you're travelling?"

"Here and there," I said uncertainly. I groped mentally for what he was driving at.

"How much do they matter to you?"

"Depends. Why don't you get to the point?"

"We're interested . . . in a lady-friend of yours."

A string of names and faces flashed through my mind.

"We'd like to contact her. And we want you to help us."

So that was it. Messieurs wanted the door held open.

"Who is it?" I asked suspiciously, trying to conceal my tension.

"You flew in with her," he said delicately.

At first I failed to understand. Then I said with unfeigned surprise:

"You mean . . . Veronika?"

3

It was the age-old game of musical chairs . . . There was no end to the tricks. Anyone could become the subject of interest; anyone from a vet to a croupier at a blackjack table. But what could they want from Veronika?

"I hope you don't take it too personally . . ." he said slowly. "Surely you're not emotionally involved?"

To hell with their emotions, I thought. Suddenly, like a thunderclap, a feeling of revulsion overwhelmed me. At the same time I knew full well that I had no right to indulge in it.

"She's purely a chance acquaintance," I said bluntly. "She's only a girl. Just happened my way and I used her as a blind, to give me a bit of back-cloth . . ." I wasn't lying. That was the only reason I'd been playing around with her. "In fact I don't even know her surname."

"So much the better," said Dupont. He was pleased. "I'd begun to get worried . . . What do you know about her?"

"She's come to Germany to get some money. From her dad. He lives near Munich. She's a lively . . ."

"Okay," he interrupted. "You'll introduce her to our man."

"I don't know if it'll be all that easy and discreet," I said quickly. But I knew it would obviously be easy and discreet. In the West people are so naive. Things weren't like this on the other side. What was I going to get her mixed up in?

"What do you want from her?"

"Not much."

Not much. Of course. A trifle.

"Tomorrow," he said. "All right?"

"What's your man like?" I asked grudgingly.

"Don't worry. Just the right age and appearance." It sounded like a criticism.

"And suppose I'd wanted to sleep with her?"

"Come, come. You said yourself that there was nothing emotional about it . . . and if you find yourself in need we'll supply a replacement . . ."

"Very kind," I said drily. "No, thank you."

"No . . . what?"

"No replacement."

"*Parfait*. Arrange to lunch with her tomorrow and ring me on this number."

I took the card with the number and slipped it into my pocket.

"When do I get your information?"

"Tomorrow. As soon as we get hand in glove."

When he got out of the car I looked at my watch. A whole hour had passed. I lit a cigarette and realised I was cold.

4

"I can't meet you anywhere outside," he had said into the phone. "You'll have to come to my place. An hour from now."

We were sitting in Barthels' flat, and already he was looking much older. His clean-shaven liberal right-wing politician's features looked positively scruffy, as if he'd spent the night playing poker and gambled away his bride. He was constrained but calm; he must have done a lot of hard thinking.

"You'll have to fly to Munich," he said. "Koerner won't come here. Not even because of me."

What he meant to say was: 'Certainly not because of you'. But that didn't worry me.

"When am I to meet him?"

"Today. Munich main station this evening at seven."

"Whereabouts?"

"Departures hall. By the flower shop. You will buy some roses."

"Is he joking?"

"I don't know," said Barthels. "He told me you were to buy some roses."

"What colour roses? Did he say?"

"He didn't mention the colour. There may not be any great choice. At this time of year . . ."

"Okay," I said. "I'll be there."

"Are you going to let me have the negatives now?" he asked.

I hesitated. "Half of them."

"And the other half?"

"After I've met him. Just imagine: I've flown to Munich, taken a taxi to the station, at seven I've bought some roses, and at eight I'm still there, waiting at the flower shop, alone. I give the flowers to the first pretty girl I see and I can't even send Nichols a funeral wreath. What do you say to that?"

"You're probably an intelligence agent. If you've got the other half of the prints on you and something happens to you, then someone else'll start blackmailing me," he said sadly.

"I'm not an agent, Herr Barthels. I'm a missionary from St Augustine's College in Kenya. My concern is the preservation of moral standards. I am looking for converts. You needn't worry; I shan't have the second half on me. They'll be in safe keeping. But whatever way you look at it, it's not something you can do anything about."

I handed him the photographs and then took out the envelope containing the negatives. I separated half of them and handed them to him.

"What if I shot you?" he asked. "Aren't you afraid I might?"

"In your own flat?" I shook my head. "Anyway, you know well enough that I don't want to trick you. At your age you should know enough about people . . ."

"All right," he said, waving his hand. "When do I get the rest?"

"Probably tomorrow. The day after at the latest. Someone will leave a sealed envelope at your flat. That all right?"

He agreed. He'd had to.

5

Peccarie was sitting in the car. I joined him and we set off towards the Intercontinental. I handed him the envelope with the rest of the negatives.

"Have them sealed and dropped in his letter-box. But

not before I ring you. And don't think of having copies made . . ."

He brushed the very thought aside.

"Shan't need to. Not now. Jens Baumgartner has been singing like an angel and we'll get our hands on Sichler in a day or two."

"One never knows," I said. "And I'm responsible for those negatives."

"Rest assured," he said.

I did. Peccarie was experienced enough not to be interested in the odd perks or gaining a bit more credit. After I left Dupont we had a long talk together, not in the car, of course, but in the operations flat near the Wall.

I didn't tell him what Dupont wanted, but we discussed at length the situation that had evolved around me, especially the fact that someone had taken a photograph of me standing in the doorway of the Am Lietzen See hotel.

Peccarie's view was that it was too much of a risk for me to surface yet and he advised using only the flat, at least until after the meeting with Koerner. We were both assuming that Koerner could not refuse Barthels' request.

"What's he likely to tell him about me?"

"Doesn't matter," Peccarie averred. "He certainly won't tell him you were threatening to milk him."

We both slept at the flat and in the morning I rang first Barthels and then Veronika.

"You nasty man," she said. "Where are you hiding?"

"I had to go to the funeral of an aged aunt. I've inherited ten marks and I want to celebrate with you. Shall we have lunch together?"

"Oh, lovely! What time?"

"After twelve. I'll pick you up at the hotel. I'll have a friend with me . . ." I checked myself. Friend? No, I wasn't going that far! "That is, someone I know. He's very funny," I added rather uncertainly.

"Couldn't we be alone?" she asked in all seriousness.

"No," I said. "I can't be with you without a duenna. With girls like you a fellow must bring a chaperon."

She laughed. Life to her seemed so much fun and full of surprises.

And now I was on my way to the hotel. Dupont had telephoned to say his 'colleague' was called de Brissac and that he would be waiting in the lobby.

— XIII —

Hope for thirty pieces of silver

I leaned against the reception desk and waited. The receptionist bent forward and muttered:

"It's room 404. But he's not there. Shall I have him paged?"

"Brissac," he said and bared his pure white teeth. He could have been thirty; he had an insolent expression, a small flabby chin, high cheekbones and a slightly turned up nose. A well-rehearsed cross between Steve McQueen and Johnny Halliday: slender fingers, well cared for, the money in his pocket probably held together by a Cartier gold clip, a career ahead of him and *carpe diem* inscribed on his forehead. He was wearing a gazelle-skin jacket, grey trousers and brown suede shoes. He looked at me as if I were his grandfather who had got drunk at the fair and had just been carried home.

"Does the chick know about me?"

"She knows I'm bringing an acquaintance along. What's your story?" I spoke as icily as I could. But the young fellow's orders were plain and he treated me like a servant.

"Racing driver. Professional. I do the lot, from Monte Carlo to Tripoli. Eighth in the World Championship year before last. We met on the plane to Paris a few years back. You're one of my fans."

It was a good story.

"I hope you don't turn out not to have a driving licence."

He smiled. "I've got three, and a Ferrari in the hotel garage. Will that do?"

"Okay, let's go."

"Wait. You go ahead and sit with her in the dining-room. I'll come over in about ten minutes. Gives you time to fill her in on me. Tell her I'm a friend of Stirling Moss and Graham Hill."

"She mightn't know who they are. What about the Rolling Stones? Don't you know any of them?"

"Tell her I've been out with Bianca," he said earnestly.

"I'll think of something," I said wearily and told the receptionist to let 216 know that her visitor was waiting in the dining-room. I also gave him five marks; I didn't want to be tripped up through not knowing Veronika's surname.

I found a place in the dining-room, ordered a Martini and lit a cigarette. The colleague had been well chosen – Veronika would be simply swept off her feet. Or would she? She walked in, wearing a grey, clinging jersey that suited her long blonde hair very nicely.

"Well then, you ugly old thing," she said and added an American, "Hi."

"If only you'd start behaving like a nice young lady from a good German middle-class family for once, instead of spouting insults like a half-caste from Greenwich Village," I said. "I don't have to be reminded every time that you prefer marijuana to Bach."

"Oh, I've nothing against Johann Sebastian. Where's this chum of yours that I have to put up with?"

"Desist from calling the maestro Bach by his Christian name and my acquaintance will be coming. Can you stand racing drivers who are still not retired?"

"Is he a racing driver, then?"

"De Brissac. Eighth in the World Championship year

before last. Enters everything from Monte Carlo to Tripoli," I recited faithfully. Turning to the waiter I ordered another Martini and three menus.

"I don't want Martini, I want gin," said Veronika.

"Respectable girls don't drink gin at lunchtime," I said and nodded to the waiter. "Martini. Sweet." I turned to look at her – in my mind's eye I could see her in bed with de Brissac under the expert surveillance of M. Dupont. "If only for my sake you ought to start acting a little less freely. I can't stand women's lib. I am an experienced male chauvinist pig and I don't intend to change."

She laughed, with that gold lamé laugh in which there was a mixture of sweet shamelessness and premature experience. A rather complex little creature this Veronika – what could they want from her?

"I've missed you."

"Oh yes," I said. "Who have you been seducing meantime? Are there no other seventy-year-olds at the hotel?"

"*Aber, mein Lieber*," came across in French German, and de Brissac slapped me on the back, winked at me, flashed his teeth and bent down towards Veronika. "De Brissac," he said and kissed her first on one cheek, then on the other, as if it were the most natural thing in the world. "So you're the discovery my friend here has fallen in love with."

I saw with glee that she was riled. Without saying anything, she rolled her eyes my way and in them was written: 'What on earth have you been telling *this awful thing*?'

"Take a seat," I said in French, and added in English, "Makes no bones about anything, this one, Veronika. Don't let it worry you."

"She's not letting it worry her; she's a happy girl," de Brissac laughed, and he pronounced that 'happy' in such an unlovely way that it sent shivers down my spine. But he had already taken her hand and turned it palm uppermost. "Happy girl, really. She loves older men, doesn't have any children and roams around the world. She doesn't play chess, but she can twist men round her little finger. Proof: for one whole minute I've thought of nothing but her." He bowed and grinned at her.

But Veronika did not bat an eyelid. She took his hand, turned it palm uppermost and said: "Lady-killer, specialising in chambermaids. Vocabulary taken from paperbacks, blood lukewarm. Ejaculation in the first couple of minutes. Ever lost a match, handsome?"

"You're telling me!" I said. "He's lost some. Lost that Bianca girl that went and married one of your Rolling Stones. Can't remember his name because I don't listen to that racket."

"I say," she said. "Mick Jagger. You were after her too?"

"No, he *got* her," I said, and swore that that was as far as I'd go. Let this Hell's Angel of a Parisian spy take care of himself. I was gratified to observe that he wouldn't have an easy job. Veronika was anything but stupid – which de Brissac had noticed for himself. He was now consulting the menu. We ordered and the conversation turned to Berlin. I had slightly under-estimated de Brissac. He was telling us about the new Berlin Mercedes centre and making it almost interesting.

"Why don't the Mercedes people produce racing cars?" I asked, to keep the conversation going, and began thinking about Peccarie, who was getting my ticket for the flight to Munich and who was to organise my contact there. When I came back from my reverie I found that Veronika had once taken part as a navigator in some minor rally and that de Brissac was telling her all about the roadholding virtues of the Ferraris.

"And if you aren't doing anything this afternoon I'll take you on a joy-ride round Berlin," he added.

"Shall I?" she asked with feigned innocence.

What could I do? True to the agreement I said:

"You must. Otherwise you'll never stop kicking yourself."

We ate and I asked her whether her father had already returned to Westphalia, or whether she had been in touch with Fritz, the family secretary from whom she was hoping to get some money in her father's absence.

"There are problems," she said. "I only spoke to Fritz today. He's at Pullach, at my uncle's flat, and he says he can only give me three thousand."

I detected a flicker of interest in de Brissac's eyes and said at once that young women like her didn't need any more anyway, but Veronika said she needed twice as much since she wanted to fly to the Seychelles for a couple of months at least and then she would like to go to London.

I followed de Brissac's glib gyrations round the money question. He did not make any specific offer – and the girl was undoubtedly worth three thousand to the French – because he obviously knew she would not take him seriously.

He'll go a long way, I thought. He's still only a cub, but he'll go a long way. Maybe even the vulgarity is only put on.

"And where's your uncle?" de Brissac was curious to know.

"He's supposed to be in Pullach, but he isn't. Fritz is at the house waiting for him. They've got some business to sort out, my travelling papa and my uncle. And Fritz is giving them a hand."

"And he won't let you have more than three thousand, the rascal," said de Brissac.

"He isn't allowed to," said Veronika sadly.

"Anyway, why are you in Berlin and not in Munich?" de Brissac asked.

"Because of him," she said, and pointed at me. "Only

because of him. I've taken a fancy to this old gent here."

"Well, well," said de Brissac. "Well, and I thought he was the one who had taken a fancy to *you*."

The banter began going round and round. I began to see that de Brissac was drawing circles round his victim. There were moments when he was full of impertinent jokes, but then he would sober down and appear to hint that all that had gone before was just frivolity, admitting in all seriousness that he was actually afraid at the beginning of every race. He'll get her, I suddenly thought, and at the same time I was ashamed that it was getting on my nerves. Veronika was sitting between us like an umpire watching two players. She must have felt that way. In fact I was merely assisting at an execution that was being performed with the ferocious self-assurance of de Brissac's youth. So far he was just a new element to Veronika, but that in itself meant that her curiosity was aroused. And the 'new element' was hard at it – who had brought him after all? I had. So he was basking in the 'seriousness' that had originally sparked off Veronika's interest in me.

After lunch Peccarie showed up in the dining-room, found a table and ordered a piece of gâteau and coffee and cognac, and sat gazing around vacantly. At least that meant all was in order and that he would be following me unobserved.

"You coming with us for the ride?" asked de Brissac, waiting for my obligatory non-acceptance and all set to get to grips with Veronika when they were left alone. I was just itching to reply: 'Delighted, I expect we'll fit in the Ferrari somehow.' But I didn't.

"No. I'm awfully sorry. I can't. I've got some business out of the city," I said. "Some other time. Mind you take care of her."

"Where are you off to, old bean?" asked Veronika tenderly in German, and without warning threw her arms round my neck. It made me cross because she only did it to provoke de Brissac.

"Geneva, but only for a day or so," I replied, and was about to pay the bill. Except that de Brissac was quicker off the mark: he put a five-hundred-mark bill on the plate. He had extracted it from a whole bundle of them, held together with a gold clip – I'd been right – and then he slipped the rest back in his pocket.

"I needed change anyway," he remarked casually, and I visualised him returning the bundle to Dupont. But he made a good show of it, that racing driver! Veronika need not have been particularly impressed, but no young female was ever insulted by a glimpse of money in the pocket of an agreeable young man – so now de Brissac had become an agreeable young man.

"Will you ring me when you get back?" she asked, but it sounded more like: 'Farewell, my tired adventurer.'

"Of course, I will," I said in my fatherly manner, consigning her soul to the Devil and assuming that that was the last I should see of her.

Then de Brissac clapped me on the back and asked jovially: "But you'll be at the Nürburgring, won't you? Everyone'll be there, including young Hunt."

Saying nothing I nodded and left. Out of the corner of my eye I saw Peccarie getting up from his table.

2

The French DST is known in intelligence circles for keeping its word. The SDECE, the French espionage organisation, is a somewhat adventurous body. Nevertheless Dupont was at Tempelhof at four o'clock.

He was wearing a beige cashmere overcoat and his face

told me de Brissac had reported that I had kept my part of the bargain.

We strolled across the concrete flagging towards the taxi rank.

"Pity you're so obstinate," said Dupont. "We could have done something for you before this. Let's hope that now . . ."

"As for now, I hope you'll give me what you promised. As for the future, I have my doubts. You fellows are a bit too much like cowboys and your purges are too frequent."

"We'll see. After all, satisfaction on both sides is the best guarantee. That Nichols of yours is in the stew. Leaving aside the question of whether he is a Soviet spy, a double agent, or just a British agent," Dupont went on, "the fact remains that we have heard that he'd got hold of information relating to the Chancellor himself."

Dupont allowed a generous pause for me to absorb this news.

"It's more than a trifle. The East Germans have been getting exact reports on everything that's going on here. The evaluation department of STASI has been dealing so thoroughly with Brandt's Ostpolitik that all the copies destined for the Presidium of the Party pass through the hands of our man – with all their bureaucracy they make two of everything! We've been watching it all for some time now . . . and that's where we hit upon Nichols. He was following things too, but from a different direction."

"You mean . . . ?"

"What I'm saying is that they know what's going on inside Brandt's head. That's exaggerating a bit, but not much."

"Could you prove it?"

"Possibly. If we felt like it. The question is, prove it to *whom*? The main problem is that someone else can prove it too."

"And presumably that someone else is Nichols?"

"Right."

I lit a cigarette and suffered Dupont's scrutiny. I tried not to let him see how perturbed I was at what he had said.

"What else do you know?" I asked, playing for time.

"Nichols had got further than us," said Dupont, and he sounded frosty. "He had got so far that STASI contacted the Russians and, at first, it was decided to liquidate him."

"But–"

"Yes, he is alive. Complications, don't you see? The Russians are cautious. They want him alive, they want to talk to him. They want to get back anything that might be used as evidence. That's why they quashed the decision to get rid of him."

"So you don't believe Nichols could have been a Soviet agent?" I said quickly.

"Why not? Suppose he was, but decided to turn a quick penny and sell out to the Americans?" Dupont smiled. "I refuse to *believe* a thing. I am merely saying that Nichols *knows*. The rest isn't up to me. Nichols isn't our man. As you know, the Western intelligence services don't do much coordinating – that's why we're so much worse off than the Russians. To say nothing of the American Congress and Senate."

"So they pulled a fast one on him?"

"Yes. They pulled a fast one on him and played him into the hands of Koerner and Groller."

"And they put him away and now they're keeping him under wraps."

"They put him away, and now they want to do a swap, because Groller has a brother. His name is Heinrich."

"And that brother is working for STASI?"

"No – he works for the BND and he's now in the cooler in East Berlin and the East Germans are offering a deal with the West Germans. And because he's the brother of

Adalbert Groller, Koerner's right-hand man, they didn't even have to use much pressure – it was enough to drop a hint that Heinrich Groller might meet with an accident in East Berlin if they didn't get 'their' man – Nichols – by return post. Do I have to go on?"

I shook my head. Nichols was in a stew. Definitely.

"And in a squeeze like that a quick swap is the easiest way out for Koerner: he wouldn't let his deputy's brother go to the wall, would he?"

"Especially if it's not going to cost him anything. When are they going to do the swap?" I asked.

"Kagin started negotiating today. It'll take a day or two."

"Where is Nichols?"

"They've taken him to Hamburg."

"Where to, do you know?"

"I will soon. Very soon."

"Why don't you tell Koerner?"

"Why should we?" he asked. "Because the British want Nichols back? Or because the Russians want him? Besides that, our relations *avec les Boches* are a bit too official. We've never approved of Gehlen's system, it's riddled with East German agents."

"You mean to say you believe that even Brandt . . . ?"

"I've already said I don't believe anything. We might have a few scraps of evidence, but we certainly don't know as much as Nichols. We've got to be cautious. It's all too high up. On top of that . . . it's not very likely. True, Brandt used to be an alcoholic, his Ostpolitik may be sheer madness, but to think of him working for STASI, or for the Russians, that's taking things a bit too far. So we're biding our time."

"In the meantime the East Germans will swap Heinrich Groller for Nichols. And STASI will grill him – to a turn – and shoot afterwards."

"You know the rules of the game."

I heaved a sigh. Dupont was right. Even if the French did decide to pass the information on, it would be hard to decide to whom. The BND? The Federal Office for the Defence of the Constitution? Strauss? Or the President? Or NATO intelligence? Meanwhile, through their contact, they were keeping an eye on the activities of STASI.

They were building up their files and trying to get a clearer picture. They were not interested in Nichols – he wasn't one of theirs. But his fate would give them an important piece of information. There was probably a file carrying some romantic code-name, but whose real subject was *Chancellor Brandt*.

"What do you know about Koerner?" I asked.

"That doesn't come under our agreement," said Dupont. He turned and we began to move back towards the airport. "But he's a great hunter. And his Sonderabteilung is widely respected."

I looked at him enquiringly. What did he mean?

"And Groller?"

"Groller is two years older than Koerner. They were in the Abwehr together. But they were both very young then." Dupont cleared his throat, his way of laughing. "They're a bunch of has-beens. Ageing has-beens with their prostates removed."

Munich

Are meetings at railway stations safe? In France or Italy, maybe . . . but in Germany? Koerner, of course, wasn't concerned with my safety, otherwise he wouldn't have chosen a station. Germans aren't given to hanging about on stations. They buy their tickets and hurry off to catch their train. So any decently dressed foreigner is conspicuous; he can't help but stand out among the groups of quaintly dressed, dark-haired, olive-complexioned men with moustaches who chatter away in all languages of the south and look suspicious. Here, it is the Balkans who hold sway.

As in Hamburg, or Cologne, or Frankfurt, the main station in Munich is dominated by Jugoslavs, Turks and Greeks. They live there. They meet there, they hold their endless debates, do a little bartering – God only knows what in – find each other jobs, and sometimes, but only rarely, they also travel.

It was five to seven. I bought roses – two of every available colour – and watched one of these little groups nearby. They were standing in a circle, some of them with Jugoslav newspapers – Serbian it looked like – and they were talking.

A little way off stood Williams, my contact, who had met me at the airport. He was smoking and pretending to read the *Süddeutsche Zeitung* – ready to follow. If possible.

I did not expect Koerner in person. I was right: the man

was on the stout side, squat, with brown eyes and a smile, an all but forgotten remnant of past servitude.

"Are you expecting someone?" he asked politely, looking meaningly at the roses in my hand.

"I'm waiting for Herr K." I thought of Kafka.

"Is there an O in his name?"

"Yes," I confirmed.

"Come on then," said the man.

2

The car was an Audi, black and ordinary. The driver was wearing a sweater; he was the strong, silent type. My guide spoke briefly to him in a Bavarian dialect, compared to which the Belfast brogue is promisingly melodious. So they were locals. To my surprise, we were entering Schwabing, the centre of Munich's night-life. After only a short drive we pulled up outside a restaurant.

"*Bitte schön*," said my guide, and led me to a modern building next door. A plain, dull entrance, certainly unlike an entrance to the premises of a Sonderabteilung. But just inside the door two men frisked me (with an apology), then one of them picked up a phone from a small table and said "Your visitor's here." Then he gave a nod, hung up and said, "You may go on up." My guide said "*Bitte schön*" once more and grudgingly bowed me across to the lift, which was too small for both of us, and we were carried to the third floor.

When the door opened, we entered a room with a deep carpet and heavy panelling, leather-upholstered armchairs and two overhead cameras. I did not doubt for a minute that Colonel Koerner was scrutinising me already – and probably having a few photographs taken as well. Was this the headquarters of the Sonderabteilung? Or just an annexe? Either way they were well-equipped.

My guide sat me in a leather armchair, went to a door in the rear wall, knocked and left the room.

In a moment he re-emerged and left the door open. "*Bitte schön*," he said predictably and I went into a spacious office, where everything was neat and geometrical – from the desk, a safe that looked like a bunker, and two filing cabinets to the telephones, automatic callmakers and other appliances.

I was at once certain that Colonel Koerner recorded all his calls and either stored them or erased them as the fancy took him. I looked at him and said, "*Guten Abend, Herr Oberst.*"

He was about fifty-five, slim, with an elongated skull. His expression was that of an ill-tempered and spoilt only child. His hands were those of a schoolboy, with thin fingers and nails cut straight across. He was the type who hasn't been beaten enough by his teachers and the world has been paying for it ever since.

"*Guten Abend,*" he responded in a quiet voice, as if he were in a forest and afraid of waking a hedgehog. I found him just as repellent as a gang of youths kicking in shop windows after a football match. Except that this one had people to do it for him.

My extra sense told me that this spycatcher was neither a patriot nor a man of any particular philosophical persuasion, but a dyed-in-the-wool careerist who makes notches in the butt of his revolver.

"Why don't you take a seat?" he asked, and I took one. For a moment we looked at each other. I knew I hadn't a dog's chance.

3

After some twenty seconds – a very long time in the circumstances – he looked at his watch and then back at me. In excellent German, he said:

"It is the custom for visitors to explain the reason for their presence. Herr Barthels did not tell me the reason for yours."

"Nichols," I said, equally quietly.

We looked each other straight in the eye, and found each other loathsome. Each would condemn the other to death by ripping open his belly.

"Who are you?"

"My passport is in the name of Therrick. As you know, in the present case I am representing British intelligence. The section headed by Mr Queeney."

"I know nothing of the sort. No one has telephoned me, no one has written to me, no one has said anything to me."

"So the gentleman you sent to me at the Intercontinental must have been a ghost and he must have thought I was St Peter, is that it?"

His eyes narrowed. But only for a twinkling thereof.

"You're off the point."

He didn't have to try. He knew his strength.

"You'll have to let Nichols go," I said.

"Have to?"

"You understood, Colonel."

He took a metal cigarette-box from the table and held it towards me.

"Cigarette?"

I looked at the box. It was smooth, polished, tawdry.

"If part of your job is to collect finger-prints, I've left mine on the counter of the flower-stall in the station hall. You can go and fetch them."

Without a word he opened a drawer and tossed in the box. He closed it noiselessly.

"Matters like this are decided by the BND and the State Prosecutor," he said.

"Not in this case. We both know that."

"Why didn't you approach the BND? If we'd received orders from Wessels . . ."

Wessels was the new head of the West German Secret Service. Koerner was mocking me.

"They would have made enquiries at the State Prosecutor's Office to see if diplomatic approaches had been made. The Prosecutor's Office would have said no, because, although Nichols is behind bars, there's been no formal committal or charge, and so they couldn't know anything about it . . . and by the time things had been cleared up Nichols would have been swapped."

"That is a real possibility," he conceded with irony.

"Colonel Koerner," I began respectfully, "be so good as to exchange your own for your own. But not for ours."

"Nichols is a Soviet agent, Mr Therrick."

"I've already heard that nonsense. I am authorised to state that he is our, British, agent."

"What's your account of his activities on the territory of the German Federal Republic?"

"He was ensuring coordination between our operatives and the intelligence organisations of NATO."

"Does it not strike you as odd that NATO hasn't intervened?"

He was now wearing an expression of innocence, and his heart was bursting with sheer delight.

"No, it does *not* strike me as odd."

A pause.

"The English haven't got used to the idea that the war ended twenty years ago and that the German Federal Republic is a sovereign state on whose territory foreign agents are not welcome. Least of all those who are working for the Russians."

"It's not them I'm talking about," I replied, "but Nichols. And you're forgetting that you arrested him in Berlin, which is not part of the German Federal Republic, but comes under the four-power Military Administration. It was a kidnap, Colonel. Why?"

"I admit you may be acting for the British, which I can verify anyway . . ."

"Verify away," I broke in, "I'll be glad to wait."

He gestured with his hand that there was time enough.

". . . Suppose I do accept that much," he went on, "why didn't the British Military Mission approach the proper German authority, in this case the Berlin City Council?"

He was still making fun of me. But I couldn't say: 'This is getting us nowhere,' because he didn't need to get anywhere, nor did he want to.

"It would be too late for that. I'm telling you Nichols is a British agent. We accept full responsibility for all his actions."

"Diplomatic responsibility?" he returned sarcastically.

"Responsibility at the level of cooperation among the intelligence services of the NATO countries. You are still in NATO, Colonel, as far as I know. And should Herr Brandt consider leaving NATO in the future, it ought not to take effect retrospectively according to international law."

"What you're telling me is a *locus communis*," he said caustically, and added in a schoolmasterly way, "That is, a platitude. Not germane to the case before us."

"You are willing to let Nichols be murdered," I said calmly.

You could read his thoughts: 'Nichols is as good as a corpse, you idiot Therrick, and you know that as well as I do. Why are you trying so hard, you clown?'

"The Russians hardly ever murder their agents," he said.

"Usually only when they intend to defect. Why not have a word with them? I can let you have Colonel Kagin's phone number."

"I see you're inclined to jest," I said. "What should I offer him for Heinrich Groller? You?"

It went home. And stuck. He sat up a little, then regained control and said with a hint of a smile:

"British agents are not to be under-estimated. However, at least you'll appreciate that given the chance to get back such a brilliant operative . . ."

". . . that STASI pulled in just so they could demand Nichols from you. On whose orders was Nichols kidnapped?"

"I gave the order."

"Well, Herr Oberst . . . suppose I drew the conclusion from that that you were working for STASI?"

"Then I would recommend you to enter a criminal charge against Colonel Koerner either at the Federal Court, or through the Verfassenungsschutz Amt."

"Heinrich Groller is the brother of Adalbert Groller, your right-hand man. You are exceeding your authority. That much will interest the Verfassenungsschutz in any case. And the Christian Democrats in Parliament."

"Help yourself. Have you got Strauss's telephone number?"

"Any difficulties you might have won't bring Nichols back to life."

"You're about as interested in Nichols' life," said Koerner, "as I am in who wins the Saturday lottery. You want to interrogate a double agent and then lock him away. Do you think I can't see what game you're playing?"

If this was sincerity, what had suddenly brought it on?

"Nichols is a British agent," I said stubbornly. "Even if your double agent theory were correct, he would be a British agent working for the Russians with British knowledge and consent. All the more reason for wanting to get him back."

"That's your affair, Mr Therrick," he said airily. "I expect you'll find a way out of the mess you're in – you can always suggest him for a DSO in memoriam to the Prime Minister, can't you? Ever since Philby's day your Prime Ministers have preferred dead agents to live ones. We'll hand Nichols over to the East German authorities, and they'll hand him to the Russians. What the Russians do with him, as you surely appreciate, is hardly my responsibility. Next time you have an agent on Federal German territory with a Soviet passport and good friends in Odessa, and the job of ensuring coordination between British and NATO intelligence operatives, warn the BND, or us personally, in good time and I assure you there will be no difficulties."

He smiled like a vivisectionist completing a tricky operation on a quarter-inch worm, and stood up.

"We are living in a world," he added, walking round the desk, "which suffers from an utmost lack of discipline, order and that very coordination I mentioned. The German Federal Republic is supporting almost a third of the so-called developed countries of the West. It is we who are keeping the EEC afloat – and you are hoping to join it. Don't you think it would be a good idea if we showed each other more respect and stopped waiting for some emergency to arise before deigning to consult one another?"

It wasn't a bad speech – from the lips of a minister in Brussels.

"I want to speak to Nichols," I said as I stood up.

"Nichols isn't here. Did you really think we would bring him here for you?"

"I can be in Hamburg by tomorrow."

His features took on exactly the same expression as when

I had mentioned Heinrich Groller. And just as before he regained control at once.

"I don't see what good that would do." He paused and then he suddenly smiled. "All right, Mr Therrick. You shall speak to him. I'll give you half an hour. Is that long enough?"

By and large, you don't knock down experienced intelligence agents with feathers, but if Koerner had hit me with one at that moment I don't think I'd have been on my feet before the count of ten.

But I replied, as calmly as I could, that half an hour would indeed be adequate.

He gave a magnanimous nod.

"You will take the first morning plane," he said. "You'll be picked up at Hamburg airport."

— XV —

Nichols

It was dark by the time I was let out of the Sonderabteilung
building. The lights of Schwabing were shining and it was
cold. My next job was to contact Peccarie and give him
instructions for the following day. Book the flight first and
let him know to give his men a better chance to tail me.
Fix the time and place to meet them in Hamburg. I did
not doubt that I would be followed and that they would
try to tap any phone call. That meant getting through to
Peccarie so quickly that Koerner's henchmen would not
have time to rig a phone tap.

At the end of my talk with Koerner I had had an idea,
not a very original one, but one that struck me like an
electric shock. On the way down in the lift I came to a
firm decision.

Once out of the door, I was pleased to discover that I
was not to be taken back by car. The street, with its little
local park, was busy. I supposed that I was now being
watched by more than one pair of eyes, that two or three
cars were parked somewhere, linked by radio-telephone,
and that the customary six fellows with walkie-talkies were
hanging around.

Was Peccarie at the safe-house? I could reasonably
hope that he was. Speed was essential. I decided not to
ring from the hotel, but from a call-box. I walked a few
paces and entered a bar, the door of which was plastered
with pictures of busty blondes. It was just the sort of

place which pimps retire to in the intervals between collecting their cash, and where they might now and again bring a select customer to try some speciality. There were a number of girls hovering behind the bar, one a Titian-esque lady with a magnificent bust without visible means of support. The air was filled with the frightful squeal of electric guitars, and the room was stuffy.

I ordered a *Korn*, that disgusting beverage beloved of Germany's hard-working labour force and left-wing intel-lectuals, and asked for some small change and for the phone. The lady behind the bar looked at some point beyond me and then in Bavarian said it was not working. I nodded and finished my drink. In the corner of the room there was a glass door and behind that a telephone. A man was holding the receiver and speaking.

I turned. Behind me stood a beefy hulk of about thirty in a brown anorak, with his hands in his pockets as if he were ashamed of their size; he looked like a stevedore from Piraeus, except that he was fair-haired and had grey eyes that looked straight through me at the bar lady with an expression that said he had not finished counting all the bottles.

I walked round him, opened the door and went outside. I stood a moment by the door, but he did not come out. Even so it was obvious that I was still too close to the head office of the Sonderabteilung.

When I crossed the street I spotted him at once: Williams, my Munich contact, hunched on a bench, and looking in my direction. I walked slowly towards him, passed him without a word and strode into the park where I had seen the yellow of a phone-box.

I went in, lifted the receiver and put in the first of the five loose marks I had. The instrument was dead. The mark courteously fell back out. I was still too close to the head office or perhaps I was unlucky.

I walked towards the University and Leopoldstrasse. I felt chilly, but I was glad – anyone who has experienced the warm and enervating Föhn wind of Munich will appreciate even a cold spring. There were a lot of people in the streets and somewhere among them was Williams. What would be in Williams' mind? Probably the worry of losing me. What was in my mind at that moment was that here I was long past forty and roaming the world in someone else's employ, without pension, without a family, without a future. I was scouring Munich for a phone-box to help the British save one of their agents. Later, I might become a regular agent for them and, when this flap was over, they would settle down once again to keeping a meek watch on their trade unions' anti-state activities and reading about horse racing, cricket and Wimbledon in the papers. I had preferred the British to the CIA because with the CIA you never knew what senator would make it his mission to destroy the one organisation, *without* which America would disintegrate into fifty fragments.

Then I spotted another booth. It was on a street corner and someone was in it. So it was working. I lit a cigarette and waited. It was a girl in jeans and a strange smock thing, and she was earnestly gesticulating to someone at the other end. In due course she finished and I entered the illuminated phone-box, took out some change, inserted two marks and began to dial the Berlin code.

I heard the door open behind me and then someone's hand cut the connection. I turned. It was a nasty, young, thin person with freckles and an impertinent grin on its face. Not one of God's best efforts.

"You surely don't want to use the phone," it said. His hand still lay on the hook and mine still held the receiver.

The coins bounced back out. The youth opened the door a little further and grinned again. Behind him in the doorway stood another bum, and a little to the side, through the glass, I could see the face of the blond fellow in the leather anorak, the one who had been standing behind me in the bar. A few seconds passed. There was no sign of Williams, and anyway a fight just wasn't on.

"No, I don't think I do need the phone after all," I said and raked back my coins.

"That's good," said the youth. "Public phones get spluttered into by thousands of old people and you could easily catch flu. Or clap," he added, exploding into laughter.

He was a classic specimen of the Lumpenproletariat in the service of a state organisation, and he was enjoying his tiny measure of power.

He stepped backwards out of the booth and held the door open for me.

3

Koerner hadn't bothered to tell me the conditions of our deal. Clearly, it wasn't during our conversation that he had decided to let me meet Nichols. He had kept it up his sleeve as a kind of trump card and now here I was in a trap, crawling through the streets of Munich with three louts hanging on to me and pretty certain that soon others would materialise.

They allowed me to stop for another drink and stood around outside. One of them, the leather anorak, had a drink as well. They were no longer grinning, just watching me, and when we came out onto Leopoldstrasse I saw another two, less conspicuously loutish, who came and joined them. The new pair came into the hotel with me;

one of them booked my flight, and the other accompanied me to and into my room.

"Have a good sleep, and no arsing around," he said matter-of-factly.

"Why don't you just lock me up till tomorrow?"

"No need," he replied, and he was right. I might just as well pay for my prison accommodation myself.

When he left I sprawled on the bed and reached for the phone. The line was not dead and the operator asked what I wanted.

"Nothing," I said, because I knew that they were listening in. Or that they would cut me off in mid-sentence. Or something else. I put the receiver back and lit a cigarette. Then I heard a groping noise at the door. When it opened Williams was standing there.

He put a finger to his lips and closed the door behind him. My guardian angel – all the way to the hotel there had been no sign of him, but then I had not had much chance to look around without my escorts noticing.

Williams, slightly awkward and obviously worn out by the waiting, went across to the television and switched it on. It was long past midnight and there was only the third channel with a female in round glasses à la Trotsky reading from Marx, not loudly enough for us to be able to talk. I followed him into the bathroom. I started running the bath and turned on the taps in the wash basin as well.

"Before we get flooded," I said softly to Williams, who was watching me, cool and detached, "tell me where they are."

"One's in the vestibule, and one's arranging something with the bloke in reception," he replied equally softly and also in English. "I've got a room on the floor above," he added.

"You'll have to go and phone from outside the hotel," I said. "You must contact Berlin on this number." I gave it to him, together with the number of my flight to Hamburg and added, "Tell Peccarie he can deliver the envelope as agreed. And secondly, a tail in Hamburg first thing in the morning. They must stick close to me."

"I'm not sure I'll be able to arrange that," said Williams. "We're not in England and he won't have enough time. If your plane's at six forty-five and you're in Hamburg at eight in the morning . . . and our people in Hamburg don't even know what you look like . . ."

"They'll have to make do with a description," I said. "I'll be carrying the *Daily Telegraph*."

I could tell he was making mental notes. He was probably feeling sorry for Peccarie at the same time.

The details were all-important now.

How high was the probability that Williams would be caught when leaving the hotel?

How high was the probability that I'd be able to shake off the surveillance?

Even with the best planning I could produce, an unhealthy amount of improvisation was involved and we were not a practised team.

"They must follow every move I make. I expect to be seeing Nichols sometime in the morning. Have them contact me straight afterwards. If I am still tailed, the rendezvous is on Carolinestrasse at four, up in the restaurant tower. I shall need at least four men, maybe more. And get Peccarie to give you a phone number I can use in an emergency – with Koerner you never know. Then come back here. I'll leave the door unlocked."

Williams gave two more nods for good measure and I began turning off the taps.

4

I was alone in the plane. That is to say, I could not see any of my friends from the night before. I had not slept much; Williams had returned in the night to say Peccarie would do what he could and to give me the phone number of someone called Wollrath.

"Peccarie will be sending one of his best operatives," he had added softly, while all the taps in the bathroom were again turned on at full blast. The eavesdroppers must have reached the conclusion that I suffered from a cleanliness mania, or that I wanted to make the best of my modern German bathroom with its high-grade mixer taps and proper water pressure – not to be found in England. "He's called Greifner and he's extremely competent. The only snag is that your flight reaches Hamburg almost an hour before his – there's nothing before that from Bonn to Hamburg. But Wollrath and another chap called Kunze will be at the airport and they've got your description." He sounded not much more promising than a bank manager saying he'd see what he could do. "I hope you'll manage to get your *Daily Telegraph* at the airport," he said as he left. I did get it and now I was reading the editorials.

We landed at Hamburg just after eight. I walked through customs, my small case in one hand, and the *Daily Telegraph* in the other.

There was only a handful of people in the arrivals hall. I hoped that 'mine' were among them. Before long I was approached by a man wearing a grey overcoat and a Tyrolean hat, a strong-bodied, red-faced man, aged about fifty.

"Welcome to Hamburg, Mr Therrick."

He led me to a Mercedes parked nearby and asked, quite pleasantly, what kind of journey I had had. I assured him it had been a good one and in return I expressed my polite regret that he had had to get up early on my account.

The Mercedes had a chauffeur and we set off at once. In the wing mirror I saw a BMW pull out behind us, which in due course was replaced by an Opel Commodore. My guides were not in the least like those of the night before. The driver was preoccupied with his job, because it was early morning and the streets of Hamburg were very busy. We drove through Winterhude and headed in the direction of the Central Station. But soon we turned off towards Altona.

Only later did I learn that Wollrath and Kunze had had a rough time of it; their driver was ill and Wollrath himself had to drive and at the same time keep talking to the team in the Opel, which also consisted of two men; and, because none of them had the slightest inkling of where we were going, they had their work cut out for them not to lose the Mercedes.

I had expected them to blindfold me at some point, but nothing of the sort happened. My guide talked about the Hamburg opera and what a pity it was that the Director, Liebermann, had gone to Paris.

My guide lit a cigarette and fell silent. We were passing westwards through posh residential areas and we were heading for Blankenese, that suburb of Hamburg that sits perched on the Elbe and is the nest of some of the richest and most conservative citizens.

Soon we were descending a long serpentine road between yellow and white houses reminiscent of the South of France.

The sun was getting warmer and Blankenese glittered. It all had a slightly magical aura: the German cleanliness, the houses, the spring and the Mercedes with a driver, and a guide from the German secret service who was taking me to visit a condemned man, as if he were taking me to the zoo to visit a wounded tiger before its operation.

5

The house stood almost at the water's edge.

As I got out of the car I saw the BMW coming slowly down towards us and wondered how 'my' men would manage now: it was a very lonely spot despite the other houses all around.

Near the entrance stood a slim fellow who did not look like a gunman, but undoubtedly was one. He nodded to my guide and we entered the small garden through a wrought-iron gate. Only then did I notice the two television cameras covering both entrances.

The door into the house opened automatically. The hall-way had deer antlers on every wall like a hunting lodge. Two men, looking like Pat and Patachon, came down the stairs, which were covered by a thick carmine carpet.

"This is Mr Therrick," announced my guide and retreated.

The men shook hands with me and then, with an apology, did a body-search. It was extremely thorough: they checked absolutely everything, including my papers and my backside. If I had been trying to get some poison through I would have failed; they did not even overlook my teeth. Then they apologised once more and the small one said, with a glance at his watch, that I should have to wait another ten minutes. They led me into a small lounge on the ground floor, with barred windows. We sat down and the small man left. I began to realise how well organised this all was. There must have been many more people in the house, but I did not have the chance to glimpse them.

Then the small man returned and said he had to ring Munich once more to get final confirmation that I was to see Nichols, since things might have changed in the meantime. They took everything into account. So we went on waiting and, since the trip to Blankenese had taken almost three-quarters of an hour through the morning rush, it was half past nine when he came back and said that everything was in order and that I had thirty minutes for my undisturbed conversation. Undisturbed, I thought, except that you lot will be all ears to the microphone and be taking damn good care to see no one disturbs you while you're listening in! Did they take me for an utter idiot? Or was it a trick? An experiment? Just what was Koerner trying to do?

We went up the stairs to the first floor, down a corridor which had windows – all barred – along one side, and four doors along the other. A civilian was patrolling the corridor, a machine-gun in his hand. In the midst of all the luxury and apparent unconcern he seemed incongruous. He ignored us and the small man stopped in front of the second door, which he unlocked and opened.

"*Bitte schön*," he said, and I entered a small room, elegantly furnished, with a vast bed in the middle, a small book-case and dining-table, the whole lot mock Biedermeier. In the corners were cameras (of course), and the adjoining bathroom had no door, but photo-electric cells instead. The door closed behind me and the key turned in the lock.

"They even watch me shitting," said Nichols as he got up and took a step towards me.

— XVI —

A conversation

Nichols was fairly tall and had light-brown hair. His face testified to the good intellectual diet he had been given, but differed slightly from his photograph; there were tiny downward wrinkles round his mouth and eyes – not a photogenic type. His mouth was that of a man of experience who does not squander his kisses. Even now, in captivity, hardly that, if it were a prison, he retained a steady gaze and resolute movements.

When I entered he was sitting smoking in a corner by a barred window. What had he been thinking about? How fully did he appreciate his predicament? Had he been expecting me? Or had they told him nothing? How were we going to talk when every word was being picked up by other ears?

"My name is Therrick," I said, and offered him my hand. He gripped it firmly, but with a certain restraint. I tried to imagine what it felt like to be in his position; could he trust me, or was he determined not to trust anyone because he didn't dare? In the latter case how would I get rid of his distrust? I had no idea. He was under threat of death, because he knew too much, a classic situation. Given that, what sort of risks was he prepared to take?

"Sit down," he said.

I sat down on the bed, and he sat down again in his corner.

"I assume," I began, "you don't know who I am. But

that you do know that every word is being listened to."

"I was told a British representative was coming. You're not English, are you?"

"Not even British."

"And you're nothing diplomatic either, are you?"

"Right."

We looked at each other.

"Why didn't they send someone I know?"

I couldn't tell him they'd sent me because they knew I would have to take action visibly outside the German law – they expected it of me. They knew that if the worst came to the worst and there were no other way, I would liquidate Nichols.

They'd sent a mercenary.

"No one ever assumed," I said, "that I should have the chance to talk to you directly."

"What did they assume then? That you'd come to my funeral?"

"They assumed I'd be dealing with the German authorities. That's what I am doing. And it's got me this far." It sounded trite, true though it was. But I knew that it was a trick of Koerner's, or an impressive goodwill gesture at a stage when Koerner felt it no longer mattered. I added, "Perhaps you could tell me about things that are known to those who are listening, but not to me. There's no risk in that, is there?"

He gave a feeble smile, like a butterfly fluttering past unexpectedly.

"Have you spoken to Koerner?" I asked.

"No."

"No?" I was surprised.

"No."

Why hadn't Koerner interrogated him? Were they not interested in what a 'Soviet' agent had to say?

"I did talk to some third-rate twits," Nichols said

slowly, and the words carried the resignation of a condemned man, ignored by all except the priest and the
hangman. "They didn't ask me much. Just told me that I
was a Soviet agent, that they had proof, but that I was
lucky to escape trial and long years in prison, because I
was to be swapped."

He gave me another of those looks and smirked. "Charming, isn't it? Escape trial and long years in prison."

He looked up as if to make sure I knew what that meant.

"How long have you been here?"

"This is my third day. They brought me over in a
military plane."

He was wearing a light grey suit, but no tie of course
and his shirt was none too clean. He was clean-shaven, but
I was certain there would be no razor-blade in the bathroom – they had doubtless provided the latest Braun
electric.

I would have liked to have asked him how many men
there were in the house, or at least how many he had seen –
but our hidden audience would have guessed at once what
I was driving at.

"Just what did they ask you?"

"Nothing, really. It makes me feel as if I were an
untouchable. One little fellow asked me the same question
twice: whether there wasn't anything I'd like to tell him.
But he wasn't very persistent."

"Weren't you puzzled that no one tried to debrief you?"

"Aren't *you* puzzled?" He gave a bitter laugh.

I did not reply.

In a tone of exaggerated indifference he added:

"They aren't interested in what I know. It's only the
other side that's interested. All I can tell you is that I am
not a Soviet agent. I assume you know that. Several times
I've asked to see the German Public Prosecutor. Nothing
doing, of course. I told them umpteen times I was a British

citizen. They looked at me as if I'd come from outer space. It's a rigged game. And I can't prove anything because they stole my passport. Anyway, there's no one to prove it to, even if I could."

"Have you asked to see the British Consul?"

"No."

He said it harshly: he knew he was not entitled to contact the official British. The Foreign Office would have repudiated him. It would have taken ages before they agreed to find out about his British citizenship, if they had been forced into it, because he didn't have a British passport. And if not ages, then a week or ten days, which for Nichols amounted to the same thing. They would have done it in the end, but not soon enough to save Nichols' bacon. He was at a distinct disadvantage; and he knew it. But would it have been any help to him to pretend things were different?

"What passport did you have on you when they arrested you?"

"None," he replied simply. "They got hold of it the night after my arrest. But it was the Soviet one."

"Genuine?"

"Sure. I'd been to Odessa on it. It was in the name of Nikolayev, and it was valid for Germany, even for West Berlin. They are now claiming that I *am* Nikolayev. Colonel Nikolayev. He was about the same age as me. But he defected and in the end was shot – somewhere in America, I think, although he'd originally defected to us. He used to be with the UN in Geneva. Anyway, one thing's sure, I'm not Nikolayev, although I do speak Russian."

"Fluently?"

"As well as I speak German. I went to good schools."

I did not know what schools he meant, whether university or espionage training, but it sounded ironical whatever the case. I tried to feel neither admiration nor sympathy for

146

him. I tried to behave like a doctor talking to a patient suffering from a mild form of cancer. But I felt more like a grave-digger.

"Time is against us. But I may be able to do something for you."

"Save yourself the trouble," he said. "I know I'm as good as dead."

It was the reaction of a man rebelling against his own impotence. I took out a cigarette and lit it. He did not trust me but he handed me the ashtray.

"It's all a farce," he said. "They'll never have me up before the Federal public prosecutor. They have other plans for me. They know damn well what they're after."

"So do we, Nichols." There was a sharpness in my voice, but it was intended for our audience, not for him. But he missed the point and gestured with his hand as if to say: 'Balls, old son, I know the score all right.'

"They've eliminated Nighton," I said.

He looked at me in astonishment, then dejection.

"Cyril . . . He's dead?" he asked as if seeking assurance that the world was a filthy hole full of filthy goings-on.

"Forever," I said. "You've no idea who could have done it?"

"No," he said through clenched teeth. He still had that sorrowful expression in his eyes. "But most likely the same bunch who are so interested in me."

"There are many people interested in you at the moment."

"And they all want the same thing: me dead. Don't you?"

I did not reply. But he was no fool, not in the slightest. I looked at my watch. We had barely ten minutes left. I had to keep up the conversation. Not that I believed it would do any good; there is a time for words, and another when all that matters is action – but I had to put on a convincing performance for our audience.

"Does the name Groller mean anything to you?"

"There are two of them," he said. "Adalbert and Heinrich. Which one do you mean?"

"Adalbert, the one who works with Koerner. Heinrich's in East Berlin. They arrested him. It's him they want to exchange you for."

Listlessly he said, "I don't believe that. He's only small fry."

"But he's Adalbert's brother."

"They could easily swap him for somebody else. It's me they're after. If they have arrested him, it's only for appearance's sake. Can't you see that?"

Of course I could see it. But I wanted to reassure him that I really was who I was claiming to be. So I chose the old method of identification that had fortunately occurred to me in London and that I could make use of now, although all I hoped to achieve by it was to boost his morale.

"I've spoken to your wife. She's doing all right, but of course . . . she's very worried about you." Then I described to him the house, our meeting and the photos she had shown me. I was as detailed as possible and seemed to have convinced him. He knew that I could't have got through to his wife without approval from his superiors, and that she, without their approval, would certainly not have shown the family photos to a stranger.

"Do you know of anything," I then said, "that they can, and I ought to hear?"

He smiled. "I'm beginning to believe you were sent by our side, but I can't tell you any more than that it seems the East Germans have a mole right in the heart of Bonn. It's assumed that I know who it is and, what's more important, that I can prove it. That's why the East Germans are so keen to get me. And it's also why this lot here want to get rid of me so quickly."

"And they're breaking the law in the process," I countered. "Strange, isn't it? The German Federal Republic is meticulous in its observance of law; they're so scared of someone calling them Fascists that they can't even smash the Baader-Meinhof gang. While here . . ."

"They aren't literally breaking the law," he said, "they're just ignoring it. They're turning a deaf ear to anything I tell them, because it suits them. It's nothing but backstage junketings of the old school."

"Still, wouldn't Koerner want to know who's working for the East Germans in Bonn?"

"Koerner may well put the odd thing down in his notebook," said Nichols, "but, first and foremost, he believes I'm a Soviet agent. Or wants to believe it, which amounts to the same thing. And then of course he's under pressure from Adalbert Groller who wants to help his brother. At least, that's how I see it. The East Germans seem – from what you have told me – to have made one simple condition: either the Russians get 'their man', that is me, back, or Adalbert's brother will meet with a road accident or fall out of a moving train. That's all."

"I'll try and see Adalbert Groller, today. As far as I know he's in Hamburg. Possibly in this very house."

"You don't think he'll leave his own brother in the shit just because of you?" he mocked; he didn't realise that my mention of Groller had been meant for the ears of our unseen audience.

"We can try to find a way out, Colonel Koerner and I. If he only would forget his *idée fixe* that you are Nikolayev."

"There's a way out all right: get hold of some top-notch Soviet or East German agent."

"Paradoxically, that's partly in your hands," I objected. "I've heard that that highly placed East German agent is actually close to the Chancellor. If what is being assumed about you is true – that you know who it is and can prove it – and if I had that information I would go straight to the Minister, today. Wild horses . . ."

"You wouldn't go anywhere to see anyone," he interrupted sadly but firmly. "If I could tell you – that is if I knew" – *he* was speaking to the unseen ears now – "I would tell you only on British territory or somewhere where I could make sure you're one of us. It wouldn't be a matter of trust, I'd have to be certain. But even if I were sure of you at this very moment, it wouldn't do a scrap of good. Rather the reverse – you'd end up in the same boat as me."

But his eyes shone and his face looked excited; he had lost his detachment, his resignation. He had revealed to me something that he might not be *certain* of, but of which he was intuitively convinced – that it was the truth that really mattered.

"You think . . ." I began, and broke off.

He nodded. Slowly. Gravely.

In whose hands was he? In whose hands were we?

The possibility that I realised I had only toyed with until now suddenly rose up like a nightmare.

I was almost – for a passing instant – sick with shock.

Koerner was working for the Soviets!

— XVII —

Action

"We can't go and attack the house like gangsters," said Wollrath. He was stout, earnest, used to the occasional unpleasantness, but not to attacking houses in Blankenese in Hamburg.

"I'm afraid that's exactly what we shall be doing," I said, with an attempt at a chilly smile.

Wollrath looked at the others. We were sitting round the table in their Hamburg safe-house where they had brought me after they had made contact with me on Mönckebergerstrasse. After leaving Nichols, I had been handed back by Pat and Patachon to my guide, and he had driven me back to the city centre. No one asked me anything and it was as though they had completely lost interest in me.

Now we were sitting here, Wollrath looking dissatisfied and drinking his beer, Kunze cracking his finger-joints, Bristow gazing out of the window as if it were nothing to do with him, and Greifner thinking. My team. Greifner was tall and as cold as steel. He had grey eyes and international experience and no uncertain dislike of special agents who come into a friendly country, throw the normal run of things into total chaos, and, after they have stretched the whole network to near breaking-point, go away and leave it to the residents to patch things up again. I could read his thoughts.

'I've got to obey you, but I can make life awkward for

you if you make life awkward for me. You are responsible for your special mission, but we here are responsible for the steady and uninterrupted flow of information. Who's more important, you or us? Special agents come and go; we remain. We're badly paid. Many of us aren't even British. None of us believes any longer that we are defending something, since governments do not take the proper measures on the basis of our information. They're afraid of being unpopular, although they're unpopular anyway. They don't know how to lead people, they don't know how to inform them. When you disappear leaving the wreckage behind you, we shan't even be able to protect ourselves. Any kind of scandal is our enemy. We want to transmit information, not to attack houses. But we have to obey your orders.'

That's what Greifner was thinking. Aloud he said:

"I don't doubt you've considered the consequences. We shall be shooting at members of the German Secret Service."

"I'm not trying to persuade you."

After a moment's silence, Greifner said, "It's an order, then."

He looked at me, and I looked at Wollrath, who was gazing into his glass of beer, as if at any moment a submarine were about to surface there to take him off to South America.

"Of course. Hasn't my authority been verified?"

Greifner gave a sigh. "It has." Then he added calmly, "Unfortunately."

"Subordination doesn't carry much weight here, does it?" I remarked, because I knew it was now up to me to get the situation fully in hand and because Greifner was a potential 'representative of the opposition'.

"Subordination," he repeated, and shrugged. "You're talking about a hold-up. And those guys are going to shoot back. So you're talking about corpses as well. And then the scandal. Or is there going to be a Rolls waiting for Nichols to take him straight off to the Embassy in Bonn? Subordination! You're thinking like a bloody cowboy! I'll obey your orders, but first you've got to convince me."

Which meant: 'Convince *me* and my men will follow. Otherwise – complications.'

Time was running out. I had to drive him into a corner, even if it meant foul play.

"This isn't a democratic debating society," I assured him politely. "I give the orders around here, and you carry them out. Or you'll have to say you're going on strike," I added with irony. "It's quite the fashion, you know, but even if London makes allowances for strikes among the British electorate, they're not likely to for a strike by their own agents in Germany. Do you want me to contact London and tell them I'm through, because Herr Greifner has decided he's got cold feet?"

"I wouldn't do that if I were you," said Greifner mildly, "because I've said nothing of the sort, and your interpretation of what I said just won't wash. I am not impressed by your political simplification." He smiled, as if he had just solved an elementary bit of algebra. "I've told you my objections. If you were to order me to go off and shoot the President of the Republic, I'd be just as unwilling. And what you're asking is only slightly less loony."

"Herr Greifner," I said sharply, "while we sit here blathering, Nichols might be on the way to Russia. Either we get moving in an hour from now, or I want to be put through to London with the scrambler."

Greifner thought for a moment. Then he spoke calmly – and when a German decides, on mature reflection, to appeal to the bureaucracy, not even wild horses will make him budge.

"I'm not refusing to obey your orders, but I demand that London expressly confirms them through our chief of station. Have them ring him in Bonn."

2

I dialled the London number that Bride had given me for emergencies. It jangled for a while – in England the telephone rings differently than on the Continent, always giving a double grunt – and a somewhat surly female voice came on.

"Yes . . ."

"Darling, I've left my shirt at home," I said.

"The one I took to the laundry yesterday?" she asked indifferently.

"No, the one that's on the settee," I snapped out the rest of the code.

"Where are you calling from, son?" she asked, more affably now, and when I told her from a long way away she added, "Hang on a moment then, I'll have a look."

There was a pipping noise as she looked for the right extension indicated in the second sentence of my coded message. When she finally found it, which took her nearly a minute, she reassured me she would put me through, and it began to crackle again. I waited. I was alone with the scrambler on the little table in front of me and I doodled dirty pictures on it with my finger.

It was past twelve. Suppose Queeney were at lunch. Or seeing the Minister. Or seeing C himself. Or simply off sick. Would Bride be able to settle something that had turned into a problem? My experience had taught me that if something that had originally been cut and dried reverts by force of circumstances to being a question, no subordinate will come up with an answer; he'll just raise another.

"Receiving you," came through the telephone.

"Me too," I said. "But I'd like to be receiving Victoria."

"Who's speaking?" asked the voice.

"Velasquez. At my destination. On a public line, but the what's-it's here handy." I was still doodling my dirty pictures all over the what's-it.

"I'm afraid," the voice said, "that Victoria is in conference. Speak to someone else."

"I don't want anyone else," I said angrily, but relieved because that meant that Queeney was there after all. "I want Victoria. It's to do with the Confessor."

"What else could it be to do with, since it's you?" the voice complained, as though I were trying to make a fool of him. "Nevertheless, Victoria is in conference," he repeated stubbornly.

"Listen to me, you silly little shit: tell Victoria *at once*, and I mean *at once*, that I'm on the line or you'll cop the bollocking of a lifetime and Victoria will possibly have a *heart attack*. Can you figure *that*?"

Unlike the Germans, the English are not impressed by a raised voice. He said calmly:

"The meeting is in the rear wing. Even if I put you through, Victoria won't have a what's-it there. Call back in an hour."

"And you'll tell me he's at lunch, eh? In an hour will be too late. I'll tell you what you'll do: you'll take the what's-it along to Victoria personally and you'll tell him I know where the Confessor is and that I've spoken to him. Well . . . get a move on."

He gave up.

"Call back in ten minutes. But a different number – 230 1200. Got it?"

"Is that a direct line?"

"That's none of your business," and he rang off.

It was a long ten minutes. I knew I should have to tell Queeney my plan. I would have preferred just to create the situation and let the consequences take their course. And then appeal to his clear instructions, which had said 'At all costs!' Everything would have been settled and London would just have to sweat it out. But they would have got Nichols. As it was, Queeney was going to be sweating the whole time. Someone was bound to curse him. In the end it would be up to C himself to defend him. But I couldn't care less. I wasn't going to change *all* their nappies for them.

When I dialled the number, a man's voice answered and told me in a Cockney accent the frequency we were going to use, then added: "Wait ten seconds." I set the scrambler to the frequency and mounted it on the phone. After ten seconds, I said: "Hello, Velasquez speaking . . ." and waited a moment. A wild whizzing noise came through the receiver, like a speeded-up tape-recording.

Frantically I tried to remember what I had done wrong, but I could think of nothing. I took the scrambler off and put my ear to the bare receiver. Again I got the wild whizzing noise, but this time it was at a lower pitch and slower. At the other end of the line they were still trying to talk into the scrambler, but on a different frequency from the one I had set.

I waited for about a minute, until there was a plop in the ear-piece, something like the noise you get uncorking a bottle of ten-year-old claret – whereupon I began to hear in all clearness Queeney's Oxbridge English.

"Can you hear me?"

The question was a joy to hear.

I said I could, and that I was Velasquez, to which he said he was Victoria and gave me a frequency quite different from the one given me by the Cockney. So I repeated the manoeuvre with the scrambler, and in about ten seconds I was listening blissfully to Queeney saying:

"They say you've spoken to the Confessor?"

At last I was speaking to the one who mattered. Cautiously I said:

"Yes. Under certain circumstances I can lay my hands on him in a couple of hours."

"Marvellous," he said, "I can see we sized you up correctly." There was a moment's silence. "What circumstances do you envisage?"

"We'll have to use force."

"Of course," he said. "Of course. Is anything wrong?"

"Before we begin the action, your men want my authority verified again. Through the station."

"That's easily done."

"I'm glad. Can you do it at once? Time isn't on our side."

He hesitated for a moment. Then he told me to change the scrambler one degree. When we could hear each other again, he asked slyly: "Is it going to be an extra tricky action?"

"Bit of violence, some shooting perhaps."

"That all?"

"Maybe. There's no telling in advance. I might have to use hostages. A plane and a clear take-off and all that. Got it?"

"Do you mean you're going to negotiate with Bonn?" he asked drily.

"That, hopefully, won't be necessary. I think there are a number of people involved who wouldn't welcome any fuss."

"Who are you going to deal with, then?"

"The relevant authorities," I said tersely.

I almost heard him thinking. Then he said, "You've got the all-clear. I'm phoning the station now. But . . ." he added almost beseechingly, "try not to break all the china in sight."

In the age of terrorism and in a case of top priority, even a man like Queeney was willing to help me face up to my own responsibility. I had begun to be really alone.

3

The five of us were sitting together again. We had to wait another hour. In the meantime I explained my plan to them.

"You don't know exactly how many men are at the house," said Greifner. It was the only remark he tendered.

"I know there may be six . . . perhaps ten. No more than that."

"There are five of us," Wollrath remarked.

"Determined attackers," I said in the best German I could muster. "The surprise element is what counts. We'll easily deal with the one outside the house. As for the driver, he won't be prepared for any shooting. Nor will my guide. That's three. Pat and Patachon are not likely to carry more than pistols. The only snag is the one with the machine-gun in the passage outside Nichols' door. To make the odds in our favour remember one thing: no arsing about."

Finally, the phone rang and Greifner answered it. I heard him say, "Repeat it once more."

Then he hung up and looked round the room.

"Kunze," he said, "pop down to the cellar with Wollrath and bring up five machine-guns. And handcuffs. Wollrath's got the keys. And plenty of ammo."

4

Both cars drove quietly. I was with Kunze and Greifner in the Commodore, Bristow and Wollrath followed us in the BMW. We stopped a few yards from the house, got out and left the doors ajar.

It was three o'clock in the afternoon.

At that hour Blankenese was deserted. There was not a soul in the side street. I went first, because the guard knew my face. I handed my machine-gun to Wollrath. We followed the wall right up to the gate. It was closed, but when I beckoned to the man on the other side, he came over. The rest was the work of seconds. The levelled machine-guns convinced him and he opened the gate.

Wollrath handed me back my machine-gun, and Greifner asked:

"You got television circuit in there?" The man nodded. "How many watching it?"

"Schindler," the man said, and added, "but he's having lunch now." The guard had only a pistol, which Wollrath stuffed in his pocket. When he had handcuffed him, he unlocked the door with the guard's key and we went into the hall. No one was there.

"Where's the closed circuit screen?" Greifner asked, and the guard nodded towards a door. "Is it switched through upstairs?" The guard nodded. He was a bit hazy, and you could tell he was not going to let himself be killed for his bosses' sake. "Hurry up," said Greifner. "Where's the kitchen?"

We split up. Wollrath and Kunze stayed in the hall with the handcuffed guard and their machine-guns at the ready, covering the sitting-room door.

Schindler was eating in the kitchen with Pat and Patachon. Schindler dropped his knife and fork and Pat and

Patachon raised their hands. That was all. Bristow led them into the hall, where Wollrath handcuffed them and reported that the entire ground floor was empty.

I led the way up the stairs to the first floor and peeped cautiously down the passage. There was no sign of the man with the machine-gun. There was just a door half-open, at the end of the passage.

I felt as though I were back in Cyprus in sixty-four or before that in Algeria, or even earlier as a volunteer in the FFI at the end of the war . . . Except that now I was much older and felt far from heroic.

I said softly, "The man with the machine-gun was here."

Greifner said, "Three doors in all, including that half-opened one. He could be behind any of them."

"Or behind none of them," I said. "And he has the key to Nichols' room. Bristow, go down and squeeze it out of those jokers."

We were standing in cover, Greifner and I, at the head of the stairs. We waited. No sign of life anywhere.

"He's taking his time," said Greifner.

"They must be stalling." But I didn't believe it. Then I heard steps coming up the stairs.

It was Bristow.

He didn't seem in a hurry. He didn't seem to be taking many precautions.

"Their boss is in the office at the end of the passage," he said when he reached us. "But he's alone. All the others have gone. As for the key to Nichols' room, you don't need it. They've taken him away."

— XVIII —

The action continues

"*Scheisse*," said Greifner. "Here we are armed to the teeth and we may as well do target practice shooting little mice in the cellar."

"We got here too late," I replied harshly. "Because of your bloody yacking," I added, but left it at that. It was obvious he was already furious with himself.

We entered the room. Cautiously, with the proper kick at the door and a jump to one side. But there was no one there. The room was furnished as an ante-room, and there was a wallpapered door in the wall on the right. Bristow opened it.

A man sitting behind a large desk was delving into a drawer.

Greifner spoke from behind us: "Drop that pistol, or we'll cut you to ribbons. There's three of us."

The man took his hand out of the drawer. At that moment the phone rang.

"Pick it up," said Bristow.

The man was elderly, a good fifty-five. He was wearing a grey jacket and white shirt; he looked a typical clerk, perhaps in Aliens' Department. He lifted the phone and said, "Villa Bismarck."

Then he looked back at us. He must have noticed my smirk at the code-name of the building.

I took the phone from him and heard a German voice

asking for Ernst. I told him to ring back in ten minutes and put down the phone.

The man behind the desk was silent at first. But then suddenly he said:

"You're mad, Therrick. You can't get away with this in Germany."

"People have got away with other things in Germany before this," I snapped, "and not that long ago."

"You know me because you saw me this morning through your cameras with Nichols," I said gently. "But who are you?"

He didn't answer. He had apparently decided to ignore me.

He earned himself a prompt slap in the face and Greifner gave him another.

"Any more you need will be with a machine-gun butt," I warned him. "Who are you?"

"Colonel Groller," he said, with resignation.

2

It was not yet half past three. For the moment we were masters of the situation. But for how long? And what was the situation? I watched Groller, once more sitting in silence at his desk. Greifner stood a little to one side, brandishing his machine-gun, having already carefully tucked Groller's pistol away in his pocket.

Nichols had gone; the action had effectively failed, I thought to myself. But that was typical of the whole attitude of the West. They will go on debating until the roof over their heads goes up in flames. And they won't shoot even then. No. They'll start looking for the prosecutor general to be so kind as to issue a warrant for the arrest of – person or persons unknown. Habeas corpus. Provided the prosecutor will even do it.

We could, of course, scrap the whole thing and clear out. We would find some way or other out of Germany. But Nichols would not.

"Colonel Adalbert Groller," I said aloud, slowly.

The man nodded.

No, I thought, the action hasn't failed completely. Not yet. There's still hope. But it'll be a hard fight.

When you have chosen to fight, or if you have been forced to fight, you've got to be ruthless, right from the start. I was ready.

3

We locked Groller in Nichols' prison. Kunze and Wollrath stood guard downstairs, taking turns at the closed-circuit television, Bristow ambled up and down near the door, and Greifner and I took up residence in Groller's office.

Villa Bismarck was apparently reserved for purposes that Koerner probably did not over-publicise. It was certainly nothing central – the phones did not ring often enough. When one of them did ring, I answered it and said it was Villa Bismarck and would the caller ring back at five o'clock. But that only happened three times: one of them was the voice that had been asking for Ernst.

That apart, we were undisturbed and had a full twenty minutes in which to discuss the situation.

"Point one. The telephones. Somebody's got to answer them. Otherwise there'll be a panic. Either we'll be attacked by the Sonderabteilung people or else it'll be handed over to the flying squad and so to the Ministry of the Interior. A scandal guaranteed earlier than need be. I don't think that's what is going to happen, but in any case I don't want the people from the Sonderabteilung to smell trouble too soon. I want the conflict to start when we are ready for it and on our terms."

"But it's already started!" Greifner returned.

"Not all that much," I said. "Of course, we could run for it . . . if that's what you were thinking?"

Greifner put on the expression of a man with a wife and kids. But his tone remained lightly indifferent, prudently matter-of-fact and eloquently precise:

"We could interrogate Groller. He probably knows Nichols' present whereabouts. And then try to move in . . ."

"We'll interrogate Groller all right, but even if he knew – and if he does know, he'll *have* to tell us, Greifner! – it would not get us very far. The situation won't be as straightforward as it has been. By now Nichols could be in Munich, Berlin or Frankfurt. Or somewhere in Hamburg docks, where they may be getting ready for a quick swap."

"I don't quite see how you can stop it," said Greifner.

"Listen, Greifner, I am certain Koerner is working for the East Germans. Which means the Russians. Everything points that way, but especially the fact that he refuses to negotiate with us, that he's told practically no one, that his actions are basically against the law, and that he's covering himself by claiming Nichols is a Soviet agent. I've been in this game for years, Greifner. This isn't a case of Koerner hoping to win himself a medal; it's a case of pleasing his masters on the other side, and he's taking a big risk over it. He's got to act quickly. The fact that he let me speak to Nichols was just a trick that didn't cost him anything. He had everything we said bugged anyway and Nichols couldn't tell me anything; at least not anything about the evidence I'm sure he's got or knows where to get. Evidence that the Chancellor's office has been infiltrated."

I lit a cigarette and continued.

"Koerner's cover is the fact that Adalbert Groller's brother, Heinrich, is in jail in East Berlin. Koerner would have us believe that, because of Adalbert, he's after a quick exchange of Nichols for his deputy's brother. He's pretending the muck he's hiding is not so big as it really is. He's pretending to sacrifice Nichols – and that he's convinced Nichols is a Soviet agent and that therefore he, Koerner, is acting in good faith – for the sake of Heinrich Groller. Only if that *were* the case, he would have to bring the German authorities into it, and my bet is he won't do that. Instead, he'll start negotiating with me."

"Negotiating with you . . . negotiating what?"

"I want to swap Adalbert Groller for Nichols," I said.

4

Greifner said nothing. But he was a born sceptic and was bound to be mentally projecting the eventualities.

I went on in a low voice:

"I'm prepared to shoot the hostages. One by one, if necessary. One by one, and throw their bodies out of the window, Greifner."

"You don't look the type," said Greifner, and then added pensively, "London must know why they sent you. But I would never have thought you were the type."

"London sent me here to prevent Nichols crossing the line. And he won't cross it if I'm worth my salt. You say I'm not the type. In life, there are many theories about life," I said, taking care to stress the word *life*. "One of them is that in the end you'll be shot by those that you refused to shoot."

"We were hired for information work in *peacetime*," said Greifner with ill-humour.

"You know, Greifner, we're already well into the third world war," I said in all seriousness. "One rule of this war is that the aggressor is being excused by social considerations, and the defender is ashamed of his own name. Experience has taught me that the defender's only answer is an iron fist. That alone inspires respect. And not only among the masses, but also in an aggressor. I'll take full responsibility."

He nodded.

"If Koerner isn't an East German agent, he'll hand the matter over to the Ministry of the Interior at once, and the Ministry will act. Although that'll make us look like gangsters, the consequences will be that the Germans will hand Nichols over and give us a plane. For a moment or two, Downing Street and Whitehall will be topsy-turvy but in the end it'll all be nicely settled at the level of intelligence chiefs, because they'll all be doing their damnedest to keep the press out."

"And if Koerner doesn't do that?"

"Then the situation is obvious, wouldn't you say? He'll want to keep the whole thing under wraps and find a fast, reasonable solution. For us the only reasonable solution is Nichols. Of course, I realise things could go the other way: Koerner's real bosses in East Berlin or Moscow might order him to sacrifice Adalbert Groller."

"And then?" asked Greifner, ever to the point.

"And then it will be me who'll inform the German Ministry of the Interior and the press too, if need be," I said, thinking of Whitfield, squatting in Room 315 at the Intercontinental in Berlin.

"What if they manage to smuggle Nichols out before then . . . ?"

"I shall act quickly. Today." I looked at him very carefully and said in a deliberate voice, "When you're playing blackjack you don't expect to get blackjack. Imagine the

166

dealer has nine and you twelve. It's the old question: To draw another card or not.

"Of course, you draw. You draw with the risk of drawing a ten and going bust. That's how I want to play it.

"Koerner has got to be given an even bigger fright. We've got the means to do that. The other side will have to rethink the situation. Who matters most to them: Nichols, and so the man who's working for them apparently close to Brandt, or Koerner, who's so highly placed in the security apparatus?

"Whichever way they decide, it will take them a while and they'll keep Nichols this side of the frontier for the time being. Get it?"

Greifner stood up. "Okay," he said. "It's the craziest thing I've heard these five years, but I'll grant you may be right. You give the orders, and we'll carry them out to the letter."

"Pity you didn't do that before: we could have had Nichols alive and traded Groller for a plane," I could not refrain from reminding him.

"Looks like it," Greifner replied gloomily, then he added, "What do you want to get out of Groller?"

"Where Nichols is. What they plan to do with him. Who took him away. Whether he knows what Koerner's up to. Anything about Koerner. The whole lot. Take Kunze with you – *he* looks the type. Cigarettes and pliers to his testicles. As far as possible, leave his face alone."

Greifner looked at me in silence, before asking, "Anything else?"

"Yes," I said. "Don't forget to ask him how long he's been working for the other side himself."

— XIX —

A war of nerves

We unlocked the door and went in. Groller was lying on the bed, looking at the ceiling.

Kunze picked him up like a toy – and Groller must have weighed thirteen stone – removed his jacket and shoes and put him down on a chair. Groller looked around uncertainly, wondering what was coming. When he looked up at me, I said as drily as possible:

"You're going to talk, Groller. You'll tell us everything you know, and you'll be glad you didn't tell us something you don't know.

"My colleague," I pointed to Greifner, "will be asking you questions, and I warn you in advance, we know the answers to some of them. If you lie even once . . . you'll get pliers on your testicles and they'll roast the head of your penis with cigarettes. That's a promise, Groller; I left the jokes downstairs in my coat pocket. Are you with me?"

"You can't . . ." he began. I interrupted him while Kunze was binding his arms:

"Are you with me?"

"I refuse . . . I am a counter-espionage colonel of the Federal . . ."

"Hit him," I told Kunze, and Groller was promptly hit. He did not say any more and Kunze finished the job so that Groller was practically screwed down to the chair.

"Get cracking," I said to Greifner, who sat down behind Groller with a notebook in his hand.

I left the room quietly, closing the door behind me.

I went through into the office. The inspection took me ten minutes, and one of the prizes was an address book with telephone numbers. I lit a cigarette and gave it a detailed reading.

Then I lifted the phone and dialled Koerner's Munich number. Someone picked up the receiver and I heard a terse "*Bitte.*"

"Villa Bismarck," I said. "I want to speak to Colonel Koerner."

"Who's that speaking?"

"Villa Bismarck. You heard it right."

There was a moment's pause, then the voice said "*Momentchen.*"

Eventually a cool matter-of-fact voice, slightly metallic, came on the line.

"Koerner speaking."

"I'm calling from Villa Bismarck, Koerner. If there's anyone in the office there, chuck them out. I'll wait."

He hesitated, then said, "Moment," and I heard him saying something into space, after which he returned to the phone.

"Who's that calling?"

"We spoke yesterday evening. It would be as well if you told me at once whether this is an open line. I'm sitting in Groller's office and I've got a scrambler in front of me. It might be as well for us to use it. Tell me the frequency."

"Where's Groller?"

"You really want to talk without the scrambler then?"

He hesitated. He was sure to be thinking feverishly. I waited tensely for him to decide. Then he told me the frequency.

I had not been wrong.

When we renewed contact, I said briefly:

"The house is in my hands, my men are watching your four and Groller is just being interrogated. Have you any suggestions?"

2

In the silence that followed I could hear him breathing. I could sense the intensity of his thinking.

Like me, he was certain to have lost all interest in the outside world. Like a pharmacist he was meticulously weighing the various tricks and attitudes he could take. All at lightning speed. He was an exact gamesman; he did not use the indignation tactic. He said icily:

"I want to speak to Groller first."

"By all means. He'll tell you his plight, and to be sure he's not speaking from a tape, you can ask him one question about the weather. That's all. Wait. I'll have him brought here."

"I'll wait."

They would have to unfetter Groller, and that seemed too long a process. We picked him up, chair and all, and carried him into the office.

"Groller, you will tell Koerner, who's on the line, how things stand here. He will ask you one question about the weather, and you will answer briefly. That's all. One trick and I'll douse my cigarette in your right eye-socket. Understood?"

"Yes," he said, and then I put the telephone to his ear and mouth.

With effort, he said, "Leopold . . . ?"

Koerner apparently said enough to reassure Groller as to his identity, because he added:

"I'm in Therrick's hands. They're interrogating me. They're . . . they're going to torture me."

"That'll do," I interrupted. I took the receiver and said, "Do you want to ask him a question about the weather?"

"No," said Koerner, quietly.

"Hang on then," I said, and helped Greifner and Kunze carry Groller on his chair back to Nichols' room. I suddenly wondered whether they were following what was going on from the television room, but I did not care. Before I left I whispered to Greifner, "Is he talking?"

Greifner nodded. "So far he is," he said, "but so far we've been asking about the house and so on. I'm keeping Nichols for later. Are you coming back?"

"As soon as I've finished with Koerner."

I went back to the telephone. "You there?"

"Yes," said Koerner.

"You've had plenty of time to think while I've been gone. I'm sure you've had lots of ideas. What have you worked out?"

"I'd like to know whether London gave the go-ahead for this action of yours."

"Yes, Koerner, they did. Now you know where you stand."

"It's . . . it's highly unusual," he said, and it sounded as if he were talking to himself.

"What have you worked out?" I said again, drily, ignoring his remark. I could sense how he was being gnawed by the temptation to say: '*You realise we'll surround you with police and start treating you as terrorists?*' to test my reaction and confirm that things had gone as far as he feared. But he did not say it. He knew that would seriously weaken his position, should he have to back-track on the threat.

I began to *know* how things stood, and my game acquired the rhythm of that winning streak, which at blackjack usually comes once in an evening and which you have to know how to spot so that you can raise your stakes in time. I raised mine.

"I'm not asking you where Nichols is, but I'm telling you one thing: God have mercy on you if he's no longer in your keeping."

"Suppose he's no longer mine to dispose of?"

"Groller will cop it. And you with him."

"That won't help you to get Nichols."

"Your own skin matters most, doesn't it?"

"To me. But I am sure you realise it doesn't depend just on me."

"Did you think I wasn't expecting that excuse?"

"You've no proof."

"Neither have you. And I've got Groller. Do you think he won't tell me the rest of the goings-on?"

"Are you going to torture him?"

"Certainly. I shall use every means, Koerner, every one. In the end you'll have to run. Who's that going to help?"

"Why should I run?" he protested.

"Have it your own way," I said. "If you don't want to be frank, I shan't force you. Either way you know how things stand. So, let's not prolong the agony. What's your offer?"

"I need time, Therrick."

"I want guarantees regarding Nichols."

"There's none I can give you today. Tomorrow possibly. I must have a little time."

"By this time tomorrow I shall be forced to inform the press and the Interior Ministry. In that order."

"By this time tomorrow an exchange may be possible. But only if Groller can assure me he hasn't been tortured and hasn't signed anything. You understand?"

"Nichols must be on board a plane at Hamburg airport at three p.m. tomorrow. That's the deadline. We'll all go there, including Groller and the rest. We'll board the plane. We'll fly to Heathrow, where Groller and the others will be released."

"I want Groller in Hamburg. I want to talk to him and I want him to stay here. You can take the rest as hostages."

"No, Groller's coming with us."

"Don't overdo it . . . you realise it's not just my decision."

"In your own interest you'll try to arrange things so it *is* just your decision. Or am I wrong?"

There was a silence. Then he said with resignation:

"I can't perform miracles. Where's my guarantee you won't do the dirty on me . . . afterwards?"

"Think, Koerner. I'm a mercenary. My job is to bring back Nichols. That's all I'm interested in. What you're going to do later in your own backyard is your affair."

"I'll try and stop the Nichols exchange," said Koerner, returning to his cautious official tone. He didn't even trust the scrambler, poor little lad. Probably couldn't even trust his own bed. "But I don't want you to torture Groller," he added.

"Your humanity and friendship bring tears to my eyes," I said. "But let me assure you that whatever I squeeze out of Groller, I can forget again straightaway . . . if it suits me. If you want to phone me, you know where I am."

I rang off.

3

I wondered how much time I had. Of course Koerner would order the line to be tapped, but by whom? He could not risk the BND finding out what we were on about. He would have to give the order to some of his own men, and they would need a little time. How long? Two hours? An hour?

I dialled the Berlin code and the number of the Intercontinental, and then asked for Room 315. But no one answered. I asked them to page Mr Whitfield and began to get the usual running interference with the young lady at the switchboard, the half-witted receptionist, and the head porter who insisted that Mr Whitfield must be in his room, because his key was not in his pigeon-hole.

"He carries it around with him, like a lucky charm," I told him. "Some patrons are like that, you know."

"But that's not allowed," he said with an audible shudder. "Keys should be surrendered when rooms are left unoccupied. Otherwise we wouldn't know where we were, if keys weren't surrendered!"

Keeping my self-control, I spent a while persuading him, and in the end they did get him for me, asking three times who was calling, which I patiently answered: "The American Consulate in Hamburg."

"Whitfield," came over the line at last.

"That's the ticket," I said. "Therrick. You offered me an exchange of information. I might have a scoop for you, but also I might not. Are you game to fly to Hamburg on the strength of such a hazy promise?"

"Give me a clue what it's about," he said. "Where are you ringing from?"

"Hamburg, and it's to do with the possible fall of the Chancellor himself," I said, and I had no idea that I uttered a prophetic sentence.

"Okay. When?"

"Straightaway. Put up at the Atlantic. If you can't get a room there, try the Vier Jahreszeiten. I'll ring you this evening at the hotel. But I can't guarantee anything. If I happen to be dead by then . . ."

"You won't be dead; they'll have to take an axe to you when you're a hundred and ten, otherwise you'll never die. I'll wait for your call."

Then I rang Peccarie, and told him briefly where I was and to have a handful of men ready and waiting. Peccarie asked no questions.

"It might," I added in the end, "be just a false alarm, and I might not turn up in Berlin again. But you'll get to hear."

Then I rang the Commodore.

The phone was answered by a girl who said her master was not in and that she did not know when he would be back.

"But he is in Berlin?" I wanted to be sure.

"I don't know," replied the servant mentality, and I had to make do with that.

Then the other phone rang and the same voice as before asked for Ernst. I said that Ernst had gone to Munich for two days to see Colonel Koerner, and the voice seemed content and said it was all right then. I replaced the phone and took a breather. I had won the first round. Now it was up to Groller.

4

Groller was still firmly bound to his chair, but his shirt was undone and his trousers and pants were down. Kunze was sitting in front of him with a pair of pliers in his hands.

"Doesn't our ladybird want to speak?" I asked, and closed the door behind me.

Greifner, who was sitting behind Groller with notebook in hand, said casually, "He's making heavy weather of it." He stood up and we went out into the passage together.

"Nichols is in Munich," he reported. "They want to do the exchange in Berlin. Day after tomorrow. Groller says he doesn't know why they're shunting him here and there, but he thinks it's for security reasons. Because the French secret service is showing interest."

"Which one?" I asked.

"Groller thinks two of the five. The SDECE and the DST."

"Did he say why?"

"That's just where we got to. But about this house – it belongs to the Sonderabteilung and is only used occasionally, for interrogations and negotiations. Usually there are only three people here, who live in. Here's a list of our hostages." He handed me a paper with the names. "Groller assumes we know more than we really do, but he tries to wriggle out of direct admission. He claims Koerner runs things himself and that he, Groller, only deals with certain cases. He claims there are about 5000 Soviet agents in the country, from informers to illegals. That they can't possibly keep tabs on them all . . ."

"What about the phone lines?" I asked.

"Groller says they're clean. But they may be tapped now and again he says. They do it at random."

"Like anywhere else. Is the Sonderabteilung a separate department?"

"Yes. But its finance comes under Pullach, the BND."

Groller's address book flashed through my mind. "He was serving under Gehlen, wasn't he?"

"Yes. He's been in it practically ever since forty-seven. He crossed to the Americans with information on the Abwehr."

"Koerner as well?"

"I haven't asked him that yet. We've been talking about this house, mostly. And Nichols, of course. He insists Nichols is a Soviet agent. He also insists you are mad and he's been trying to persuade us to pack it in."

"What did you say to that?"

"Kunze hit him once or twice, so *he* packed it in."

"Good. Let's go in. We've got to hurry."

Greifner went back to his post behind Groller's back and I went and stood in front of him.

"You're not talking fast enough," I said. "My friend has been complaining. Koerner, though, is trying to find a way to get you exchanged for Nichols, if that's of any interest to you."

Groller opened his eyes wide.

"You don't really believe that, do you?" I smiled. "You know there are reasons for which Koerner might leave you in the shit. We'll shoot you, Groller."

He groaned.

"You don't want to die, ducky. So say your prayers and hope Koerner will manage after all. Who's Koerner's immediate superior?"

"The head of the BND. But Koerner has wide powers of his own."

"Has he the power to arrest?"

"Yes."

"Without the approval of the Public Prosecutor?"

"He has to get the approval afterwards."

"Did he get it in this instance?"

"What instance?" Groller asked, so Kunze hit him.

"No, he didn't," said Groller.

"Did you know that?"

"Yes."

"Did you talk about it?"

"Yes."

"Get talking, you bloody idiot. What did you both say about it?"

"It was Koerner's decision."

"Who contacted you from the other side?"

He hesitated. "Teddling," he said. "He's the . . ."

"I know. STASI's unofficial representative in West Berlin. Every child in Berlin knows that. But supposing it was you who contacted Teddling yourselves . . . ?"

"No. Not us. Kagin . . ."

"So you're claiming that first you arrested Nichols . . ."

"Nikolayev. Nichols is Nikolayev . . ."

"He's not, and you've known that perfectly well for

some time. We'll talk about that later. Why did you stay here after they'd taken Nichols away?"

"I was intending to fly to Munich tonight. To Pullach."

"To report to the head of the BND that Koerner had arrested an English agent?"

"No. I live in Pullach."

"Which reminds me of one small detail, Groller. In your address book I found a Pullach number and the name Fritz under it. Nothing else, just Fritz. Do you know, that interested me." I looked at him enquiringly. "Who is that Fritz?"

"Fritz Schröder. But he's my secretary . . ."

A little shiver ran down my back and up again. That always happens whenever a hunch of mine is about to be proved right.

"Where does this secretary of yours live in Pullach?"

"Where? At my place."

"You live in a large house, don't you?"

"Yes."

"Your brother Heinrich . . . when he's not in Frankfurt, or Berlin . . . he's often at the house, eh?"

He nodded. He could not have the slightest idea what I was aiming at, and he was never to find out.

"You got children, Groller?"

His eyes popped. "I'm not married. Never have been. No, I haven't."

"But your brother Heinrich is married, isn't he?"

"No, he isn't. That is . . . he was once. But he got divorced . . ."

"You don't happen to know where his wife's living now?"

"Westphalia. Why . . . ?"

My skin turned to gooseflesh. Everything clicked. I began to see daylight. "Has your brother got any children, Groller?" I asked innocently.

"One."

"Boy or girl?"

"A girl."

I lit a cigarette. My hand was shaking slightly.

"What's her Christian name?" I asked, though I knew the answer.

He looked at me, as if I were trying to make fun of him.

"Veronika."

— XX —

Groller

It was Friday, late afternoon, time was flying, and the chips were down. I had that frantic sense of powerless rage of a man who knows how things stand and can do nothing, or almost nothing, about it. That, almost nothing, was a dangerous pair of words. In my profession it could mean a tendency to romanticise, and a tendency to romanticise in the intelligence game is being on even thinner ice than being a double agent.

Nevertheless I went back to the telephone. While Greifner carried on questioning Groller, I tried to ring Veronika. But the hotel said she was not in. What did I want to tell her? I think I just wanted to hear her voice. Once I had understood *why* the SDECE was so interested she had suddenly become a very important person. She was now more alone than I've ever been, but she didn't know it, which made her even more vulnerable.

Her innocence (and deliberate exaggeration of mine), her naivety, her conviction that she was clever and mature and knew how to cope, her spontaneity (but now the world might soon destroy it) – all that provided the perfect basis for any spooks to get her easily enmeshed in their dirty dealings.

The sharp-sighted Dupont was using de Brissac as an erotic bait with a long-term aim. He knew that Veronika, the daughter of Heinrich Groller (at present under lock and key in East Berlin as an agent of the BND), was also the niece of Colonel Adalbert Groller, who was one of the targets of French interest.

What exactly the French were after I didn't know. But I could guess that they, who always knew even more than they disclosed among themselves and are always ready to play a false ace pulled from their neighbour's pocket, were busily adding to the file on Willy Brandt.

Veronika had access to her uncle's Pullach house where she and her father apparently sometimes stayed. She was an ideal key to many things, last but not least, to the door of the house of Colonel Adalbert Groller.

On reflection I rang Pullach and spoke to Colonel Groller's secretary, Fritz Schröder, introducing myself as one of Veronika's friends.

He was a bit cagey, but in the end he did tell me that Veronika had rung the day before, Thursday, and she might be coming very soon. Then I rang off and returned to the interrogation.

2

"When did you start surveillance on Nichols?"

"He's been on the BND's list for some years."

"On whose orders did *you* start the surveillance?"

"Koerner gave the order."

"When?"

"Last January, I think."

"Who supervised the operation?"

"Koerner himself."

"Did he do that in all cases?"

"N-no."

"Look here, Groller, getting anything out of you is like getting blood out of a stone. Start talking more readily.

Why did he do it in this instance? What did he tell you about it?"

Greifner's questions rained down on Groller with professional certainty. Groller tried to dodge them where he thought there was a chance of dodging – even though he must have assumed we would notice.

"You're saying that Koerner told you Nichols was a Soviet agent. How could Koerner have known that? What did he tell you about it?"

"We had the operatives' reports."

"Did you see them?"

"N-no. I wasn't on the Nichols case."

"But since you were entrusted with holding him here . . . !"

"Only lately."

"Where are those reports?"

"Munich. Koerner's got them."

"Who was tailing Nichols before Koerner took over?"

"The BND. In a lukewarm sort of way, the way agents of NATO countries are followed."

"So the BND didn't think Nichols was a Soviet agent?"

"No."

"You're lying. Koerner didn't think so and still doesn't." I butted in on the questioning. "You'll have to get talking, Groller. Time's short. What about it then?"

"I don't understand . . ."

I nodded towards Kunze. He aimed a straight right at Groller's solar plexus.

Twenty seconds flowed by.

"Talk, Groller. When did you and Koerner make a deal about Nichols?"

"In January. Koerner . . ."

He must have felt awfully alone. Koerner was God knows how far away, Nichols' fate was in someone else's hands, and he was bound to a chair, which Greifner held steady every time Kunze went to hit him. He must have felt forsaken, alone against brute force. He must have felt the world's indifference to the destiny of an individual down on his luck.

"You joined forces long before that, Groller. Long before. Sometime in the fifties. Maybe a bit later? Was it for money? Whose idea was it? Koerner's? Or yours?"

His face was the image of despair. But I knew that that fifty-five-year-old face was that of an old, practised intelligence rat. And I was in a hurry.

"You're going to talk. Koerner won't help you. My good friend here will help you – to get talking." And again I nodded to Kunze.

"Whom did you negotiate the Nichols exchange with?"

"Teddling. He . . ."

"Which of you saw Kagin?"

"That was always Koerner . . . and Sichler. But I don't really know."

"*Sichler?*" The name rang a bell instantly. "Who's Sichler?"

"Our agent in Berlin."

"Operative, contact-man, chief-of-station . . . *what* is Sichler, Groller?"

"He ran the Benefactor operation. He's . . ."

"Does the name Jens mean anything to you, Groller?"
He shook his head.

"Then the name Barthels does mean something to you."
He swallowed.

Now I knew I was on the right track.

"What is the Sonderabteilung, Groller? Just what is it? What sort of a beanfeast were you having there? Bang in the middle of Federal Germany, bang in the middle of their security service? Do you think I can't guess? Do you think anyone's going to protect you? You're a dead man, Groller, a dead man!"

And I pressed straight on.

"The SDECE's got its hands on your niece. One of their agents is busy turning her pretty little head and is going to see Fritz at your house today as her lover. What do you keep at the house, Groller?"

"It...it's not true," he whispered. "Veronika has nothing to do with this!"

"Do you love her, Groller?" When he did not answer, I began stabbing him in the back, albeit only metaphorically. "She's young. They chose an elegant, virile agent. She'll help him, without even knowing it. Fritz can't keep his eyes on the whole house. Or the experts'll turn up; the experts will make a search, even if it costs Fritz's life. And as for your niece . . ." I made a gesture that did not need explaining. "She'll have a fuck or two. Get some money, drugs, anything . . . Groller, you're alone."

I took him by the ears and held my face to his and repeated – giving vent to the hatred I was feeling towards everything he stood for – slowly and almost gleefully:

"YOU'RE ALONE, GROLLER, YOU'RE ALONE."

Then I shook his head. "Before we exchange you for Nichols, we'll make mincemeat out of you, Groller. Who picked Sichler for operation Benefactor? You, or Koerner? Or Kagin perhaps?"

I could tell he was thinking about Veronika. He had not wanted *that*. He had not imagined *that*. Not Veronika. He must have loved her. But he had lost his bearings now. Behind him Greifner was quick off the mark.

"You won't have the time to sort out what's best for you, Groller. We won't give you any more. You're in the shit and down the sewer. A cess-pit, Groller. And now you're going to drink it." He declaimed it in a dry steady voice, like a magistrate ordering a motorist to pay a fine of a hundred marks. "You're going to pay for the damage, Groller," he added.

"*Sichler*, Groller, what do you know about Sichler? Was he with the BND? Or with the Verfassenungsschutz? Did *you* find him? Or did *they* supply him?"

And again. And again. We knew he was still resisting: the instinct for self-preservation. We did not expect answers to our questions. We kept them up, mostly me, Greifner larding them with psychological pressure: "We'll use every available means" and "When my colleague crushes what you've got between your legs, then you'll start to sing", or "Time is against you, Groller", and I came back full circle to the original questions. Groller was obviously incapable of speaking; he was tense as if caught in a spasm, he began to sweat, and occasionally a twitch of pain ran across his features. I summoned all my energy and began to stare fixedly at his naked penis while Greifner continued. Groller followed my gaze and thought I was trying to make up my mind. He was seized with panic.

3

After ten minutes, Groller was howling. Kunze was giving his testicles the works.

I opted for a short break. Kunze stopped. "Groller, burning's the next stage. Are you going to talk?"

He wanted to, but couldn't. He knew he was going head-long into an abyss. He was incapable of decision.

"The Benefactor business, Groller. Whose idea was it? Yours? Or Koerner's?"

"It . . . it was essential . . . we had to keep an eye on the private life of . . ."

I nodded to Kunze. "Not too much," I said in his direction. And in Groller's, who began to howl with pain, "You got Sichler to hire a pimp and have him photograph

Barthels' sexual jollifications? Is that what you mean?"

Groller was breathing fast by now, and shaking. Kunze gave his testicles an extra little squeeze.

"You had to *protect* Barthels from possible blackmail, Groller; is that what you mean? The pimp Jens Baumgartner and the Piermont girl. Do you think I don't know? We've had our hands on Jens for some time, and he's been talking, Groller. We'll give the stuff to the BND, be certain of that. And the balls-up over you will be forgotten. No one's going to defend you; no one's going to ask what we did to you, because everyone involved will know *why*. Sichler, Groller. Start spilling on Sichler."

"It was Koerner's plan."

"You're a little innocent. Of course, it's all Koerner's doing!"

"Koerner said a campaign was being hatched against leading politicians and that . . ."

"*He* told *you* that? He'd no need to tell you that, Groller. Who hired you? The East Germans? The Russians? Koerner? Kagin?"

Again I nodded to Kunze.

The room at once felt close as Groller began to yell.

4

Now he sat there, collapsed. He was weeping, and now and then he gave a yell as Kunze burnt him. But he was still in a state of shock.

"We'll break you, Groller," I said. "Completely and for good. I've warned you. We haven't got time. Who hired Sichler? What do you keep at your house? When did you discover Nichols suspected you? Who gave you a report on what Nichols had really discovered? What does Nichols *know*, Groller?"

Now Greifner took up the questioning again.

But Groller, or rather some power within him, still resisted. It was not an attitude, but simply an inability to speak. I realised with horror that we would have to use tougher tactics.

It was somewhat (but the other way round) like a woman who cannot reach orgasm. She all but reaches it, but is not capable of making it. You have to beat her, subject her to violence, before she loses the mental blockage that prevents her from letting herself go – but of course, while it is no good to be delicate, the violence must be applied in very precise doses, and you must never stop talking to her.

Would Kunze know how to apply this technique on Groller? I went off to the telephone.

I knew it was bound to be tapped by now, but I did not care any more. While Greifner carried on with Groller, I wanted another talk with Koerner. I decided to play the decisive hand. I was afraid of losing Nichols.

This time I mustn't be too late.

5

It took a long time before I got him on the line. Half an hour, I think.

"What do you want?" he asked impatiently and a trifle uncertainly. "I've told you already I need time."

"Put the scrambler on, Koerner. I'm going to start speaking in ten seconds, otherwise the line won't be protected and I'll be talking on an open line."

"Okay," he said quickly.

In ten seconds we began speaking. That is, I did.

"We know everything Koerner. Everything about Benefactor, Barthels, Sichler, Baumgartner." I did not care whether he wanted to warn Sichler; that was a German affair. I was only interested in putting the wind up him, and I knew that you can put the wind up *anybody* on earth, if you have the leverage. "Groller is singing, Koerner. About you and about himself. We know all about your efforts to compromise politicians so that your paymasters on the other side – or maybe they're your ideological brothers-in-arms – can steer them better along the channels of the Ostpolitik. You're finished, Koerner. I can have you arrested within an hour or two. You'll have to run for it. You'll have to live for good on the other side, and I don't suppose you find the prospect very enticing. Of course, they'll give you an official flat. And a little car. You'll be on a socialist pension, Koerner. Start packing your bags."

There was a moment's pause. Then he said, "Why are you telling me all this?"

"Because you don't matter to me any more, Koerner. You're vermin, but not in my garden. I've told you before, I'm a mercenary. For all I care, the Germans can clean out their vermin on their own. I'll give you a chance. Things can stay as they are. But – and this isn't an exchange any more, Koerner, it's an ultimatum now: I want Nichols immediately. Today. Got it?"

He said nothing. Nor did I. Seconds passed.

But I knew that he knew that he had lost.

He was working out his losses.

"What's your offer?" he asked.

"You're still being too matter-of-fact. Since last night the situation has changed. I'm laying down the law now and you'll do everything I say to the letter. Where is Nichols, Koerner?"

"What's your offer?" he repeated, almost pathetically.

"I want Nichols' address, Koerner. And I'll go and

fetch him. I'll bump off anyone who cares to object. And I'll take him to Britain. That's the verdict. Get it?"

"I want to speak to Groller... otherwise... I want proof!"

"You want proof that the Sonderabteilung is a subversive sabotage department covering for the East. Is that what you want, Koerner?"

Silence.

"If I have to run for it," he said at last, "I'll take Nichols with me. You can't stop me."

He was right.

I had driven him too hard against the wall.

The ball was back in my court.

Twist on a Friday night

Now I was thinking as fast as I could. I knew Koerner was doing precisely the same. He too knew what was at stake. He knew his predicament. It was a deadlock. I could destroy him here, but he could flee with Nichols. Crossing the German frontier from somewhere near Munich over to the Austrian side was child's play. Or he could cross in Berlin. Everything depended on how he would transport Nichols. An injection and a few hours' flight, a big crate sent as diplomatic baggage, and that would be the end. Drily I said into the telephone:

"Koerner, I don't know where Nichols is. You may manage to get him across to the other side, but you'll never get over yourself. You're being followed. And not just by my men."

"Who else knows about it?" he asked menacingly.

"The French. But they still don't know about you. They're following the Nichols case. They're on to the track he discovered. That could, of course, lead them to you. It needn't. That's where your chance, your last chance, lies."

"What's your offer?" he said again, and I knew I should have to back down from my ultimatum.

"I get Nichols and forget about you. That's all. But at once."

"That's impossible. I . . . I've already tried to negotiate.

But . . . if I'm not going to run away, I can't tell anyone the real situation. You get my meaning?"

"How couldn't I? But that weakens your bargaining power."

"That's just it."

"How do you want me to believe you, then?"

"How am *I* to believe *you*, when you're interrogating Groller?"

"You've *got* to."

It was a game of cat and mouse, except that we kept changing roles.

Not even he could know what his bosses on the other side would choose: the loss of a powerful agent close to the Chancellor, or the loss of a departmental head through whom they could carry out subversion, as well as keep tabs on the BND's knowledge of what the agents of STASI were up to in West Germany. He had to deceive them. He could not tell them that Groller was in my hands and that he was singing. And, of course, I was going to deceive him: Groller would say all he had to say into a tape-recorder, it would be transcribed, and he would sign it. Or he would transcribe it himself, to make certain. A complete confession. It would be up to the British to decide whether or not to hand it over to the BND, and when. But Koerner would gain time, which he apparently needed for some reason. That at least, I could grant him.

"I'll ring back this evening. Don't do anything," he said. "By this evening I shall know more. If you don't do anything rash, I think I might get my bosses to do what you want. In exchange for Groller," he added.

"Ring me back by nine," I said, and replaced the receiver.

I lit a cigarette and sat for a moment without stirring.

My stomach was rumbling and I could not arrange my thoughts. What was I going to tell Whitfield? Should I try to get everything ready for the bombshell to be dropped? Or play safe and go off with Nichols? Where could Nichols be? Where was the evidence on the infiltration of the Chancellor's office that he undoubtedly had? Could Nichols get at it? Or was Koerner banking on my taking Nichols without getting hold of the evidence?

I went to have a look at Groller. When I entered, Greifner gave me a silent nod: they had broken him.

I glanced briefly at the wreck that was Groller – still bound – who was now pouring out his confessions more or less coherently. He still had his trousers down – it was Kunze's way of reminding Groller that at any time it could start all over again.

"When did Koerner start working with Sichler?" Greifner was now putting his questions very deliberately, like talking to a child when it has a temperature.

"Long time ago . . . Koerner was in the BND at first and that was where he got Sichler in his team. Sichler was working in recruitment. After they lost the top agent they had in the BND – he was Gehlen's right-hand man – the Soviets came up with the idea of a separate section."

"You said Koerner began working for the NKVD at the end of the war. Did you know that at the time?"

"No," he said. He continued after a little pause: "I was young then. Koerner as well. He had gone over to the Americans on NKVD instructions – but I didn't find that out till much later. Koerner fished me out of Mercedes, where I'd found myself a quiet corner after the war. As a former officer of the Abwehr, I was easily denazified . . .

anyway how could you hope to sort out who was a Nazi and who wasn't? At the beginning of the war I think they were all Nazis, even the Communists, as long as Hitler's pact with Stalin held and until Hitler put the Barbarossa plan into action. I mean the attack on the Soviet Union."

"So Koerner simply worked his way up in the BND. And you went along with him?"

"Yes."

"Where did you have your money sent?"

"The usual places: half in dollars to Switzerland, a quarter to the account of a construction company in Lichtenstein – of course . . . Koerner and I were joint owners – and a quarter stayed in the GDR. Teddling . . ."

"We'll get to him," said Greifner. "When did Koerner first tell you about Nichols?"

"That was . . ."

I nodded to Greifner and left the room. I was hungry and I knew I would be getting a transcript of Groller's statement in due course.

I went into the television room. Wollrath was sitting on a chair, watching by turns the screens that showed the two entrances to the house, the main road, and Nichols' room.

"They gave it to him sweet and strong," he said approvingly.

"Yeah," I agreed.

The prisoners were sitting on the floor, all four in a row. Wollrath was nursing his machine-gun on his lap.

"Keep having to take 'em for a piss," he said wearily.

"That's better than letting 'em stink," I said. "Anything to eat in the kitchen?"

"Piles of tinned stuff. But not much bread. Nescafé. Beer."

"Thanks," I said, "you carry on."

But Wollrath was not looking at me. He was looking at

the television screen. His mouth was open and his eyes were popping.

I looked at the screen too.

It showed Nichols' room. Greifner and Kunze were standing over the bound figure of Groller, who was sitting powerless on his chair with his head hanging to one side.

I ran up the stairs and burst into the room.

Greifner and Kunze were just untying Groller and carrying him over to the bed. Torpid, he was even heavier, and they had their work cut out for them. He looked ridiculous, like all of us when we reach a certain age and have our trousers down.

"What happened?" I asked Greifner.

"He was singing and we'd nearly finished. I told him he was going to have to write it all out and sign it. He gave a groan and fainted."

Kunze was massaging Groller's face.

I took a long look at Greifner.

He returned my gaze and shrugged.

We both knew what the other was thinking.

Minutes passed.

Then Kunze turned to us. "I can slosh him with cold water . . ." he suggested uncertainly.

"He's had enough shocks," I said.

Greifner said, "Anyone here know anything about medicine?"

Kunze shook his head. "No. But he'll come round maybe."

"Maybe . . ." I repeated. I had no medical know-how; they did not bother with that at Gonzales' outfit.

I ran downstairs into the television room and asked the prisoners whether the Sonderabteilung had a confidential doctor in Hamburg.

The little one, the one I had called Pat, said unwillingly, "No. On the odd occasion . . ." He hesitated. "I'm a doctor. Or rather I *was*. Years back they struck me off on account of some abortions." He coughed and gave a little ironic grin.

"So we've got a gynaecologist," I said.

3

We stood around the bed and watched Pat. He finished his inspection and straightened up. "He needs hospital treatment," he said. "That's no faint; it'll be his heart." And he threw in a few Latin terms that I didn't understand.

"What about . . . a specialist?" I said, wondering whether I could wangle a heart specialist through Koerner.

But Pat said, slowly, and in English, "Intensive care unit."

And bowed to us ironically, a tiny figure resembling a nineteenth-century family doctor. Bristow took him back downstairs and Greifner and I looked at each other again. Evening was falling and all the nerves in my body were beginning to tremble.

We were in a trap.

4

We left Kunze with Groller and went into the office. I sat down at the desk. I was hungry, but I could not bring myself to eat anything. Time, I thought to myself.

"I'm afraid the dosage was a bit strong," said Greifner, as though he were reading my thoughts.

"It was me who gave the order," I said.

"We couldn't have broken him otherwise," he said, as though trying to defend me.

"Taking him to hospital means calling it a day," I said.

"That gynaecological gnome won't save him," said Greifner, somewhat unjustly. "Will Groller's corpse be any good to us?"

"He's not dead yet. We'll have to swap him as he is – sick."

"That'll be some swap!" said Greifner glumly. "How do you want to transport him?"

"I don't know yet. I might order an ambulance. Koerner probably won't refuse to supply one."

"You don't mean to scupper Koerner, do you?" He looked me in the eye. "You just want to get Nichols for Great Britain, and you don't care a monkey's what happens here. Like a racehorse with blinkers. And you're running. At the gallop. *Après vous le déluge.*"

"*Nach mir die Sintflut*, Greifner. You've got it. I try to separate what's important from what's less important. The life of Nichols from those of a couple of swine. I've made up my mind. That's why I'm here, isn't it?"

He nodded gloomily.

I dialled a number. This time it was the Commodore's own voice.

"Pretty inept girl you keep there during the day," I said, jokingly, though indeed I wasn't in a joking mood.

"She's my ward," he said in his deep melodic voice. "There's not much in the air about that mate of yours. He seems to have got lost," he added, referring to Nichols. "You still interested in him?"

"And I'm still paying for information," I said.

"I've nothing to offer."

"There's something else maybe – I need a heart man. One who'll keep his trap shut. I need him to fly straight to

Hamburg. And to forget anything he might see or hear. Do you know one that fits?"

"You seem to think that my staff includes one of everything and that all I have to do is snap my fingers and – abracadabra – there's a discreet heart specialist doing the fandango on the table!" I could hear him laughing. Then he added, more seriously, "How soon do you need him?"

"Quarter of an hour ago."

"Of course."

He was silent for a moment.

"Two thousand marks for me. I'm taking a risk. I know one, but I would get involved, wouldn't I?"

"You'll have to."

"How'll I get those two thousand marks?"

"I'll put a cheque in the post for you," I said with irony. "How can I let you have them now? Am I supposed to hop on a helicopter?"

"You're in a tight spot, if I understand rightly. Is it you who had the heart attack, or have you been tinkering with someone's health?"

"The second."

"You've got someone in Berlin, haven't you? I want to be paid first."

"Who doesn't? What about earning it first?"

"Have you ever had cause to doubt that I'd do what I've promised?"

"Have you ever had cause to doubt that I'd pay up?"

He laughed again. "No," he said. "But better safe than sorry. I've a suggestion: I'll make a phone call and you make a phone call. I'll secure a doctor and you the delivery of the money. Then you ring me and we'll come to an agreement. The moment I get the money, the doctor takes the plane to Hamburg. But make it snappy, he'll have to catch the last plane. And you'll also pay his bill in cash."

"I'll have the money delivered to you," I said. "All right?"

"Okay, but that won't be necessary. I'll tell him to accept a cheque made out to me, and I'll give him the cash myself. Don't forget to sign it." He rang off and I started dialling Peccarie's number.

Then the waiting began. Waiting for Koerner to ring and for Professor Weiss to arrive from Berlin. Waiting for the likely future.

As I ate, Greifner gave me his report on Groller's statement. The general outline I knew. Now I had the chance to hear a few interesting details.

"They were following the sexual life of politicians and their financial transactions," Greifner concluded. "They also reported on East German agents the BND was tailing or beginning to suspect. They would rub out minor agents with much to-do, so the bosses of the BND, convinced Koerner and Groller were great spy-catchers, let them have an increasingly free hand. They were put onto Nichols by the Russians. Koerner went to Berlin and met Vorontsov. It seems likely Koerner doesn't know who the man close to Brandt is. Groller certainly doesn't."

"Why didn't they rub out Nichols like they did Nighton?" I asked.

"Groller doesn't know for certain. He just assumes that the case officer of their man in Brandt's office is a Soviet. And he logically assumes the Russians don't want Koerner to know too much. On the other hand they need to know how much Nichols knows and where the evidence is. They need Nichols alive. They need to question him and then get rid of that evidence. That's only an assumption of course."

"Sounds logical," I said. "So Barthels wasn't a one-of-a-kind job?"

"No. For example, Koerner is keeping a close watch on

everything to do with Brauns. Brauns is the Bavarian CSU leader, and Koerner has an idea that the East Germans could burn his fingers for him over the purchase of Starfighters."

I raised my eyebrows. "They're very good at disinformation."

Greifner hinted a wry smile. "Anyway, there's a joke here in Germany that, unfortunately, is not far off the truth. Do you know how to buy a Starfighter cheap?"

"Cheap?" I returned.

"You buy yourself a small plot of land, and then you wait for one to fall."

He smirked.

"The Americans pay well, but with them you never know when it'll blow up. They're what we call a turbulent democracy with farcical elections rigged by all sorts of lobbies, capital, and masochistic flagellation by liberal stooges."

"You're beginning to talk like an intellectual, Greifner," I said. "In our position that's a luxury. You're going to have to write up a detailed, no-nonsense report and sign it along with Kunze. But without Groller's signature it'll have no more than good informative value for the British. The Germans would probably just be puzzled."

"Barthels could . . ."

"I don't want to get Barthels mixed up in this," I said.

"Why?" he asked. "I thought you'd cheerfully get anybody mixed up in anything, and smash as much china as you thought necessary."

"I try to separate the important from the less important," I smiled sadly. "That takes a lot of doing, Greifner. In practice it means that it is important for Groller to last out till the exchange, even if we have to exchange him on a stretcher and with intravenous feeding, and I don't care what happens to the bastard afterwards. But in the case of certain people, a word *has* to be kept. There are other people in whose case I simply *want* to keep my word."

At that point the telephone rang.

Greifner picked it up and said, "Villa Bismarck," and then handed me the phone and said, "Get the scrambler. It's Koerner."

— XXII —

Koerner

It was Friday evening. Seven o'clock.

Twenty-eight hours ago we had taken possession of Villa Bismarck.

Koerner's voice sounded muffled as though he had been drinking all night and had got through eighty cigarettes, and as though it were morning now. I would have cast him as the Pied Piper of Hamelin, marching out a column of small-time spies to the cautious applause of unseen senior officials.

"Your proposal produced the right sort of interest," he began in a roundabout way. "I think an exchange could take place. Under certain circumstances," he added.

"I've made you my last offer, Koerner," I said, "and all you're doing now is beating about the bush."

"*Schauen Sie*," he tried to protest – but it was no longer the Koerner I had met the night before; this was a Koerner in a cold sweat, a Koerner worried not only about the past, but about his future, and one who had begun to feel concern at what his own masters were capable of. "In this thing, it's not me who calls the tune. If it were up to me, it'd be all over except for the shouting. But as I've said, we've got to be reasonable."

"*You've* got to be reasonable," I said with feigned self-assurance. "I don't feel like waiting."

"They want to talk to you," he said miserably. "That's all. They want to discuss it with you themselves."

"Koerner shunted on to a siding?" I returned. "They lost faith in you already, old chap?"

"You'll discuss it together and the whole thing'll be over," he said again, in the same tone.

"The thing *is* over," I said.

"You haven't got Nichols."

"I've got Groller. And you."

"In certain circumstances they'll sacrifice Groller. Can't I get that through to you?" He was almost shouting. "I can't say more than that. But they just want to talk to you. To make a deal. An honest deal, a square one. And that'll be that."

"Why don't they telephone?"

"Therrick," he whined, "you don't know them. They're not Germans."

"I might know them. You don't know me."

We were talking like small boys, each threatening the other with his mighty father. He was right, of course: the situation had developed. Was it progress? What is progress, but a change of prison?

"They don't trust the phone even with a scrambler. They want to negotiate with you in person, you can't refuse."

"Let them come here, then. But no mucking about . . ."

"They won't come here. You'll have to come to Berlin."

"You must be mad! I'm not shifting from here until I get Nichols."

"Listen to me, for God's sake. These are top brass. I can't order them about. They said quite plainly Berlin."

"I'm saying quite plainly Hamburg. I'll talk to them here."

"No sense in that. If you do a deal . . . Nichols is in Berlin, Therrick."

"You mean we shake on it and they'll plonk him at my feet? Like that?"

"Something like that," he said.

"Something like that isn't good enough," I responded. "So what's it going to be?"

"Christ, Therrick, d'you want me to go mad? I'm in the crossfire, can't you understand?"

"For once in a while it suits you, Koerner. I have a feeling I wouldn't care if you got shot to ribbons."

"You leave your men where they are. You've got Groller and the rest. Nobody's going to try anything on. Your safety is guaranteed."

"Who by? You?" I said with irony.

"It's Kagin," he bleated. "He'll be seeing you. For you, that's a real break."

"It's not, Koerner. I've had dealings with all sorts. I know Kagin. He'd sell his own grandmother if the international struggle of the working class made it necessary. Don't take me for a fool."

"There'll be no foul play, Therrick."

"There's always foul play."

"Not this time. How can I make you believe me?"

"You can't make me believe you. We've reached stalemate. And that doesn't help you."

"Nor you."

We were going round in circles. Greifner was watching me closely, smoking slowly. Outside it was already dark and on the desk the little table lamp was shining which had lighted Groller's way through selected files.

"Therrick . . ." he began again. "They'll drop the whole thing. They'll let Groller go to the wall, and me, and all the others. The situation's . . . Christ, can't you see it?"

"I won't be forced into anything," I declared with authority, although I already knew I would have to let myself be forced. "Do they imagine that I'll just drop everything and fly to Berlin, and heigh-ho, we meet in some dive and watch the striptease?"

"If you get a move on, you'll catch the Berlin flight. I

203

could fix a car for you, but you'd be looking for the devil's hoof somewhere. Grab a taxi. We can start the ball rolling tonight. At a hotel. Or wherever you want. You can fix the place. Nobody'll try anything on, I'm telling you. Be sensible and . . ."

"Okay, Koerner. I'll come. My conditions are as follows: I shall contact my men every three hours. If I don't, if they're not satisfied, if there's the slightest suspicion, this is what will happen: the first of your men will be shot on the spot. A certain newsman, who's waiting, will get the whole story on a plate. An hour later another of your men will be shot. Did you get that: in an hour another one. There are four of them here, not counting Groller. He'll stay alive but he'll be taken in handcuffs to the BND with a machine-gun at his back, and they won't let him go until he spills out even what he doesn't know. Is that clear to you?"

"It is, perfectly. You don't have to worry . . ."

"Second thing: no one will be waiting for me anywhere. No telling. No young thugs messing around outside phone booths. No idiots at the hotel making me a present of an air-ticket. Nothing. Absolutely nothing. Make one false move and the corpses'll start piling up in Hamburg, the Interior Ministry'll get no sleep, the BND won't know whether it's coming or going, the press won't know where to start, and your friends will soon find someone to bump you off. At the very least, you'll become a burden to your bosses in Moscow, and don't you think you'll still get a dacha and a pension from them. They'll make you a back-street cheerleader in Kiev."

"I give you my promise . . ."

"You'll give me Colonel Kagin's Berlin phone number. I'll ring him myself. Without your help. You're dropping out of the game."

"I've had his number passed to your people," he said

quickly. "You won't need me . . . All you've got to do is get here. Contact your side. The rest will be plain sailing."

"I hope I never see or hear you again," I said, and replaced the receiver.

2

Give the necessary orders. Get a contact routine agreed with Greifner and settle the passwords just in case. Ring Whitfield at his hotel. Put him in touch with Greifner. Report back to the Commodore. I did all that while Greifner booked my flight. All that was left was to ring Peccarie and tell him to meet me at the airport. I did not want to leave anything to chance, which is sometimes called misfortune.

"When Professor Weiss gets here – he ought to be here within the hour – whatever he says about Groller, Groller must not leave the house," I impressed on Greifner again and for the last time. "The Professor can sleep here, he can have a nurse brought in . . . anything at all, but Groller stays until the moment of exchange. On the money side, things will be taken care of by the Commodore . . . I mean Herr Richtenhoff. I'll ring just before eleven if the plane isn't delayed. If you don't hear from me by then, check that the plane's landed, and if so, you know what you've got to do. Contact Whitfield and get the ball rolling."

The taxi arrived. I tucked a pistol into my holster. I would have to transfer it to my case at the airport and hand the case in, but for now I wanted it handy under my shoulder.

I gave Greifner my hand, got in the taxi and off we drove. No one followed us.

In fifty minutes I was at the airport.

Pan Am Flight 618 took off punctually at 20.55.

At ten o'clock I was in Berlin.

Finale

Freedom which degrades itself and the power which capitulates do not find mercy with the enemy.

CHATEAUBRIAND

MORE RUSSIAN SPIES IN U.S.
By our Washington Staff

The heads of America's domestic and foreign counter-espionage operations told a Congressional committee yesterday that Russian spying in the United States was on the increase.

Mr Griffin Bell, Attorney General, told the committee that despite this, not a single American citizen had been subject to wiretaps on national security grounds – the only ones which no longer require a court order – since he took office a year ago.

From the *Daily Telegraph*

— XXIII —

On Friday,
very late at night

I stood by the long conveyor down which our luggage was to come. There were only a couple of dozen of us travelling, we were all strangers and I barely noticed the others. Were they following me? Hardly. They knew I would be coming.

In the Tempelhof arrivals hall I swiftly and discreetly took my pistol out of my case and slipped it in my pocket. I tried to weigh up what they would gain by my death. They might think I had left instructions with Greifner. He who takes risks takes out insurance. Even the condemned man yells out his final word.

Peccarie was standing at the very end of the huge hall, leaning against a rail and smoking. I went slowly over to him.

He said, "They'll drive up outside. At ten thirty."

"That'll be any minute," I said. "You armed?"

"Yes. Do you think there'll be any shooting?"

"No, I don't. Not straight away at least. But they might try to get me over into the Soviet sector. That's only a possibility though, no more than that."

"Let's go," said Peccarie, "it's time."

We stepped outside the terminal. The wind was blowing and the moon shone. The last of the evening's passengers were boarding the coaches like phantoms returning to the graveyard from an outing. A tidy line of Mercedes cars with their glowing taxi signs stood silently to one side, the drivers reading the papers, some smoking and others chatting in a huddle.

"Whose idea was this airport?" I asked.

"Mine," said Peccarie. "I've got a few men stationed here and there and I can see what's what."

"Who have you spoken to?"

"Some German fellow. He said they'd be here on the dot."

"We'll go to my hotel," I said. "I've still got a room there and they wouldn't go near a flat. Not that I would either."

The sky was covered in clouds *à la Ruysdael* that kept blotting out the moon. I thought of my phone call to Greifner at eleven o'clock, I thought of Groller and of Whitfield, sitting in the Atlantic Hotel. Of Veronika, who must know by now. Of Nichols. Of the giddy brevity of life and of my long and fruitless past.

"Over there," said Peccarie.

A long black Zim with drawn curtains and CD plates was making slowly for the main entrance, passed it and came on towards us.

It stopped a few yards off. No one got out.

I could see the dark silhouette of the chauffeur in his cap. Whoever was behind him was concealed by the curtains.

Peccarie went over to the car and tapped on the window. A door opened slightly.

2

"They want you to join them. To talk over where we're going." Peccarie took a deep breath. "Don't do it."

I didn't fancy getting in the car. But I nodded. "If the car starts to move, shoot the driver and make a scene."

I went towards the car and opened the door.

Kagin was in uniform, with broad epaulettes. The other man was in civilian clothes. I pulled out the tip-down seat opposite them, and closed the door.

"*Vitaytye*," said Kagin solemnly. He had aged over the years, but he had the same massive features – a broad chin and long nose. Suddenly he beamed and added, "We are very glad for you to accept so quickly our invitation."

I replied, also in English. "I suggest we go to the hotel Am Lietzen See. I've got a room there and no one will notice us."

"Except for my uniform," Kagin responded good-humouredly.

"Except for your uniform," I returned. "If your friend here could manage to come in ordinary clothes . . ."

His 'friend' was slim, grey-haired and fairly old, well over sixty. He had glasses and the dried-up face of a working-class avant-garde dogmatic. He ignored me and said something to Kagin in Russian which I did not understand.

"Of course, of course," Kagin agreed. "We can go to your hotel if you will feel safe there with us." He was smiling. "Tell your people to follow us in one car if you've got two. The first one can go in front and show us the way to go. If you have not two cars, one of your people can sit by our driver and tell him which way. My chauffeur speaks German."

"We've got two cars, thank you, Colonel," I said drily, whereupon Kagin gave another of his smiles. "*Kharasho*, it is well, my friend, give the orders, let us not grow roots here."

I gave the orders and in two minutes our little convoy set out. I was still sitting opposite the two men.

"If you are not sitting very comfortably," said Kagin when the car was moving, "you may sit here between us. There is enough room."

Of course he had studied psychology, and of course I should have got out and not travelled with them. But it was too late. Kagin acted with the genial authority of one who does not want another to bother with trifles. Of course, such trifles would then be to his advantage.

I remained sitting opposite, with Kagin keeping a benevolent eye on me, while his colleague looked as though he were delivering to the Presidium of the Central Committee his proposals for increasing the budget of the security forces.

"It is a very cool spring," said Kagin. "At this time of the year when I was a boy I used to walk along Nyevsky Prospekt with a girl called Nadya. A wind like this was blowing and people did not know if they should take a coat or not. You know Leningrad, Therrick?"

"No," I said. "I've never fancied the Soviet Union for a holiday."

"I thought you did not know it," Kagin nodded with an expression of utter satisfaction. "It is a beautiful city. Do you want to know what happened to the girl?"

I hesitated between politeness and an attempt to put his psychological method out of gear.

"If it mattered to you . . ." I said in a neutral tone.

He smacked his lips and nodded twice.

"It mattered. She did not marry me." He laughed and added, "She married a thin engineer from Chemoprojekt who read Pasternak and Akhmatova and got killed during the siege of Leningrad. Fate, isn't it?" He looked at me ingenuously as if to say: 'He got killed, so what, there are many of us to one girl.'

"Destiny," I said. I could not see where we were going because the curtains were drawn.

"Indeed, destiny," Kagin repeated and kept his gaze on me. "You are very elegant, Englishman." And he laughed again. "I like elegant people. Why did you join the English, Therrick?" He did not wait for an answer but went on: "I was born in Leningrad. Now I am in Berlin. You were born in Athens and you are nowhere. No offence. It is your affair. I must admit that you know how to make problems for people. You turn up here out of the blue." He spoke like a kindly uncle reproaching his nephew for coming home late. "Grigori here knows Leningrad, but does not understand it. You do not understand Leningrad, do you, Grigori?"

"I respect Leningrad," said the other one reluctantly, "but it is not my city."

"Grigori is a great realist," Kagin continued benevolently. "He is a real Soviet. We have a problem. We must solve it. So let us solve it. Why talk about Leningrad? That is what Grigori thinks, because he is responsible. But why, tell me Grigori, why should we not talk about Leningrad in the car?"

Grigori had no objections; nobody had any objections and Kagin went on. "Destiny. They save a little boy from drowning, they dry him out and the little boy dies from pneumonia anyway. A soldier-boy deserts, runs away from the front, far away, crosses to the enemy, dear lad, but he cannot forget, the forests, the steppes, and he is so sick at heart, poor thing. A strange world. Is it not, Therrick?"

There was a shade of irony in his pronunciation of my new name.

"You're in a mournful mood, Colonel," I said grumpily.

"A philosphical mood, let us call it." He nodded contentedly. "In a philosophical mood. I have not seen you for a long time. I hear about you here and there. And you see: suddenly we are together in my car. Is that not strange?"

"I don't enjoy being in your car with you," I said.

213

"And where would you enjoy being with me? Is there anywhere?" He looked anxious to know the answer.

"There is somewhere, Kagin," I said. "I'd enjoy being with you in Leningrad, if Leningrad were St Petersburg again. You would be a Czarist officer and I would watch you losing at roulette under the bright glow of crystal candelabras, squeezed in among generously bared breasts of ladies who have long been dead. We'll go along Nyevsky Prospekt together and the spring wind will blow and you won't have a rouble left and you'll get the vodka you've drunk and the life you've lived all off your chest."

Kagin began to shake with merriment and then he roared with laughter.

The car stopped.

"You get out first," said Grigori. "We'll follow."

3

We sat in my room at a small table by the window. Kagin had taken off his military coat and put it on the bed and was seated with his back to the wall. Peccarie had taken a room on the same floor and stayed there because the two Soviets made it plain that they would not talk to me in the presence of anyone else.

Kagin took out a long Russian *papirosa* and handed it to Grigori, who lit it.

"He's not allowed to overdo the smoking, poor Grigori," Kagin remarked by way of explanation. "He gets short of breath and so I ration his cigarettes. Don't I, Grigori?"

Grigori nodded without interest and Kagin lit a Pall Mall. Then he looked up and said, "I think it's time I introduced Grigori: Major Vorontsov. We're on this case together."

Grigori Vorontsov, whose identity had been perfectly apparent to me, smoothed down his white hair and looked at me with an expression that said: 'Just how can it help you to know I'm Major Vorontsov?'

"So," Kagin began again, "that brings us *in medias res*, or to the heart of things. Well, Therrick . . . Would you care for a drop of vodka? We've got two bottles of Stolichnaya in the car . . ."

"I would prefer to remain *in medias res*. Going for vodka would only hold things up."

Kagin laughed. "But there's plenty of time." His laughter was deep-toned and resonant, the laughter of an old Cossack standing by a crackling camp-fire and looking on with pleasure as his band raped a skinny sixteen-year-old blonde on the cold grass beneath the night sky. "Surely we're in no hurry, are we? Such an important problem . . . We need to prod each other a bit. To see what we're all up to. Don't you think?"

"Groller and his henchmen are in Hamburg, in my hands," I said, "and these hands of mine can't wait to get rid of them. When and where are you going to hand over Nichols?"

Kagin let out a howl of laughter.

"Did you hear him, Grigori? A capitalist. Businesslike. Doesn't want to be prodded. No pipe of peace. Here you are, hand over – that's all he's interested in." He looked enquiringly at Vorontsov. "Come on, Grigori, what do you say to that?"

Vorontsov was looking without interest at the wardrobe, as if he were expecting the Holy Ghost or Andropov or whoever to step out of it, and he said:

"Oleg Vasilevich, perhaps you ought to explain the situation to Mr Therrick. As we see it."

Kagin turned to me. "You heard what Grigori said. I am to explain how we see the situation."

"Spare me the comic overtures, Colonel. I know you and your sort."

"But how splendid, that will help matters," Kagin said with satisfaction. "So, if you know us and our sort, you're bound to know that the first thing we want is to know with whom we have the pleasure."

"You know that perfectly well."

"Let's just take a closer look. Here we have a certain Therrick alias Berx alias Lima alias goodness-knows-who else, who is offering us a deal. A deal, that is the right word, isn't it, Therrick? The British told you: Fetch Nichols, and here you are careering round Germany on your backside trying to oblige. Permit me one little question. Why do you do it, Therrick?"

"That's my affair," I said, and took out a cigarette. Kagin took out his black japanned gold Dupont and gave me a light.

"I have two lighters, you see," he said laughing. "This one was a present from the Indonesian Ambassador at the United Nations, whom I was reproaching because the Indonesians were shooting Communist students. Do you suppose he wanted to tame me?"

"I won't give you a lighter, Colonel. Let alone Groller."

"Precisely. You are a greedy mercenary. We Soviets are capable of generosity, Therrick. Not you, though. Why? Your features tell me you are not greedy by nature. At Gonzales' agency in Lisbon one doesn't make a fortune. And the British have a small budget. So that is point one. Our partner in negotiations, Mr Therrick, doesn't have any money. How is that, Grigori?"

Vorontsov turned to Kagin and said, "Mr Therrick has an overdraft at the Lisbon branch of the Union des Banques Suisses amounting to 6456 escudos. He has an account with Neuflize-Schlumberger in Paris in which he has 8560 francs. He wanted to transfer 3000 dollars from the

Union des Banques Suisses in Geneva to the account of his girl friend, Muriel Revas, at the Athens Trapeza Elliniki, but only 2580 dollars reached Athens. We may conclude from that that there is nothing left in his numbered account in Geneva. He gets 500 dollars a month from Gonzales plus expenses plus an operation bonus. Last April the bonus came to 2000 dollars. Last year he had two bonuses. I do not yet know how much he has been offered by the British. He has no pension, no shares. The Athens flat where his girlfriend lives is mortgaged, the repayment and interest amount to 2450 drachmas a month. Could I have another cigarette now, Oleg Vasilevich?"

"In a moment, Grigori, in a moment. You've just had one." Kagin turned back to me. "Grigori hasn't managed to find out how much you were offered by the British. That is very sad, but it can be overlooked since he did not really have enough time, can't it, Therrick? And everything takes time. That is the law of nature. I hope you agree that our information is correct."

"You appear to know more of the state of my finances than I, but to say that I'm staggered by that . . . Well I'm not."

"You mean to say," said Kagin with sudden amiability, "that the state of your finances isn't staggering. So be it, at least we're agreed on that. I did say we had to prod each other a bit, didn't I? In this world of ours, everything is a matter of trust."

He grew serious and looked attentively at me.

"If you're thinking of offering money," I said, "you can think again. If I was after your money, there have been plenty of occasions when I could have got some out of you. You ought to know that, Colonel."

"Money!" Kagin gestured. "A trifling matter. We don't want to buy you. We know you can't be bought." He gave a sad smile. "Although that's not quite true – everyone has his price and maybe no one has offered you the right one yet. But that doesn't matter now. What matters now is that we understand each other."

"No, that's not what matters, Colonel. What matters is Nichols and Groller. I've been patient with you and your psychology, but I'm getting fed up. Koerner perhaps didn't explain the situation plainly enough. I'm beginning to be afraid that you under-estimate—"

"We do not under-estimate anything, Therrick," Vorontsov interrupted. I had forgotten about him. "We know just what the situation is and we are drawing the proper conclusions. That is why we are here, and you had better put aside your mercenary's self-assurance and listen to what Comrade Kagin has to say."

He stopped and stared back at the wardrobe.

Kagin's face was suddenly blank.

There was a knock at the door.

4

It was Peccarie. Apologising, he said I was wanted on the phone. I got up, excused myself and went into the corridor. "Hamburg," he said tersely as he strode beside me. "We had to wait to be connected, because I had to send my man for a scrambler."

Peccarie opened the door of his room. The telephone was off its hook. I picked up the receiver and heard Greifner's voice.

"You all right?"

"So far," I said. "Is Professor Weiss there?"

"He wants to speak to you."

"Put him on."

A moment later a strong Berlin accent came on the line.

"Weiss speaking. Are you the one makes the decisions?"

"Yes."

"Your patient must be transferred to hospital at once."

"Out of the question," I said. "You'll have to do what you can."

"He'll die," said the professor and began elaborating, mostly in Latin.

"How long before he does die?" I asked and started making mental calculations. I could feel my shirt and underpants. I could feel the knot of my tie and took in the brown of the cuff-link on the cuff of my right sleeve.

"There's no way of telling. He could last a day, perhaps two . . . three's unlikely. As a doctor—"

"Thank you, Professor," I broke in. "Please do all you can."

I handed the receiver to Peccarie.

"Tell Greifner that we'll call again in three hours. The orders stay the same."

As I made my way back down the corridor I made up my mind: I would imagine them as clowns. Kagin would be Hardy and Vorontsov would be Laurel. The whole thing's a circus, and Nichols is in a Mercedes, dashing along a French motorway in the direction of Boulogne. In half an hour he'll be boarding the hovercraft. But suppose he's heading for Dunkerque? We're only in the closing scene of a circus performance: Laurel has just shot the clown Fregolli with a wooden pistol and Hardy is weeping in the middle of the arena and grown-up children are merrily clapping. In a moment they will all go behind the canvas of the big top to their caravans, the clown Fregolli will turn into Nichols, alive and well, and he'll say: 'A very good audience we had today.' And Laurel and Hardy won't know a thing about Muriel in the tiny Athens flat. They'll be just two tired clowns with make-up running down their cheeks.

When I entered the room I sensed that the pair had not used my absence to talk. They had not needed to.

Vorontsov was sitting in the armchair by the coffee-table, smoking a Russian cigarette.

"I've let some fresh air in," said Kagin. He was standing by the open window. Outside spread the dark hotel grounds and the waters of Lietzen See shone in the moonlight. Further off behind the trees lay Berlin.

"Take a seat, Therrick," said Kagin calmly. He closed the window and drew the curtains and stood in front of me, running his hand down the row of shining buttons on his tunic. He was wearing a white shirt and black tie. The tunic was khaki and on the left breast he wore a number of ribbons. It made him seem even huger. 'The clown Hardy,' I repeated to myself, 'Comrade Clown Hardy.'

I sat down and Kagin began to speak with conspicuous simplicity in his voice, as if he were talking of pollination.

"You got Groller by a trick that wasn't carried out quickly enough for you to get Nichols as well. I can imagine that you squeezed all you could out of Groller. You've made Koerner nervous. When paid hands like Koerner get nervous, it's never pleasant. Koerners lack faith, and if they get afraid they cease to be reliable. They usually end in the way described by the CIA as 'termination with extreme prejudice'. But, Therrick, is all this important? You can hand Groller over and spoil our whole game with the Sonderabteilung in the *end*. We enter it under our 'losses'." He smiled. "Don't you believe me? Okay. It would be a most unfortunate loss. But no more than that. You don't know the name of the agent who's perched there with Brandt. And you've no proof. You want Nichols, because Nichols knows where the evidence is. Nichols knows all that's needed to scupper our squirrel in Brandt's oak tree."

He walked round the table and put his hand on Vorontsov's shoulder, as if to prevent him making some remark.

"But is *that* really why you want Nichols? Is it of such concern to you personally that our squirrel should fall? Or do you want Nichols just because the British have given you a chance and because the British long so much to have him? Let's be clear about your interest, Therrick. Could it not perhaps be a professional interest, your need to make a living?" He waved a hand as if driving away a fly. "*Passons*," he said. "Of course the British don't want us to hear Nichols' confessions in Moscow! But we were quicker, and with the continuing courtesy of the Sonderabteilung we can make a very neat exchange with the West Germans. And you think you will stop us." He looked at me like a senior nanny at a feeble newborn child. "Poor Therrick!"

I killed my cigarette and said nothing. I waited.

"Groller . . ." he went on. "Groller. Well. So what . . . ? Koerner. The Sonderabteilung. It's worked for long enough. It will stop working. So what . . . ? Our squirrel in Brandt's oak tree? Very important, I admit. But with the French DST on our squirrel's track anyway, because it hopped to Marseilles too often, it'll be dealt with sooner or later at NATO level. And you think that will change the Germans' Ostpolitik? Do you think there'll be some awful crash like on the stock exchange? Germany calling Strauss to its aid? Withdrawing the German Ambassador from Moscow? Poor Therrick! At worst they'll lock our squirrel-agent up and put him on trial behind closed doors. They'll start poking about in the files of the secret services, chairs will get moved round the table, there'll be embarrassment and red faces all round and Brandt will have to go . . . but that will be all. Officially the culprit will be the German Democratic Republic. Why else do we keep it? *Et voilà* : a loss. But allowances are made for losses. Would we lose the whole game? Not at all. The energy expended has already paid for itself; our squirrel-agent has carried out his mission. He has kept us informed in advance and in detail of Brandt's thinking and of all his intentions and weaknesses throughout our negotiations with Germany on the Ostpolitik!"

Was there towering over me, arms folded, a trained party professional, sure of his backing, proud of his affiliation to something that reached far above him? Or was this a man jaded with the ever-same of human striving, a skilled player trying out primitive little tricks for his own amusement, knowing they don't matter anyway?

"You're trying to get me to believe," I said, "that Nichols isn't important any more, because you've simply written off your squirrel-agent. Don't try that one."

"Mr Therrick," Vorontsov suddenly put in, "that squirrel is only a spy."

5

There was a moment's hiatus. Kagin was watching me with an expression if not mocking, then inscrutable.

"But that's just it, isn't it?" I said. "A spy of yours."

"Not so, Therrick." Kagin spoke drily.

"I don't understand," I said.

Vorontsov said, "That is why we are here. Comrade Colonel Kagin will explain."

6

Kagin took out another Pall Mall and slowly lit it, looking me in the eye. It was a look full of pity for the lone wolf in the borderless Siberian steppes; the look of the sophisticated cynic of international games who scorns the odd weed in his garden-realm until he decides from which side to start rooting it out.

"You, Therrick, are an intelligence mercenary without allegiance. And we, the KGB, are the avant-garde of the working class. We are its fist. We were, and we remain, the steel fist of Stalin. Stalin means 'man of steel' in Russian. Make sure you appreciate that and don't try to think for a moment that I am giving you our usual ideological lecture." He nodded, as if to himself. "I would never lecture *you*. You – you can be told the truth, because there is no one you can go running to with it. You are quite alone and we know that. You cannot betray us because you are of the old world, and everyone is ashamed of the old world. You are an intelligence mercenary with an excess of common sense that makes you a condemned man. I'll tell you your verdict."

Slowly he drew the smoke from his cigarette, a long, epicurean pull, as if he had been waiting years for it.

"It's not spies any more, Therrick. Spies don't matter to us now." He blew out the smoke and went on in the tone of a psychiatrist explaining to a younger female colleague that orgasm was not the result of love, but of the forbidden craving to murder, that which we need in order no longer to be subjugated by it.

"In the fifties, and even into the sixties, spies did matter quite a lot. We collected information and prepared for the moment of attack. But, even in those days, what mattered more to us was compromising people who were in a position to influence Western strategy. But Western strategy has ceased to exist, in case you didn't know. We can get most information by reading your papers, or your specialist periodicals, the rest we can get for money or by blackmail. The importance of espionage has shrunk to the minimum, thanks to our vast military potential. There's nothing left to spy on. All your side is interested in is counter-espionage, and on our side it's . . . disinformation of the masses and individuals, political sabotage, psychological defeatism and plain subversion, carried out through front organisations."

He paused briefly.

"There is one secret file known to several hundred people in the entire world, but they are our people and they won't talk, and it is closely guarded. It is known to the members of our Politburo, to the heads of the states you call satellites and we call the peace camp. It is known to the top-ranking officers in charge of intelligence and operations. It has 3000 pages. It has neither number nor colour. It has a name. Between ourselves we call it Plan A. But that's our code name for it. Officially it is called DOCUMENT ON THE THEORY OF THE EXPORTATION OF REVOLUTION AND ITS APPLICATION ON A WORLD–WIDE SCALE."

— XXIV —

Kagin

Kagin took several paces around the room. He stopped in the middle and wiped the point of his shoe on the carpet.

"Most pages are written by Stalin who went back to Trotsky for some of them and worked out the rest with Beria in the late forties. Stalin lived in the present, but he moved in the future. Then came other authors – Suslov, Shelyepin, later Andropov and Castro though not much of him . . ."

I interrupted him: "What about Che Guevara?"

"You must be joking. He was just a Patagonian robber. No, there were serious authors like Molotov, Mikoyan, Kozlov. Even I contributed a handful of sentences . . ." Kagin gave a semi-ironic smile and bowed towards me. Then he fell serious and came to sit down opposite me. He was speaking very quietly now and as fast as his English would let him:

"The contents of the document describe the advance of Soviet power right up to the final stage of taking over the so-called hybrid world, because by then the capitalist world will have ceased to exist. All that will exist will be hybrid capitalism, with a suicidal fear of its own name. The second half of the seventies will be years of active progress in the war of subversion that we have called the Struggle for Peace. We are not interested in a major war, because we simply don't need one. By the nineties all that will be left on the capitalist side will be the United States. For how long? That the Document doesn't say. We then might use a surgery."

He gave a slightly apologetic smile and I broke in:

"Sounds interesting, Kagin. So somewhere in the Kremlin there is some such document. However, it's rather an abstract affair whereas I, out of necessity perhaps, am a practical man. As I see it, there's no evidence of any downgrading of the pawns on the espionage chessboard."

"We've always found James Bond highly amusing, Therrick, and one or two of those spy thrillers of yours are quite decently written. We're pleased to think of your people reading them. It keeps their minds occupied and makes them believe that somewhere in the outside world, there is a clash of two forces in the spy war. If anything were to happen, it won't be during *their* lifetime. At least it doesn't seem so, which is a comforting thought. Indeed, what could happen? Soviet troops in England? Not even *I* believe that. So there you are. It shows the wisdom of taking things easy and holding in leash the various communist parties. You must not alarm them. Treat them like . . . ah . . . you would treat a stupid girl whom you want because of her rich body – ah, golubushka, you snow-white dove! – first stroke her knee, quite casually; but politely kiss her hand at the same time. Compliment her on her complexion. Don't rip her knickers, Therrick. Raping and strangling will be done only when the victim has already tied *herself* up. Of course, you stuff a gag in her mouth, but only as an act of charity to spare your own eardrums."

A spark of puckish benevolence darted across his fleshy features like sudden torchlight on the face of a Rubens soldier. But it didn't last.

"In plain terms, Therrick, we have the following situation. We're in 1973 and we know we're going to win. The Warsaw Pact armies are fully a match for NATO. In training and discipline our forces are far superior. In four or five years' time our conventional weapons will easily outstrip yours. Don't imagine that the laments of NATO commanders are going to persuade European governments to dip into their electors' pockets, even in the electors' own interests. On the contrary, the popular thing to do will be to cut arms expenditure, raise subsidies for unemployment, and give more nourishment to left-wing elements in the West who have no inclination to compete for higher living standards by working hard or inventing things, only by raising their voices with new demands. Half the people out of work would refuse a job if you offered it them.

"In a few years from now factory managers won't be managing anything – they'll be too scared to fire anyone as they stagger between picket-lines and industrial tribunals. Especially in England. She was once the soundest country in Europe, where you found the best characters and the best education. We dare not subject her to any outward threat – those Britons can be very tough and stick together. But it's a prime objective of ours to neutralise Britain, precisely because of her prestige in the Anglo-Saxon world and her key importance as a means of changing America's position.

"We shall use 'agents of influence' in the Labour party and elsewhere to debilitate industry; we shall destroy respect for the élite and thereby wreck the educational system and the ability of the media to transmit information responsibly. Their counter-intelligence staff will fight a hopeless battle: the laws will be against them, the prime minister will see them as an enemy. Nobody will be allowed to work who is not in a union. The police will be paid as badly as possible, so that they feel themselves treated as scum by the country they are supposed to defend. Corruption will set in. There'll be scandals and we shall use them to paint your police still blacker. Do I have to go on?"

He didn't wait for an answer, but continued firmly and persistently, with soothing gestures, occasionally raising his voice. I pictured him stepping out of his Zin limousine, or his Chayka, disappearing up a broad marble staircase in the huge complex of public offices lining the north-eastern side of the Dzerzhinsky Square at one end of the Karl Marx Prospekt. Was it summertime? Which year was it? There he was, sitting in the planning-room of the Political Philosophy Committee listening to the fair-haired, smooth-featured speaker who, in this innermost sanctum of the KGB, continued to elaborate his thesis:

". . . Which means, comrades, that society will gradually sink into anarchy. Welfare workers and liberal-minded people will put pressure on the courts to treat criminals as innocent lambs and set them free to step up violence and create an atmosphere of personal insecurity and fear. Ground will gradually be prepared for union control over the press: newspapers will only appear by courtesy of the unions; in other words there will be censorship exercised by the so-called working class. But since this is a capitalist system, the right-wing press will start to anticipate the process by putting out softer-toned commentaries and carefully phrased reports. On television we shall go in for documentary half truths. In the schools we shall brainwash the young by teaching Marxism and giving everything ideological labels, like 'imperialism' – *always Western, of course* – or 'humanism' – *compulsory humanism, that is; love the niggers because we're all equal and the best example of humanism is the Soviet Union; their teachers will never tell them we're not quite sure whether we've liquidated sixty million souls since the Great October Revolution or only forty million* . . . then there's 'liberalism', a milder and more acceptable version of capitalism on the lines of '*socialism means progress'* and *'after all, there's something to be said for it, it all depends how it's done, fascism is the real enemy'* . . . and we shall use the younger generation at the same time as a means of pressurising the man-in-the-street. Eighteen-year-old clowns with voting rights will go around shouting slogans and ordinary people will make excuses for them – they're young, it'll pass off. Psychology, comrades! In a few years' time the normal citizen will view the approach of socialism as something perfectly natural, so bemused will he be by the cries of 'We're not after the Soviet brand of socialism, we want our own!'

"Left-wing activist groups, regarded by liberals as a possible tool for splitting the communists, will in fact become an effective instrument for splitting the establishment, or what's left of it – the family, marriage, the church. In our country, if a student turned up at a lecture in jeans he'd be out on his ear and spend the rest of his life in a factory or down a mine. But in your country we shall encourage contempt for the material gains of capitalism, whether it's abstract art or just dressing badly – we shall nurture a cult of the ugly, a cult of puking on one's own civilisation and so ensuring that it's condemned."

The speaker paused to contemplate the glass of water in front of him. There were twenty or thirty men sitting around him, as I imagined the scene – all of them select examples of the clever and assiduous, the ones who had survived the Party schooling, the lectures and exercises, the surveillance and the purges . . . Did I really picture Kagin taking notes, hoping the speaker would notice? Who was he, this orator? Andropov? Or Comrade Ignatiev, the KGB political linkman with Suslov and the Politburo? Or would Kagin have been fully sure of himself by now, long in possession of a Grundig radiogram in his flat with JVC speakers bought abroad, or in the hard-currency shops? I could imagine him passing through the Vnukovo airport controls: "*Timofey Petrovich,*" he is saying to the official sent to receive him, "*I've got one or two things in my luggage for myself, h'm . . .*" "*Quite, quite, Comrade Kagin . . . Incidentally, did you bring any of those saucy pictures for Katov?*"

Or is he thinking about his wife just now? And while the fair-haired orator pursues his theme, where are Kagin's thoughts? With the Western middle classes that he is talking about? Weighing the strategy of destroying the hierarchy of values because this is what holds together the state, law and order, and – instead of so called progress – the real development of the nation?

"We all appreciate, comrades, that a single well-trained Party member or left-winger is a match for a couple of hundred run-of-the-mill people. Run-of-the-mill, I say, meaning people who console themselves with percentages and other statistics.

"As soon as the union pickets, under our influence, start bashing in the heads of their police and calling them fascists, and their magistrates, too scared to put them away for five years, just let them off with a fine and three months on remand . . . that will improve police morale no end! Remember what Lenin called the liberals and suchlike? Useful idiots! And there are useful idiots galore in the West. People don't, after all, enjoy thinking. What they secretly admire is strength. But the idea of the West exercising strength is something no one will dare to advocate. Fascism, they'll cry! Gestapo! Imperialism, social injustice! It is the old Coué method. Repeat *We're idiots*! forty times a day, and soon you'll be convinced that you really are weak in the head.

"All-pervading fear – there's a mighty weapon for us."

I could almost hear the speaker smack his lips. His tongue clicked with dry and well-balanced joy, like the crack of a whip.

"All-pervading fear. The public will no longer trust the state and the laws to protect them."

How many Kagins have learned to grasp the psychology of subversion? How has Kagin propagated his kind? By the patient cell-division of cynical analysis and the language of euphemism?

Was that where his thoughts lay as he climbed into his car and sped off down the 'Chayka lane' reserved in the middle of every Moscow highway for the use of *aparatchiks*? *He* knew what the masses were like. What did they call them in Russia? *Our mighty working class?* Of course, under the leadership of the avant garde, i.e. the Party, i.e. Kagin and those above him.

Did he feel affection for Stalin, or just admiration for his iron fist? Or was he like those Germans after the war who had 'had no idea'?

The speaker tosses a pile of scripts across the table.

"Comrade Kapitonov will hand round these notes I have made about the race problem and how to exploit it. After all, a dark skin stays dark. The blacks are potentially some of our best allies. Over a third of their intelligentsia – as against the masses, of whom four out of five will always vote left – over a third of their intelligentsia are our own lads who've enjoyed the benefits of our political schooling at the Lumumba University."

The speaker closed his file and melted from my sight.

Kagin took out a cigarette and gave me a contemptuous stare.

"You under-rate the importance of the minorities, as you've always done. A coloured minority is a time-bomb. For one thing, Therrick, it multiplies very merrily. And for another, it has an inferiority complex. Those blacks will teach you a thing or two. No one will dare hold a referendum on whether the British want a multi-racial state or not. Quite the contrary: our agents and their do-gooding intermediaries will sooner or later bring in a system of positive discrimination, a sort of reserved job schedule where an unqualified black candidate has to be given preference over a skilled white. We shall use your own intellectuals to instil a neat little sense of guilt into you. By the early eighties press freedom of our opponents will be considerably pared down. Meanwhile . . ." He lit a cigarette and took a drink.

"Meanwhile we shall move on to direct terrorism. The early experiments we've witnessed to date, plane hijackings and attacks on embassies, will spread during the eighties into an uncontrollable network of internal aggression. So far it's been just a few groups, though you haven't managed to shoot up even those. Just a handful of Arabs, Baader-Meinhof people, the IRA . . . We give them weapons, our own or Czech stuff. Cash they can usually lay hands on themselves. We train them . . . Few of them – like Carlos – we give even a thorough schooling but nevertheless the general impression is that of a bunch of anarchists. We realise that we mustn't get your public scared.

"But by the late seventies we shall be kidnapping and shooting prominent businessmen and industrialists. Some Jews, of course. In the following decade we shall be taking on journalists, commentators, politicians. Little by little, Therrick, not all at once. Before you've realised it, the thing will be a daily occurrence. Then you'll be faced with complete lawlessness. Judges will be afraid to judge, newspapermen afraid to write. And ordinary people?" He burst into laughter. "If you were to tell them the facts now, we should simply let your liberals accuse you of seeing reds everywhere. 'Cheap anti-communism' it would be called. And to dismiss it as a renewal of the Cold War.

"Then, one day, it will be too late. No one will want to risk his neck to save a civilisation that has exchanged God for pornography. The Roman Empire took four centuries to decline, but there's no comparison. We shall have to liquidate Israel and discipline the Jewish diaspora, of course. It'll take some doing, but people are always happy to leave the Jews in the lurch, you know. Either because they just envy them their brains and their ability to fight for a living, or because they're failures themselves and feel bitter about Jewish success. As for the Vatican, ruined by sectarian splits and battles over doctrine, they will realise too late that it is Israel which in its way is a symbol of Western freedom. And the Jews themselves, having learnt that no outside help can be expected and that everyone will abandon them in a crisis, they will always be opposed – except in their own state, perhaps – to authoritarian governments, even if they might be necessary for survival, because they like to believe about the liberal ones, however suicidal they've become nowadays, that they are the only ones to offer them assurance of physical freedom.

"Already today we're labelling Israel as an aggressor. Have you seen those huge graffiti on German university buildings? It's the Arabs that young German students admire now. Who are they really modelling themselves on, these heirs to the pinnacle of civilisation? Well, they're all growing up, they'll all want to have their say. Germany, instead of redeeming past crimes by standing firmly on the side of your famous Western freedoms, is again preparing to lick the jackboot – this time on our Soviet foot! And since the West has no ideology to offer and is incapable of creating one – it dreads the very thought of it! – real knowledge will be restricted to a few suppressed intellectuals who we are pleased to call rightists and reactionaries and who in any case won't have access to the media. And even if they did – the large public would not understand what they were saying after all we've done to propagate Equality, Liberty, Democracy and Socialism – and that appeals to the masses. The masses don't read complicated books, but they do have the right to vote about complex issues. In your country, they listen to the Rolling Stones.

"That leaves America, or rather the United States. And they're not going to help you. Why should they? Ever since the war ended you've been yelling, 'Yanks Go Home!' Taking the mickey out of them or denouncing them as imperialists whenever they do something responsible, or treating them like a crowd of mafiosi. They may be naive, they may be juvenile. Europe is perhaps really a little beyond them. But they had the guts to wrestle with life, they can be efficient beyond measure, they're not afraid of obstacles and they work hard. What they needed was your sincere friendship, your experience and your good taste. Well, you've lost your good taste, you're ashamed of your experience, and when they fight against us in Vietnam you spit in their faces till they start spitting in their own.

"Now they're going to give Nixon the push. That'll mean the loss of Vietnam and Cambodia too. Whoever replaces Nixon will be a man nobody's voted for. And who'll be President after that? Some do-gooding figurehead under pressure from the minorities, some likeable portrait of the honest hard-working American with puritanical anxieties and dishonest stubbornness, lacking speed, decision and international shrewdness, someone driven by the need to be popular and compelled to break up the CIA for us. That'll be the main thrust of our attack.

"The CIA, which was trained by the British, is still dangerous. It operates with all the inventive skill of the Americans. *They* had discovered Philby. Angleton, their head of counter-espionage, did. He's the sceptical one, he's the skilled and the foreseeing one; and his men and men alike, those from their old school. Those who knew that man has to have the courage to make his hand dirty if his family is at stake. Well, we shall smash the CIA. We'll turn

234

it into a Salvation Army. Do you know what American college campuses are like, Therrick?"

I did not reply. I didn't even *want to know*.

"Let's call it a day," he said. "Otherwise I'll go on for hours, and you've got my point now anyway. The Americans will pull out of Europe and turn to isolationism. Their Kennans will serve it up to them without our having to bother. And you'll have no cause to be surprised at them.

"It *will* surprise you, though, when we let Solzhenitsyn out. You'll kid yourselves that we've become more liberal. Crap, Therrick. Nowadays we can well afford to let him go, because in a few years' time the West will see him as an 'embittered emigré' – a nuisance. Just a nuisance. And it will help the theory of convergence which we like so much – after all it was created by our disinformation department.

"You'll be surprised at the ease with which people swallow our propaganda, at the way they will find any excuse to destroy themselves.

"You will think up all sorts of explanations. But it's quite simple. People don't feel a desire to destroy themselves. They are just envious. Their paramount desire, next to self-preservation, is to feel important. It's all connected with sex.

"You've provided your people with cars, refrigerators, washing-machines, decent material standards. And your up-and-coming generation moans about alienation. About the emptiness of life. In reality the youngsters only dimly discern the oppressiveness of a life-style which deprives you, once material comforts are assured, of the great struggle for basic things and sets you face to face with death, futility and uncertainty about God. And with the certainty, on the other hand, that even if they are earning good money, others are earning more and yet others are even presidents and ministers, which is more than they themselves are even remotely capable of. You have nothing to offer to the worker or the black or the student – only work, at best. That still leaves them feeling unimportant. But we offer them the chance to destroy. The chance to be dangerous. To be feared.

"There are plenty of countries where we've already given such people the authority to destroy, the authority to send others to prison. And in countries like that there was no need for us to raise the wages, say, of a caretaker's wife. Oh no! What we gave her was the right to inform against the people living in her building, keep records of who visited whom and have the prestige of serving on a street committee that the have-beens are so afraid of . . .

"One of the most secret divisions of the KGB is the Executive Action Department. The Department of *mokrye dyela*, as we say 'wet affairs', 'wet work' if you like. That department is in charge of subversion and assassinations – which we're planning ahead for.

"But sometimes it turns out that at a given moment the caretaker's wife can be just as effective."

He looked at me and added, "It's hot in here." With his strong fingers he began to unbutton the jacket of his uniform.

"You've under-rated the 'little man' and his capacity for destruction. You've under-rated his admiration for power, his sneaking regard for Hitler and Stalin and Mao. People feel that men like that offer them some sort of guarantee. *You* can't guarantee them a thing. In the forties it was your Englishmen who made Stalin a present of two million Soviet citizens – thereby sending them to their death. Their Foreign Office *wanted* to believe the powerful dictator. One in five of them we shot on arrival, the remainder when they reached the camps. Only a few thousand survived. No, Therrick, here we've got to the heart of the matter. Who can trust you? Who can rely on you? What sort of people are you? A crowd of wretches who tell themselves lies and are scared to box the ears of their own children.

"And what about *you* in all that?" He paused.

"You'll never win the confidence of the English, Therrick. You'll always be a foreigner to them. You can never be their man. *Their* men have certain advantages: for one thing, their authorities can't always bring themselves to lock up their traitors. They *let* Philby escape. Knowing who he was, Therrick – knowing who he was. But they'll never trust a foreigner."

"They trusted Blake," I had to object.

"But they locked him up, didn't they? That was one man they *did* lock up." He smiled. "We had to get him out, of course. So as to show that we don't let our own people down. An English prison is a bit of a joke, of course. Prisoners arrive by taxi and any time now they'll be having their own trade unions and colour TV in every cell. Quite ridiculous."

"Makes up for all the free injections you stuff *your* prisoners with."

"My own brother," Vorontsov broke in drily, "is commanding officer at the Lubyanka prison. Mention my name to him when you find yourself inside there and you'll get colour TV too.

"Your young folk are an arrogant lot," Vorontsov went on. "You'll find yourselves having socialist children. Give me a *papirosa*, Oleg Vasilyevich."

European women, happy to sleep with District Party Secretaries. Rows of children in white shirts and blouses and red Pioneer scarves, singing the Internationale and raising their little right fists. Denouncing their own parents for anti-socialist thoughts. I shuddered.

"You're like these country women," Vorontsov sighed faintly. "We tell you how we adore you and you go on panting about love, love even when we're squeezing your breasts and your throats. But in the end you'll shut up and submit."

Vorontsov lit his Russian cigarette and leaned towards me.

"And now for your case, Therrick. Do you still imagine we will be exchanging Nichols with you?"

He looked at me enquiringly.

"What else would you have come for?" I said. "I mean, you're here, aren't you?"

There was a knock.

Peccarie walked in, silently handed me a slip of paper and left. On it was written:

Greifner has just rung. Groller died ten minutes ago.

2

Laurel and Hardy. The clown Grock is dead. What happens now to the clown Fregolli?

Life . . .

I folded the paper and put it in my pocket. I did not know what to say, I did not know what to do – all that was left was that old gambling routine, the poker face, from which the fears have been squeezed long ago, a robot face, a face of lost eyes, the face of an illusionist.

Kagin and Vorontsov were watching me. Vorontsov had long lost his interest in the wardrobe, Kagin was far from asking ironically whether the news was good, both ignored Peccarie's arrival and departure, they were both equally certain that all they needed to do now was to smash the ball straight at the legs of this sweat-stained opponent.

"We came," said Kagin, "to see you. At close quarters. You imp."

"To tell you about the situation," said Vorontsov. "Now you know it, if you hadn't guessed it before."

"We used to play spy games, Therrick," Kagin went on. "But today? You surely don't think that we will give you Nichols for Groller? You'll create a scandal. It will embarrass only the West Germans. You can do what you like with Groller. That won't get you a pension. The British won't be pleased. You know, Therrick, we and you – it's like a toy dog barking at a Great Dane."

He came up to me and put his hand on my shoulder.

"You can get Nichols, Therrick. You can win the favour of the British and get a permanent engagement with them." He smiled at the word engagement, slightly grudgingly, as if to mitigate what was to come. But I knew full well what was to come. I'd been in the game for too long. Whatever they cared to say, they could never grow out of those spy games, the shooting at empty goals, the pouring of powdered glass into a soufflé destined for the school meal.

"We'll give you Nichols," said Kagin. "In exchange for you."

3

"Come, come, Mr Therrick," said Vorontsov. "Pull yourself together. I don't have to do much more explaining, do I? You desperately need to solve the Nichols case to the satisfaction of the British. But not even that will secure you a pension – you're alone and abandoned. You'll be fifty soon. We surely don't need to go into details. I'd find that embarrassing. How long is that Muriel of yours going to go on waiting in Athens? How often do you see her? And what are her prospects? Sharing misery with you. She'll get old, get wrinkles on her neck and start putting aside extra money for a facelift. Is that the future you're preparing for her? What sort of a man are you? You trundle around the world without money and, despite your intelligence, ability and experience, you're short of logic, too. Around a world that is not of your making, and that is up to the eyeballs in its own excrement. Do you owe more to what you call your world, or to that woman, who I suppose you love and who loves you? Not to mention Nichols . . .

"You know enough not to go burning your fingers: for people like you there's a lifebelt on your Titanic. It's called a healthy dose of cynicism."

"Sooner or later," Kagin took over, "every man gets his knife. I mean he gets it put against his throat. You can have Nichols tomorrow. I'm not talking about money, but, of course, we would like you to be as big a hit as possible with the British. We will give you a couple of our men to toss to them. A couple of trade unionists, a couple of students . . . bit by bit. You'll get a very decent case-officer. And it won't be for life. Ten years, let's say. You'll earn some 15,000 dollars a year and for every sizeable piece of information you'll get a bonus. When the ten years are up we'll give you a fifty to a hundred-thousand-dollar handshake. We can discuss the details. Just think of it clearly – and I haven't even mentioned the possibilities that might crop up during those ten years. Suppose you were to work up to a really good position . . . But you don't want me to give you a briefing here, do you? If we shake on it, you can have Nichols tomorrow afternoon, we'll collect the people in Hamburg and then we'll sit back and wait. A few months later we'll let you blow Koerner and his little game to get them to trust you and to get you a medal."

"It's quite clear, Kagin," I broke in. "For God's sake don't wear yourself out drawing pictures of the future. Believe me, it's been clear a good while."

We were silent and I lit a cigarette. What was I to do? What was left for me to do? What more had I to lose?

"You're trapped," said Kagin, as if he could read my thoughts. "You needn't be ashamed, though. Others have let themselves be caught and then started bragging about it. Others who needn't have. Who had money and a station in life, who were something in their capitalist society. Who enjoyed its trust. Come on, Therrick. There are all sorts of agents. The Americans divide them into four lots."

Now he was talking almost with compassion as if he didn't want to hurt what was left of my pride, as if unwilling to remind me of my status as a mercenary whose convictions interest no one and whose honesty is no earthly use to him.

"The first type of agent is one discovered by our recruiter and gradually trained. That wouldn't be your case. The second type is the so-called walk-in, the type who offers himself, bringing some information. The third is what the Americans call the Philby type, a long-term agent recruited in youth. But not even the fourth type fits you, because those are agents who, although they are working for us, firmly believe that they are working for somebody quite different. False flag agents."

"So for me you'd have a new category that would help me ideologically?" I asked wearily.

"We have given you much close thought," said Vorontsov. "We and others. Because you are well-trained, you know a lot of details and you know a lot of people. We've also looked at your political views, as far as we know them."

I smirked. "I've had no political views for a long time. I have a feeling of political hopelessness, if that's of any interest. For me, you are and always will be barbarians."

For the first time a hint of a smile flickered across Vorontsov's face.

He nodded as if he had just diagnosed gangrene and

ordered amputation, and said, without taking offence, "We do have a special category for you, Mr Therrick. A most unusual one, but one that fits the logic of history." He made a tiny theatrical pause. "You will be our agent from despair."

4

As in a speeded-up film, the characters in my life filed before me. And those of Hamburg. Greifner. Groller. And Nichols, saying: 'Save yourself the trouble, I know I'm as good as dead.'

Were we all dead now?

"I won't be your agent from despair, Major Vorontsov. I'll *never* be your agent." I was speaking mechanically, as if groping for a light switch in the dark. "I know all the tricks. Yours and ours. I know you're right. That, failing a miracle – and who deserves a miracle? – you'll swallow up the world with the help of your front men and victims. But I'm not going to help. Not because of pride. I probably haven't got any left. You've guessed right. I've seen too much misery and suffering, too much business and ruthlessness, too much naive apathy and too much exploitation of all sorts to be able to stay clean or, as you put it, to use the lifebelt of cynicism. But just as you hold that there's a price to everything, I hold that there's a limit to everything. There are minor sins and greater sins. And very great sins. But to my mind the greatest sin is that committed by a man who knows he's an intelligent man. Maybe it's the last bit of the Catholic in me, maybe it's plainly and simply the fact that I am not willing to kill my parents. I don't believe in equality among men. Like you. But that is just why I believe that what may be forgiven in a naive man, one who doesn't know – that is to be browbeaten, to yield to it and to be abused – could never be forgiven in me. I cannot *be* abused, I would have to take part in the abuse. I am capable of various kinds of foul play, but not of this. All that's left to me is fear of the future, contempt for you and loathing for those in the West who are helping you. And that, as you appreciate, is not for sale."

5

I stood up.

Kagin said uncertainly, "That is your last word?"

"It is. Whatever happens I shall die a bad death. But your way I would be dying every day and one day it would be even worse."

Vorontsov said with severity, "Surely hatred isn't a Christian quality."

"One day somebody's going to be sick all over you, Vorontsov. I'd do it myself if I didn't have such a callous stomach."

"Enough!" Kagin spoke. "Wait, Therrick. Major Vorontsov has got to go now anyway, and I want to tell you a little more about the situation. Those few minutes..." He glanced at Vorontsov, who stood up, bowed towards me and said to Kagin, "Shall I wait here?"

"No," said Kagin, adding something in Russian.

After Vorontsov had left, Kagin buttoned up his tunic, picked up his coat and said,

"For an old hand, you put a nice lot of feeling into it, Therrick. Did you really feel so hard-pressed?"

I looked at him without understanding what he meant.

"Have you decided you do want Groller after all?"

He shook his head and smiled. "No. Not for Nichols. Not a chance."

"That's as well," I said. "Because if you did want him after all . . ." I reached into my pocket and handed him the paper Peccarie had given me. Kagin glanced at it and looked back at me despondently. He said nothing, merely handed me back the paper. I slipped it into my pocket.

"What more do you want?"

Kagin watched me for a moment and then said dully, "You've got good nerves. Or maybe you haven't any left at all. Maybe you too are . . . drained . . . can you say it like that?"

When I said nothing, he added, "Come on, let's go for a stroll in the garden. There's still one way you can get Nichols."

6

He went down the stairs ahead of me. A robust figure in a Soviet uniform. A Kutuzov without ideals, a Suvorov without a Czar. Whose battles was he really fighting?

"The hotel's asleep," he remarked as we crossed the hallway.

"It's only a small hotel," I said for something to say.

The garden was swathed in darkness and it took us a while to get used to the dark, now the moon had gone behind the clouds.

Kagin strode on ahead of me down towards the water. He leaned on the railings and took out a cigarette.

"Do you fancy a Pall Mall?"

"No," I said. My head was ringing and I felt completely exhausted. Decades of exhaustion for nothing. The futility of the hunt. "No," I repeated, but it applied to something else.

"As you like," said Kagin. He gazed into the water for a

moment. I could not see his face properly and I did not care what he was thinking.

"What's the last chance, Kagin? What else have you cooked up? Are you thinking of kidnapping Muriel in Athens and blackmailing me?"

He half-turned towards me. "Shhh," he whispered and added, "You're talking too loud. Sounds carry over water. Blackmailing you is the last thing I'd do." He took a drag and slowly released the smoke in the cool night air.

"There is still one way you can save Nichols, Therrick. And it won't cost you a thing. Just speed and dependability! Nothing that you couldn't or wouldn't care to do." He turned his back to the railings and rested his hands on them. "A short while ago we made you an offer. You turned it down. Did I expect you to? I don't know." He looked steadily at me. "But maybe I wanted you to."

"I don't get it," I said.

"You will in a moment," he assured me and gave a slightly mocking laugh. But this time it sounded theatrical. Then he added, quickly, as if someone were forcing him into it:

"You make the same offer to me now as I made to you, right? And I'll take you up on it."

— XXV —

Saturday morning, very early

Kagin was smoking slowly and waiting. Of course he knew beforehand how many questions would flood my brain.

"If it's a trick . . ." I began slowly, "then it's the stupidest one I ever heard of. So it probably isn't a trick."

"Speak quietly," he cautioned. "Not that I think there is any danger . . . Grigori thinks I am blackmailing you. We had already agreed on that. You were not far from the truth: I thought you would refuse our offer. I don't know why. But I thought so. Perhaps because of that business in Cyprus, in sixty-four. In order to set up the chance of talking alone together I used some information that we got from Athens yesterday about your account. Your Muriel isn't in Athens at the moment, she's in Salonika at her father's place. If you'd wanted to ring Athens, you wouldn't have got through to her. I told Gregori that I would try to force you to accept our offer because you'd have thought that we were holding her."

"Which Grigori agreed to, of course, eh?" I said

"Would it *really* have worked?"

I shrugged. I was too tired. Even clowns can die lethargically.

"I can't say. I would have wanted evidence. I might even have shot you . . ."

"Out of despair . . . ?"

I nodded. Then I said, "Why did you choose me of all people to ..."

"Defect?" He tossed the cigarette into the water. "I've known you for some time and decided that if you refused our proposal you were the right man. It may not be so. We'll soon find out. You know, Therrick, I've got quite high up our ladder. I barely ever see our opponents. I read about them, make suggestions, study reports. But if I do meet them I'm never alone. Either Vorontsov or some-one else is always with me. I've been thinking about it for over a year. I expect it has been in me for much longer. But when you're setting up a sale . . ." He nodded and looked at me earnestly, as if to say: 'Here we go again. Back to spy-games. Back to persuading fate to change its name.'

"Everything I told you upstairs was true. We are poles apart, Therrick. I wouldn't give twopence for your cow-ardly civilisation. I don't trust it. I'm equally convinced that you didn't give me the whole truth in your answer. That bit about loathing, for instance. Who do you hate more? Us, or your cosy little liberal businessmen and politicians, armchair communists, Marxist students and left-wing film stars? Us or them?"

"I should answer: 'You, Kagin'. Them I despise."

He laughed. "Not a bad answer, that." He waved dis-missively. "But enough of that, let's get down to business. I've never wanted simply to transfuge and offer myself on a plate: 'Here I am and this is what I've got'. That goes without saying. You don't take me for a fool. My con-ditions are very precise."

I interrupted him. "Before you tell me, Kagin. Why you and why now?"

"Isn't that beside the point?"

"It looks as if I'm to organise your coming over. That is one question I'll be asked."

"Not necessarily, not once the other side knows what I'm offering."

"But I want your whys and wherefores."

"You won't be able to verify any of your theories on me. I've long since stopped believing in our Soviet ideology and that what we are doing is right. I know we shall succeed. Even if I were there when it happens, and I won't be, what comfort is it supposed to be to me? That Rome is burning and Russian is compulsory in the schools? That the theatres put on optimistic plays and the word 'death' is outlawed along with God? What good to me would our optimism be? Me, a star performer in Soviet espionage and a long-standing party member? Me, a comrade who has done his stint for the party?" He laughed. "When a man gets old and has seen a lot, his ideas change. He looks for something to grasp, something personal. I have nothing, Therrick. Where you are desperate, I am disenchanted. I am a disenchanted ex-devil and I don't believe in what I have done. Unlike you, I don't even believe in your civilisation; I'm not sorry for it. I was brought up in Leningrad, and when, before the war, I came to Moscow, my life hovered between Belorussia Street and Dzherzhinsky Square. On a Sunday I'd take the Circle Line of the metro to Gorky Park where I'd meet Young Pioneers and militiamen and women who looked like bears. What did I care about the Sistine Chapel?" He took out another cigarette and this time, I had one, too. He fondled his gold Dupont and gave me a light.

"In those days there were no dollar shops in Moscow and there was no going to the Aragvi Restaurant in Gorky Square. There were purges and I knew it. I put my faith in Stalin not because I didn't know he was a murderer. My boss at the time had worked on the assassination of Kirov and knew why they were all shot. He drank pure alcohol – vodka was like mineral water to him. He used to tell me:

'Oleg Vasilyevich, you must learn to live your way into Communism!' I put my faith in Stalin *because* he was a murderer. Because he was probably the greatest murderer history has known. I wanted to see the broken eggs without which you can't make an omelette, as our Cheka man used to say. I wanted to see the splinters flying when the trees were chopped down, as our beloved Lenin used to say. He relied on the envy of the elderly and on the cruelty of the young. He was right: we didn't murder out of sadism or cynicism, we murdered to be in on the *action*. We were liquidators and blood was our reward, the assurance that it was *the done thing*. Destruction, Therrick, just what your left-wingers are hatching for you at the moment. We'll bring them to heel later, but for now let them get on with the blood-letting." He sighed as if he could not believe it possible to explain to people that two and two make four.

"And then I moved into action in the West. Living there, Geneva, New York. Paris sometimes. My wife began to strike me as fat and clumsy, do you understand?" He wet his lips. "I haven't slept with her for twenty years. She's in Moscow and goes to the dollar shops and fingers the glossy capitalist products. She's a member of the Central Committee and votes for every resolution. She's a member of the Central Committee of the Council of Women. And I am supposed to love her!"

He spluttered with laughter.

"You can pile gypsies into a palace in Venice. They'll light the stoves with Renaissance canvasses and stoke up with the parquet floors. Do you imagine I haven't come to see that over the years? You see, I've always wanted to go to Venice, but I never got there. I want to take a look now. In a year's time, after all this is settled. When I'm ... free, Therrick. Relatively free. My wife is an unhappy cow and my son is an expert chess-player, married to a ballet-dancer who is unfaithful to him with a bi-sexual. What's that to me? It is the family of my mistake. It's the family of my Stalin. Not my family. I shall have to retire in a year. They'd give me a dacha and there I'd have my wife and the friends who spend their weekends whispering in corners about Andropov's latest directive. What am I supposed to do there? Play billiards and wear medals on my coat? Surely not. I want to die with capitalism and under capitalism. I know how you'll go and it serves you right, but I'll have time to take a look at the world between Venice and Rio de Janeiro once the excitement dies down, once I get a new face from the hands of your expert surgeons and a perfect new identity. And girls, Therrick. I haven't had much fun in life, mostly just ordinary sex with a sheath. We're puritanical at home, and abroad I had to be careful so I've got plenty of spunk left for squirting around. Does that suit you?"

"Perfectly," I said. "What are your conditions and what do you have to offer?"

"There we are, the little chap has recovered," Kagin said patronisingly, then added in a businesslike way: "Firstly, I'm not interested in going to the British. Their MI5 are national heroes without money and without rights – and I have nothing to offer them. But I do have something to offer the Americans. The CIA is under threat. Not only do I know why – but I made the liberal senators, my dear Therrick. Same method as with Roosevelt's adviser at Yalta, Alger Hiss. He was a homosexual; these are madmen. We've got several of our own men among them, and until recently I was the case-officer for the whole business. There's still time to stop this demolition of the CIA. There'll be hell to pay. Especially at a time like this – a swipe at the American liberals won't be very popular. I shall really enjoy watching the rumpus, my friend."

"What are your financial terms?"

"That needn't worry you, I can handle that myself. Your

job is this: I want to see some top CIA man this evening. And on Sunday at 16.00 Nichols will get in your car and I'll get into an American one. That's the deal, as they say in Langley. Who do you know at the CIA?"

"Ferguson," I said. "He's—"

"He's in Geneva negotiating with the Arabs. All to no purpose, but that's none of my business. Anyone else?"

"Owen, Ellenword. Or—"

"Ellenword's stuck in the Plans Division. I think he'd be just the man. He was in operations for a long time. And he must have it in for those idiots. You know him well?"

"I've known him for years. We've never been exactly close. Don't forget, I worked for Gonzales. We've met several times, and we've worked together several times . . . Just now it's late at night in Washington, suppose I don't catch him? Can't you really make do with someone here?"

"You only give explosives to the house-boy if the butler has been pensioned off," Kagin remarked. "Forget it. Ellenword or Owen. Let's go and phone. The Washington code is 202, and the CIA's number is 351-1100. I expect you remember the extension."

"Naturally. And, of course, Ellenword is just waiting for my call on that extension because he has nothing else to do. No, really . . . if they get him to the phone at all, it'll be great fun explaining to him that he should drop everything, jump on a plane to give me a kiss in Berlin even if, talking on an open line, I can't tell him why."

"You'll manage, Therrick. Tomorrow at 16.00 the Germans will be officially handing Nichols over to us. I'm to receive him. I'll send him to your car under the conditions I have set. Ellenword must have time to give me certain guarantees. I'll make my own arrangements just in case. So try hard."

My weariness vanished. I knew now that there was a

chance. And that Kagin, that bear, gambler, cynic, Mephisto all rolled into one, had resolutely set off after his goal and that we were in the thick of it and that the false Hardy would be abandoning the false Laurel and clown Fregolli would be saved.

We went into the hotel vestibule. Kagin sat down in an armchair and began looking through *Quick*. The phone booth was next to reception.

2

"Central Intelligence. What can I do for you, sir?"

There was disturbance and the odd crackle on the line, but the girl had a pleasant voice, without the usual American accent.

"I'm calling from Berlin on an open line. I want extension 2660."

After a moment's pause a man's voice came on.

"You're calling from Berlin on an open line. Right?"

"Yes. I need to speak urgently to Mr Ellenword. If he's not there can you get him?"

"Who's speaking?"

"Tell him that it's Berx." I used the name by which Ellenword could identify me most readily.

"Mr Ellenword isn't here. Can anyone else handle it?"

"I'm afraid not. Is his secretary there?"

"That's me."

"Is your chief in Washington?"

"I can't give you any information. All I can do is try to see he gets your message. Will you ring back in half an hour?"

3

Kagin kept checking his wrist-watch. His face was calm and relaxed, but there was no doubt that he was thinking of Vorontsov. Vigilance and caution.

"Suppose I can't persuade him?" I asked.

"Arrange to talk on a protected line. But I warn you: don't go talking about liberal senators. You mustn't mention me by name. Understand?"

"I do," I said. "That's just it. Unfortunately, I do understand."

4

"Call New York: 586–9449," said the man on extension 2660. I did so and someone murmured, "International Fruit Limited. What do you want?"

"Berx here. Does that mean anything to you?"

"Hang on."

Then: "Berx . . . ?"

I let out a sigh of relief. It was him.

"Ellenword," I said. "I'm ringing from a hotel in Berlin. I can't give you the details. You'll have to take my word for it all. Are you game?"

"Go ahead," he said, and I caught the characteristic sound of his laugh.

"You've got to get on a plane and in eight or nine hours be at the Hotel Am Lietzen See in Berlin. That's all."

"Can I ask you something as you're paying?" he said.

"As long as you don't ask what it's all about . . ."

"No. I ask you: In whose interest? Yours? Mine? Ours? Who are you working for? Lisbon? You must tell me something at least."

"It's not Lisbon. It's London. And although I'm deeply interested personally, it's definitely in your interest too. Try trusting to my experience. Your credit there will soar. Very high. But no telephone conversation can carry it, not even on a different line, and there is an absolute time limit."

"Berx, I can send one of my men. Someone I fully trust who can take all decisions. Is that enough?"

"No. Not because of me; it would be all right by me. But because of my client. He wants you. Or Owen. Can you send Owen?"

"Owen's in Washington." He hesitated. "No way, son. Wait a moment." I heard him telephoning the airport from another phone.

"I'll scratch your eyes out and make you eat them," he said after a moment, "if you're dragging me off to Berlin to hand out leaflets."

"They won't be my eyes, Ellenword. They'll be the eyes of quite different people. And you'll be glad you had the chance to do it."

"I'll take your word for it," he said. "I'll be at that hotel of yours about eight in the evening your time. Make sure you've got your client handy."

"He'll be handy."

— XXVI —

Saturday evening
at eight and later

I first met him about fifteen years ago, when he was working
as a CIA operative in Havana, just before the fall of
Batista. It had been my first active mission: I was supposed
to sell some arms to Castro. An embarrassing mistake occurred: I had kidnapped and locked away in a cellar that
selfsame Whitfield who was now sitting in the Atlantic
Hotel in Hamburg. Ellenword had doubtless got to hear
of it, but he had never mentioned it.

Later, we had met often. Nicosia, Marseilles, Prague,
Amsterdam . . . Sometimes working against each other.
Even though I had once, on instructions from Gonzales,
worked indirectly for Ellenword himself, he had always
maintained a certain courteous reserve towards me, such
as representatives of the big services always display in
contact with their clients, informers or even their 'wild'
colleagues from parallel organisations.

Now he was looking around in the vestibule. He was well
on the way to becoming grey-haired, and in his black and
white finely striped jacket and black knitted tie he looked
more like an American trade rep for printing machinery
than a former operative who now held an important position
in the CIA.

When he saw me, he gave a slight smile and nodded. He
carried a lightweight coat over his arm with an attaché case

in the same hand. He stepped towards me and we shook hands.

"I can stay at the Consulate," he said. "Or do you think I ought to take a room here?"

"Take a room here just in case," I said. "Here's where you'll be talking anyway."

When he came back from Reception with his key he said, "I'm hungry. Can we talk over food? Where's your client?"

"I think we can talk over food," I replied. "My client will be along a bit later, to give me time to fill you in. Do you want to take your things upstairs?"

Shortly afterwards, as we sat in the glass-fronted dining-room with a view over the Lietzen See and the waiter poured out the Moselle to go with our smoked salmon, he looked at me as if he had last seen me two days before and asked, "Whose chestnuts are you pulling out of the fire this time?"

I swallowed and drank. The wine was very cold and it was Trocken Beerenauslese, really a little sweeter than I liked. But Ellenword seemed to enjoy it.

"I'm changing jobs, I think," I said uncertainly. "Caetano won't last much longer and I've got to think of the days to come."

"You didn't make us an offer, Berx," said Ellenword with mock reproach.

"My name's Therrick now."

He nodded. "Why didn't you make us an offer?"

"Because you'd only put me in with the daredevils, and I feel I'm getting on a bit for that. I wouldn't go into Cambodia. And you haven't got an empty seat for me in the administration."

He gave a short laugh. "I wonder who will have one for you. Well, what's cooking?"

"Colonel Kagin of the First Directorate wants to cross

over to you." I said it in a very low voice, and in a very low voice he said:

"Where is he?"

"He'll be coming here."

Ellenword nodded. "How did you get near him?"

"That needn't concern you."

"Where's his family?"

"He's forgotten they even exist."

"Do you believe him?"

I tried to reproduce in a nutshell what Kagin had said early that morning in the garden. I tried to be as accurate as possible, because I knew how much depended, at least initially, on motivation.

Ellenword watched me expressionlessly; he had put on his international-spy face, that posthumous mask of curiosity that belongs to experts in leafing through personal files.

When I finished, Ellenword said nothing. The waiter was busy clearing away the remnants of the salmon, in which Ellenword had lost interest.

"Did he give you any details?" he asked as soon as we were alone again.

"I only know that he was case-officer in charge of manipulating certain liberal senators," I said briefly.

"You mean to say . . ."

I'd got him.

"They're getting set to demolish the CIA. Until recently he was in charge of the thing himself. That's all I mean to say."

Silence fell for a moment.

"He didn't tell me his terms . . ."

Ellenword gestured. "He'll tell them to me and I'll accept them. I'll have to inform Langley, but – as long as he doesn't want a hundred million . . ." He smiled. It was an excited smile.

"There is just one more condition, Ellenword."

"Yes?"

"This business is part of a certain agreement. That's where I come in. It's nothing to do with you, and I won't tell you anything about it, of course. He insists that you come for him to a certain street here in Berlin tomorrow afternoon at 16.00 precisely. There must be no hitch, understand?"

He looked at me as if trying to guess whether it might not be worth trying to pry something out of me. But he had second thoughts and said tersely:

"No problem. But where is he?"

Automatically I looked round the dining-room, which was lit mostly by candles.

Kagin was striding down the central aisle between the tables. He was in civilian dress: a dark-grey suit. He came to our table, pulled out a vacant chair and sat down.

"I have twenty minutes," he said in English, without formal greeting.

"That's not much," said Ellenword affably. "But it will have to do in the circumstances."

"I assume your attitude is positive," said Kagin.

"You assume correctly."

Kagin nodded. "I won't speak in front of Therrick. I have a car parked outside the hotel. My apologies, but I must allow for everything."

"That'll be all right," said Ellenword quickly, and with authority. Then he turned to me. "I'll be back in twenty minutes."

"In twenty minutes," said Kagin, "Therrick will come to the car. I have to settle a certain detail with him about tomorrow – that is if we can agree."

"We will agree," replied Ellenword.

"We shall see," said Kagin. "It's a blue Audi, Therrick.

If you come out to the car park, it is about a hundred metres on the left of the exit."

I looked at my watch. "Twenty minutes," I said.

They departed across the dining-room, different in every respect, from figure to clothes, from gait to bearing, but both like old and hungry dogs that have just discovered a bone.

2

After lunch I ordered a mounie and slowly turned the glass round in my hand.

It was as if I could hear them whispering in the blue Audi a hundred metres to the left of the hotel. Ellenword in the role of purchaser, closely checking the condition of the goods being offered; Kagin, using scraps of information he was prepared to sell as chess pieces, knowing from experience that the more important the defector, the more threatened feels the service he is selling himself to. An important defector is not unlike an experienced whore – everybody wants her but everybody is afraid of what she might do to his life. Kagin, trampling mercilessly on his past, like a Byzantine carpet dealer some of whose samples had lost their colour, while their secret weave was now all he had. Part of the secret would have to be surrendered in the present interview, the rest later, during the long, long weeks of debriefing.

Or were they perhaps sitting there as two fences, belonging to an international ring of thieves, traitors and traducers, cautious and anxious. Ellenword, in the knowledge that Kagin's information would cause cracks in the routine of his service – certainly some names used by Kagin had already brought sweat to his brow; Kagin, in the knowledge that he has to disclose enough but keep enough back. At this moment he must be watching Ellenword closely for any signs of response.

I could guess which way Kagin's information was pointing and thus I could imagine Ellenword making mental projections of the standing and lobbying strength of those senators of the Eastern liberal establishment. Perhaps one or two of them had been manipulated directly by Kagin himself, while others had been unwitting instruments of Soviet foreign policy, so-called agents of influence, exploitable because of their political do-goodery, personal ambition or financial interest. There was also a whole bunch of well-known people who were professional defeatists.

They were sitting in the Audi, each of them nursing his predicament: Ellenword pushed for time which he counted in days if not hours, simultaneously working out the practical aspects of the 'Kagin defection'. In any case by now he must have realised that he'd have to contact the CIA bigwigs.

And Kagin. Kagin who knew as much.

I paid and left the dining-room, crossed the vestibule and went out of the hotel. I turned to the left and walked for a hundred metres.

The blue Audi stood by the kerb.

Ellenword opened a door and got out.

He nodded to me and said, "When they start shooting drifting freelancers, remember I owe you a favour." He shook me by the hand and added, "See you tomorrow at 16.00 when I come to collect him. But I don't think there'll be time for us to have another talk." He smiled. "Get in touch some day, okay? You never know, we might find a vacant seat in the porter's lodge . . ."

He patted me on the shoulder, quickly, almost coyly it seemed, and hurried off.

I sat down beside Kagin, who was leaning on the steering wheel and smoking. I shut the car door.

"Strikes me that Ellenword's going whip and spur. That's what you wanted, isn't it?"

Kagin did not reply. He exhaled against the windscreen and watched the smoke curl and disperse across the smooth surface. Then he reached for the ignition key and switched it on. He put his right hand on the gear lever, which was in neutral, and moved it absently from side to side.

"Tomorrow at 16.00," he said with effort. "Friedrichstrasse."

"Checkpoint Charlie," I blurted. "Isn't that . . . isn't that taking the romantics a bit far? I'd rather . . ."

". . . something deep in the heart of the American sector," he interrupted me. "Except that what you'd rather just doesn't count. Even if I agreed, I wouldn't dare to suggest it. It would make me look suspicious. You see, I won't be alone, Therrick." His large eyes in the Broderick Crawford mould fixed me with mournful disdain. "Our car will arrive from the Eastern sector, as you call it, and besides the driver, Vorontsov will be in it, and someone from STASI, and I don't even know who that'll be. But he's bound to be armed. He'll be less likely to shoot when I start crossing over to the American car once Nichols is sitting pretty in yours, see?"

"We'll be armed, of course," I said quickly, "if that's what you mean."

"What I mean is absolute precision. Everything must be to the split second. I explained it quite plainly to Ellenword, and he saw my point. By the way, I had to hint that you'll be getting a British agent. I hope you don't mind."

"Mind or not, when the apple falls we stop fussing about the branch and start looking to see that the apple hasn't got maggots. I hope Nichols won't be brought over on a stretcher, Kagin."

"No, he'll be on his own two feet. From car to car. But . . . I've made my own arrangements, just in case. Not that I'll tell you what they are. I'm not sticking my neck out for the hell of it."

"I never dreamed you might! But I've done all my part of the bargain."

"Look here, Therrick, *I* don't give a damn about Nichols," he said mournfully. "For me, you go together with Ellenword, and the two of you and your precision are the guarantee of my safety. I don't burn bridges, you know."

He looked at me almost menacingly.

"I'm not one of those defectors who have to go and hide away among the heroin-pushing Chinese in Holland because something doesn't come off. Ellenword's jubilation and the whole Western attitude is a load of bull where I'm concerned. I've made my own arrangements: one false step and Nichols is a corpse and my defection is a fiasco for America. *Poni ál?*"

"You mean you'd shoot him a few yards from the American sentries?"

Kagin didn't answer but continued.

"The plan is this. At 15.45 precisely you'll arrive in one car, plus the driver and one of your men. Nobody else. You'll park facing the exit from Friedrichstrasse into the American sector, twenty metres from the American sentry-box. Ellenword will see to it that there's enough space. Five minutes later, at 15.50, we'll drive up and park close behind your car. Vorontsov, the German and the driver will stay in the car. I'll get out and so will you. We walk towards each other. At 15.55 the West German car arrives, from the Sonderabteilung. That will contain Nichols, two men and the driver. It will park on our level, but across the street. Nichols will be allowed out of the car at 16.00 precisely. At 15.58 Ellenword and his men will arrive, but they won't park. Their car will stop in the middle of the street on the line Nichols has to cross. Ellenword will come for me and I will give the signal for Nichols to be let out of the car. At the same time three uniformed American military police will surround my car and will position themselves during a polite inspection of documents so that neither Vorontsov nor the German can start shooting at me, if the idea occurs to them."

"Or at Nichols," I said quickly.

"They will not shoot at Nichols," said Kagin.

We looked at one another.

"You're certain about that?"

"I am certain about it."

I heaved a sigh. "Okay, Kagin. What then?"

"The door of your car will be open and Nichols will take his seat. You, Ellenword and I will be by the American car at that moment and I will give you a small personal memento. That will be four o'clock and a few seconds. You can drive off then wherever you want. I doubt we shall ever meet again. Repeat the plan."

I repeated it slowly.

He listened without interrupting, then he engaged first gear and began slowly letting out the clutch.

"At three o'clock set your watch by RIAS Berlin. You'd better get out now. I've got to go."

He did not offer a hand and I got out.

I banged the door and Kagin pulled slowly away from the kerb and his Audi was lost among the rest of the traffic in a few seconds.

All that was left was to give Greifner the order to hand the whole business over to the German Office for the Protection of the Constitution. And to give him the word to inform the waiting Whitfield.

To give Peccarie his instructions.

To secure two single air tickets to London, for Nichols and myself.

And then to pray, most earnestly.

I turned and headed back into the hotel.

It had begun to drizzle again.

— XXVII —

The exchange

It was overcast, but it was warm. We were reversing slowly into Friedrichstrasse. It was half-empty.

"It's Sunday," said Peccarie. "Those who've got visitors' passes to the Eastern sector are already there and won't start coming back till after seven. There won't be a square inch to spare here then."

Our driver turned towards the kerb and reversed slowly to a halt. We had stopped twenty metres from the American guard hut, a longish wooden building freshly painted white. One MP was gaping about outside, but otherwise there was no one to be seen. They must all have been inside, keeping an eye on their watches and following progress through the window.

It was 15.45.

Peccarie sat in the middle of the back seat and slightly opened the rear left door. I nodded to him and got out.

I stood by the car and watched a grey Mercedes as it slowly entered the narrow street; at the wheel was an elderly bespectacled woman in an incredible hat. She nodded towards the American guard and drove on unconcernedly towards the red and white barrier, about a hundred metres from the Western sector. Beyond it the street stretched away towards the Wall, the barbed wire, the lookout towers and the Vopos, armed to the teeth.

The American guard paid no attention to me, merely glanced at his watch and then disappeared into the hut.

I lit a cigarette.

Then a small Volkswagen drove past, full of children and parcels.

Above Friedrichstrasse behind us shone the windows of the Springer skyscraper. It was 15.48. On the other side the first barrier went up. At that distance I could not make out the car properly, but it was a large limousine. Black. It reached the second barrier and a Vopo went up to the window. He saluted and the barrier came down.

Almost at once I made out it to be a large black Zim with diplomatic plates. It drove on towards the guard hut and stopped a few metres behind our car. I could see the driver gazing vacantly at a point somewhere behind me. The others were probably in the back seat.

Then the door opened and Kagin got out. He was in civilian clothes. He leaned into the car and said something, then closed the door and came slowly those few metres towards me.

He did not offer his hand, merely bowed slightly, and I returned the bow: if this was a comedy show put on for the benefit of those in the Russian car, it was convincing. He stood beside me and looked towards the end of the street. He took care to present a left profile to the Zim so that they could see he was not speaking to me.

"One more minute," he suddenly hissed quietly.

"Yes, of course," I said, and resisted the temptation to look at my watch.

A large raindrop fell on the kerb, and then several more. But that was all, as if the rain could not make up its mind.

It was 15.50 and I saw the blue Audi. It drove fairly smartly into the street, eased up and reached the pavement on the other side. It stopped on a level with our two cars, facing the Eastern sector.

I could see the driver. A man sat next to him. Another was in the back, I could not see Nichols.

"Where's Nichols?" I whispered.

"Inside," Kagin whispered back. "Don't worry."

He stood motionless beside me, like a statue that has been moved from a park onto a dusty street and has not got used to the change.

Then there was some movement in the blue Audi and a face swam into the window. I knew it at once. It was Nichols. He was looking in my direction. There was a bare twenty metres between us and I could have been mistaken, but he seemed to open his mouth as if trying to tell me something.

I made an involuntary gesture of the hand which was meant to encourage: 'Just five minutes, old son, five minutes and you'll be out of it.'

But Nichols kept staring at me and began to move his lips again. But I was no lip-reader, certainly not in English. I winked at Kagin, but he was not paying attention. He was looking intensely to the end of the street.

I glanced at my watch. It was 15.58 and 20 seconds. The second hand kept leaping forward.

I sensed rather than saw that Kagin was taking out a cigarette. I heard the click of his Dupont. It was 15.59.

"A minute late," escaped me. "I expect they've been held up at the lights."

Kagin offered no reply.

Slowly, very slowly, it began to rain. It was a warm rain, sparse rain, rain in big drops, it fell on and around us, spring rain, Berlin rain, undecided rain.

Peccarie, sitting in our car, opened the rear left door wide. It stuck out into the street like a challenge.

"I don't understand," I said. For Christ's sake, where was Ellenword?

"I do," said Kagin. "It's twenty seconds to 16.00. You shall have what you deserve."

There was movement at the guard hut. Three American

military police came out and strode over to the black Zim. They surrounded it, two on the pavement and one in the roadway, who tapped on the driver's window.

"It's exactly four o'clock, Therrick," said Kagin.

"Look here, he's bound to come," I said. "He's bound to come."

I was taken aback when Kagin replied, "It's seconds that count now," and simultaneously raised a hand.

That instant the door of the blue Audi opened and, though I had no idea of the reason that had made Kagin decide, I knew he had given the signal.

First his legs appeared, groping for the roadway, and then his hands.

Then his face appeared, and Nichols stood up uncertainly. His knees seemed to be failing him. His mouth was open, but the lips had stopped moving. His face was like that of a sightless deaf-mute. He took one step forward, then another. He began to walk slowly towards our car, gaping ahead of him.

I moved, but Kagin's voice checked me.

"It's been finely timed, Therrick. He's had twenty milligrams of Tubocurarine. That's an alkaloid extracted curare. If he isn't given the antidote in seven or eight minutes, that's an equal dose of neostigmine and one milligram of atropine sulphate, he'll die. He's already had the first symptoms: haziness of vision, ptosis, relaxation of the face and jaw muscles, sensation of tightness in the throat, difficulty in swallowing and talking, weakness of the neck muscles. He'll reach your car, but that will be all he'll manage. Then with increasing speed he'll get weakness and paralysis of the limbs and abdominal muscles, then the respiratory muscles will be affected, last coming shallowness of breathing and death."

Nichols was in the middle of the road. He dragged himself on.

There was a screaming of tyres at the end of the street. A huge American limousine hurled itself into Friedrich-strasse and stopped a few metres from Nichols.

Ellenword jumped out of the car.

"You've done the dirty on me, Kagin," I said. "You've given us a corpse. You won't get to Ellenword." I drew my pistol.

"Come on, Therrick," he said. He set off in Ellenword's direction and said, "I haven't done the dirty on you. I promised you a little gift. Only I had to take precautions. We drugged Nichols yesterday and interrogated him. But I haven't handed the report over. I've got it on me. This was just in case Ellenword didn't get here in time, so that I could go back, because we don't need Nichols any more, and exchanging him would only strengthen the evidence against the Sonderabteilung."

Nichols climbed, or rather collapsed, into our car. I saw Peccarie helping him. The Audi started up and set off towards the Eastern sector.

"Therrick," said Ellenword. He was looking at me and at Kagin, who had stopped behind me. Ellenword also seemed to have difficulty breathing.

Three or four seconds passed. Or was it five?

Then he said in a single breath, "I was held up because I had to wait for clearance up to the last minute. And – I didn't get it."

Kagin stepped back a few paces.

"We can't take you." Ellenword was on the verge of angry tears. "We can't. We can't because we're on the run. They want to believe in Fedora and Angleton is lost . . . he's become a leper. That means we will be destroyed . . ."

I realised what, in perspective, this moment meant.

Fedora was the most highly placed Soviet defector on whose credibility a powerful group in the CIA and beyond had staked everything. Angleton, the best man on the CIA

Soviet Desk, maintained Fedora was a Soviet plant.

The liberals were winning another battle for the Soviet Union.

We both looked at Kagin.

He was standing about two metres from us, and a scowl crossed his features, full of disdain. He said nothing, just reached into his pocket and took out an oblong box, which he opened for me to see.

It contained a syringe, filled with a light brown liquid.

"That was to have been your gift, Therrick – you would have used it to save Nichols. I haven't done the dirty on you. You can go and settle accounts now with whom you like."

Before I could stop him, he dropped the syringe on the pavement. It landed without breaking. And Kagin quickly stamped on it, shattering the glass so that the golden-brown liquid burst out of it and ran away, merging with the rain.

Then he turned round and walked steadily back to the black Zim, where the three MPs were still standing, awkward and not knowing what to do.

Epilogue

It was an ordinary day once more. It was Monday. The sun hung above the skyscraper with its Mercedes symbol and gave warmth: Spring had come to Berlin.

I slammed the car door. I picked my case up from the pavement and tossed my coat over my arm. Then I waved briefly to Peccarie in the driver's seat. He gave a nod and started the car. I turned without waiting for him to drive off and walked over to the Tempelhof terminal building.

I handed in my case, received the ticket and went over to BEA, where I presented the other ticket.

The girl in uniform looked at me. "Mr Nichols won't be flying?"

"No," I said.

"The ticket is for yesterday. But we can't cash it for you if you're not Mr Nichols. You're not Mr Nichols, are you?"

"No," I said.

"We'll forward the money to him."

"But it was me who bought the ticket," I said.

"If you could provide evidence of purchase, I might be able . . . Otherwise . . . Can you let me have his address?"

I did not have his address. I waved her away and took back the ticket.

"Wait," she said. "We must do something about it . . ." She smiled as though it mattered a great deal. She was the efficient sort without being ungracious. They had plenty of cancellations; Nichols' was not the only one.

"I'll deal with it in London," I said. "I've got to go now."

"Strictly speaking, cancellations have to be made in the country where the ticket was bought," she called out after me.

I went through customs. I went through the body-check. It was quickly over: I was not carrying a pistol.

I went through passport control.

In the departure lounge I checked my take-off and the gate number.

I had ten minutes to spare. I went up to the bar and ordered a Martini. And then I spotted her.

She stood two metres away from me, leaning on the bar, with a travelling bag at her feet.

"Veronika . . ." I said.

She glanced at me. Her expression didn't change. Then she turned away, picked up the bag and slowly detached herself from the bar counter. She walked away and I followed her with my eyes, knowing that I should never learn where she was bound and why. Nor what would become of her.

But do we ever learn what will become of us all? Us, who in life have not followed the beaten track, either because we chose not to, or because there simply wasn't a choice . . .

I would be reporting to Queeney that afternoon. He would be pleased Nichols had not crossed the line. Should I tell him what Kagin had said? That they had interrogated him and that Kagin would now be handing in his report?

I was the only one who knew.

And I was alone.

Who can be relied on? Who could still be called dependable? Where were the friendships of my younger days?

How will I die when the time comes? Like Nichols, in an alien city, in an alien car, opening my mouth in vain, as if I had something of importance to say, but desperately gasping for breath?

The Office for the Defence of the Constitution will settle the Sonderabteilung's hash and the French from the DST will probably finish off Nichols' job; all as had been foretold by Kagin, who will be going to the Aragvi Restaurant in Moscow and playing billiards with his pensioned-off soulmates.

Brandt will resign and nothing will come of it: the decline will go on.

I finished my Martini and headed for the exit.

There was only one thing in the world that I was sure of: when I am dying, Jack Parnell's orchestra in their white dinner-jackets will not be playing me out with *Smoke Gets in your Eyes*.

And we are all going to be dead for a long, long time.